D1522095

Dedication

In Memory of Challis Gibbs.

*You were well and widely loved,
and you made a difference.*

Midwinter Sun

A Love Story

Carol Ervin

Printed by CreateSpace, an Amazon Company

LONGWOOD PUBLIC LIBRARY

MIDWINTER SUN

Copyright © 2014 by Carol L. Ervin
All rights reserved.

This publication may not be reproduced in part or whole, distributed,
transmitted or stored in a database or retrieval system without prior written
permission of the author, except as permitted under the U.S. Copyright Act of
1976.
Characters, events, and places portrayed in this book are fictitious. Any
resemblance or similarity of name to persons living or dead is coincidental and
not intended by the author.

Cover design by Victorine E. Lieske, http://www.victorinelieske.com
Learn more about author Carol Ervin at http://www.carolervin.com

ALSO BY CAROL ERVIN

The Girl on the Mountain

Cold Comfort

The Women's War

The Boardinghouse

Ridgetop

Dell Zero

Midwinter Sun

1

MAY ROSE

On the train and during layovers, May Rose sleeps sitting up, no more than minutes at a time. She takes account of other travelers without openly watching, and like them, guards her privacy. In public places, men may converse with strangers. Women should not.

She has seen pairs and groups of female travelers, but no other woman traveling without a man, not even a woman alone with a child. May Rose has Evie, and being responsible for the girl gives her courage. But bringing Evie on this trip also causes worry, because Evie's mother doesn't know.

Chicago's Grand Central Station is well-lit, and late at night it's nearly empty. May Rose and a few others are politely-spaced on benches throughout the waiting room. Two men push wide brooms back and forth across the marble floor. A distant gong strikes eleven. It's too late to sleep.

One arm hugs the straps of her valise; the other lies over Evie, who is stretched beside her on the bench. Evie is patient and well-behaved, convinced they'll soon see her ma, who is supposed to be somewhere in West Virginia. They've heard nothing since she left.

Her sense of ordinary time has been distorted by lack of sleep and replaced by train schedules. In an hour, they'll catch the B&O eastbound passenger for the last portion of their trip. Tomorrow night they should arrive at their journey's end—Grafton, West Virginia.

Two telegrams lie folded in her pocket. One is from her old friend, Hester Townsend: "Come soon. We need you." The other telegram, from Hester's brother, tells why. "Hester is dying."

Her memory fills with Hester's disapproving stare, quick hands, and the click-click of her heels on polished wood floors. Hester Townsend, a short, stern protector, wound tight in her own rules. She gave and withheld, betrayed and saved.

"*We*," Hester's telegram said. Not "*I*." The *we* might refer only to Hester and her daughter. She hasn't seen them for fifteen years, since the girl was a toddler.

She and Evie left Fargo, North Dakota, the same day the boy delivered the telegrams. She doesn't remember what she put in the valise. Evie's clothes. Hopefully something for herself. She opens the clasp, touches a day dress as well as the black, enough for a short stay.

Hester and Barlow Townsend: sister and brother. They still live together, but now in Grafton, not Winkler. Fifteen years ago, Barlow managed the Winkler Logging and Lumber Company, and Hester operated a boardinghouse. For part of a year—a time of many troubles—May Rose lived and worked with them. Before she left for Fargo in 1901, she and Hester reconciled. She and Barlow did not.

At no other time in their fifteen years of correspondence has Hester asked for anything, and on no other occasion has her brother Barlow sent a word. Hester wrote when he married and when his wife delivered a stillborn child. Hester's regular letters were full of details about the guesthouse she managed after they moved to Grafton, "not quite a boardinghouse, not quite a hotel," and news of her adopted daughter. In turn, May Rose sent letters about the orphanage and news of Evie's family. Neither May Rose nor Hester has a husband to write about. Neither has a child of her own.

Hester is dying. The idea is not yet real, only the compulsion to come as she asked. Help and consolation come first. There will be time later for grieving.

A man enters the waiting room, stands along a wall and opens a newspaper. He seems watchful, perhaps not a traveler but a thief, alert for opportunity. Rumpled travelers enter from doors on the track side of the station. Some go toward the restrooms; others line up at ticket windows then drop onto benches throughout the room. A man chooses the bench opposite May Rose. She tightens her grip on the valise.

"Someone supposed to come for you?" Suspenders hold the speaker's pants over his broad belly; he wears no jacket, and his shirt collar is unbuttoned.

She does not like his question. "Soon."

"Me and my wife are going home to New Orleans," he says. "We just buried her sister." At that moment a stout young woman plops down beside the man on the bench, and May Rose's suspicions ease.

"Her sister worked for Western Electric," the man says. "Was on that ferry that tipped over. The Eastland, did you hear of it?"

May Rose smiles a sympathetic greeting to the wife. "I did. How terrible."

The woman shakes her head in wonderment. "They was on their way to a company picnic. She worked for Western since she come north. She loved that job, but she was going to quit 'cause she was getting married. More'n eight hundred drowned. We was going to come for the wedding."

"I'm sorry for your loss."

"Thank you. Folks has been kind. A newspaper man got our story." The woman reaches into a carpetbag, pulls out a kerchief and swipes her eyes. "He said somebody should pay. At least my sister left no orphans." She sniffs and nods toward Evie. "Is that your girl?"

"My granddaughter," May Rose says.

"Couldn't be! You don't look no older'n me."

"Her mother is my stepdaughter. Evie is nine."

Evie sits up. "My ma is Wanda Wyatt. My pa is dead."

May Rose gives her a squeeze. "She's a good traveler."

On the night express, May Rose dozes part of every hour. Given the rocking of the train, she doubts she'd rest better in a sleeping car.

Nothing bad ever happens at a good time, like when she is rested and unburdened by the needs of others. But there are few times like that, and she cannot ignore the urgency of the telegram's request. Hester would not ask her to leave the orphanage and make this long trip just to say goodbye.

At Wheeling, she and Evie have a few hours' layover. "You're good company," she tells Evie. The girl is more than good company. Having someone to guide and protect has helped May Rose endure the trip.

During the layover, they walk in the sunshine, buy apple muffins from a depot vendor, then sit inside for shade and air moved slowly by a ceiling fan. Mid-afternoon, they board again for the last and shortest portion of their trip.

Near dusk, the conductor passes through the car, calling Grafton, West Virginia. She gives Evie the last clean kerchief to wipe her face and hands. Soot lies over everything, because it's been another stifling day and passengers have kept their windows open. May Rose's skirt is damp, wrinkled, and stuck to the seat. She tries to pin up hair that's come undone.

Evie gives back the kerchief. "When will we find Ma?"

It's reasonable for the girl to hope. "I'm not sure," May Rose says. "Your ma may be on her way home. Maybe our trains have passed."

As the train slows, Evie stands at the window. "Maybe she's here, waiting for us."

Their train rattles past loaded coal cars and rail yard sheds. May Rose pulls on her cleaner pair of gloves, then sits on the edge of her seat and watches like Evie, though she doesn't expect to see anyone she knows.

Then she has a glimpse of someone she does know, and her heart catches. She rises to see better and quickly sits back, so as not to be seen. It's Hester's brother, Barlow Townsend. The train's brakes squeal.

They have to meet sometime. She's not ready, no more than she's ready to see Hester on her death bed. She hopes he's there to meet someone on railroad business. Even so, she's relieved to see him, like the worst encounter is now over. *Fifteen years.* If he's cold or distant, she'll bear it, for Hester's sake.

Every passenger in their car seems to be preparing to get off here. She and Evie can blend into the platform crowd and avoid Barlow for now. But when she steps from the train and turns to give Evie her hand, there he is, striding to them with long-legged determination. She fixes a smile and braces herself for their meeting. Even in the heat of midsummer, he's wearing the kind of trim suit and high white collar she remembers, though in place of the old bowler, a summer straw hat.

Barlow takes the hat off, revealing gray at his temples. He places the hat under his arm and covers her hand with both of his.

His eyes widen and his cheeks rise. "May Rose." His tone says everything is forgotten, forgiven, or of no importance in this sad time. "I'm..." His voice breaks.

She fears the worst. "Barlow. Have I come too late?"

"No, no. She's hanging on, waiting for you."

"Excuse me," someone says.

Evie tugs her sleeve, Barlow releases her hand and they move aside so a passenger on the steps can get down from the train.

Still alive. *Hanging on.* She and Hester will have time together, though the quality of that time is unclear. She cannot imagine Hester passing away without a struggle.

It's a relief to be met and not have to find her way in another strange place. They stand on the platform with the crowd passing around them. Barlow seems transfixed.

"This is Evie," she says, suddenly breathless. "Wanda's daughter. I couldn't leave her."

She expects the kind of nodding acknowledgement adults give a child, but he shakes Evie's limp hand. "Evie. I'm Barlow Townsend, and I'm pleased to meet you."

"Thank you, Sir. I'm pleased to meet you too."

Evie's response diverts May Rose's thoughts and makes her smile. The girl is so different from her mother. She's been with her these two months, playing with the orphanage children and imitating how they must speak to their elders. *Yes, Ma'am. Yes, Sir. Please. Thank you.*

Barlow picks up her valise and ushers them through the crowd.

She's glad to be moving toward a common goal: whatever they can do for Hester. "Thank you for meeting us; it's very helpful. But I know you're busy. We'd have found you."

"I've met every eastbound train since we got your telegram."

Whether he came at Hester's urging or of his own accord, she's moved by this confession.

"Our automobile is on the street. We've only a short drive."

"I don't want to impose. I thought we'd stay in a hotel or boardinghouse."

"Hester wants you with us." He pauses. "It's perfectly proper."

The word *proper* hangs between them, an uncomfortable reminder.

"My wife is there, naturally, and Glory."

Barlow's discomfort is plain. He was May Rose's employer, her friend, and her suitor. Before they parted in anger, he made a proposal that was not proper, but one she finally accepted.

Most memories fade, but never those she regrets. How he bowed his head, trying to make amends, the last time they met. What she said. How he pushed her away.

It was long ago. He seems to be saying they can go on as friends. Witnessing Hester's decline will be difficult for both of them. And what will it do to Glory, a girl of eighteen? According to Hester's letters, her daughter is artistic, beautiful, and strong-willed. May Rose hopes she's also strong.

"If Hester wants us, of course we'll oblige," she says. "But I don't want to intrude or cause more work. I hope to be of some use."

"Hester attempts to manage, even now. She needs a friend." He directs her into the pillared terminal, through its cool, high-ceilinged waiting room, past benches of rich, polished wood, shining marble and brass decor.

They come out onto a narrow street of shops. The automobile is a black roadster with four doors and a canvas top. "Here we are." He opens their doors and sets the valise on the back seat.

He drives slowly along the street, as though inviting her to admire the brick paving and sidewalks, lighted shop windows, the banks, hotels, the trolley line. The street lights come on.

"Grafton appears to be prospering," she says.

They turn beyond the business district and stop at railroad tracks where a watchman swings a red lantern. A long train passes in front of them. Though she keeps her eyes focused on the freight cars rolling past, she sees how Barlow glances her way and how his hands grip the steering wheel.

"Grafton is the most important station on the Baltimore and Ohio line," he says. "All due to the B&O shipping business, mainly coal and lumber. How does the town compare with Fargo?"

She looks above the train to a skyline of plump green mountains and tree tops. "Fargo is flat and spread out, and its streets are wide. I'm glad to see hills and valleys again. Curving lines are always more pleasant to view than straight ones, don't you think?"

A train whistle smothers his words. She waits, but he shakes his head and does not repeat them.

She tries another explanation. "On flat land everything feels exposed. But structures in valleys are set close and built uphill. I like the look of Grafton; it feels sheltered, like Winkler."

"Ah," he says, speaking over the rattle of the train. "Grafton is nothing like Winkler, though it may have been, in the beginning."

A second challenge has been met, both naming the place that connects them. They may never need to speak of it again.

"And how are your cousins?"

There's no trace of bitterness in his words, but she glances to see if his expression has changed. The question about her cousins may be only polite, with no reference to events that forced them apart. If anything, his face seems only sad.

"As far as I know, two of my cousins are fine. The oldest died in childbirth; I think I wrote to Hester about it. The other two married and moved away. I believe they're busy with families."

Evie leans over the front seat. "My ma is here."

"In Grafton?"

"Here in West Virginia," May Rose says, relieved for the change of topic. "Somewhere near Winkler, we believe."

The caboose clears the tracks, and the watchman waves them on.

"We're closer to Winkler than you might think," he says. "You came through Wheeling? It's about the same distance. South, of course."

"Good," Evie says.

May Rose says nothing, hesitant to encourage or discourage her.

Barlow turns onto a well-lit street of houses with wide lawns. "Here we are, McGraw Avenue."

"It looks lovely," she says.

"We have a bit of river view, but are not close enough to be bothered by flooding."

A driveway circles the house. He stops under a roofed entrance, opens the passenger door, extends his hand to May Rose and helps her out. She waits while he opens Evie's door and takes the valise.

Hester's house has lights in every screened window, and through one of these drifts a faint sound of piano music. It's sprightly ragtime, perhaps from a Victrola recording. As they climb the steps to a broad porch, a woman rises from a chair. Not Hester.

"My dear," he says. "Here they are. Come inside, so you may see and meet properly." He opens the door.

The woman who must be his wife goes ahead without comment. Inside, she turns and greets May Rose with eyes of startling blue. Alice Townsend has a delicate face, a slender neck and a tiny waist. She stands beside her husband with perfect posture, head erect, as though to see past the visitors. Her stance makes her look elegant.

The house is elegant too, much grander than the old boardinghouse, yet she can imagine Hester here. The entry room has a marble floor, a broad center staircase, and stained glass windows on the landing.

The piano recording ends.

"Alice," Barlow says, "this is Hester's good friend, May Rose Long."

"How do you do?" May Rose removes a soiled glove to shake her hand. Alice's clasp is quick and light.

Barlow draws Evie forward. "And this is her young charge, Evie...?"

"Wyatt," May Rose says. "Wanda's daughter."

"Ah, yes, Wanda," Alice says. "We've heard no end of stories about Wanda." She says this to Barlow and does not look at Evie.

Like a good orphanage child who does not speak unless spoken to, Evie says nothing. May Rose squeezes her hand.

The clatter of quick steps turns them to the stairway and the young woman skipping down. Like Alice Townsend, she wears a pale, gauzy dress, but unlike Alice, her face is pink with pleasure. She calls out before reaching them. "Is this Aunt May Rose?"

Alice steps back. "Apparently so."

May Rose blinks back tears. The young woman's face, dark hair and eyes are identical to her brother's when he was a boy. This is Glory, Hester's adopted daughter. Charlie's baby sister.

Glory falls on May Rose in a hug. "You're so good to come."

"Seeing you, I wish I'd come years ago." She's loved and missed the Herff children, a family neglected and divided when their mother died. Hester claimed Glory. As a little boy, Charlie went to Fargo with May Rose and lived with her until he was fifteen. The fact that she hasn't heard from him since then is a constant sorrow.

"This is Evie," she says.

"How wonderful!" Glory stoops and kisses Evie's cheek, then stands and takes a deep breath. "Let's go see Mother."

Alice Townsend frowns at her traveling clothes as though she's trailing dust. "Perhaps May Rose should have an opportunity to freshen."

"Mother said bring her directly."

Barlow clears his throat. Alice's lips are set. The moment may represent a shift of power in the house. If Hester dies, Alice Townsend will rule here. Perhaps this is why Hester wanted her to come. For Glory.

She and Evie must not be another source of discord. "A change and a few minutes' wash will make us more presentable."

"Then please excuse me," Alice says. "I'm not at all well today."

Barlow sends his wife an anxious look and offers his arm, but she lowers her gaze to the luggage at his feet. "I'm capable of reaching my room. Please have Banovic clear this away." With a brief nod for May Rose, Alice Townsend glides to a door off the foyer and shuts herself from view.

At the orphanage, May Rose sometimes must serve the children's needs by letting administrators and patrons think they know best. Her path here seems clear. To help Hester and Glory and save Barlow from further embarrassment, she'll have to pretend his wife is perfectly polite.

2

BARLOW

Barlow is tired of keeping the peace between his sister and his wife. Since the onset of Hester's illness, he's refused to be manipulated by Alice's tantrums. She often breaks away from the family like this, her show of displeasure. Unfortunately for Alice, no one seems to miss her company.

In the wake of his wife's departure, May Rose smiles and gives Evie a squeeze. Evie stands very still, but her eyes move like she's uncertain she's in a safe place. The child's discomfort embarrasses him and makes him angry with Alice. Even a child knows when she's unwelcome.

He meets Evie's eyes. "We're very glad to have you here." He'd like to tell May Rose that his wife's behavior has nothing to do with her visit to their house, but he can't. He knows it does.

Alice may not love him, but she reads him well. During this visit, he must hide how May Rose captures his attention. He lifts her valise and gestures to the stairs. "Shall we go up?"

Her face is fuller, less girlish, and her golden hair is done up in the same kind of pompadour that Alice wears. Otherwise, she's exactly as she was. Mid-thirties, now, he believes, and never re-married. He finds that a marvel and a consolation. He hopes she's changed in one respect. He's tried, all these years, to be the kind of man she might love. Just in time, he retracts the arm that almost touched her back.

He follows them up the stairs. They can be friends; old feelings don't have to get in the way. But he wishes he'd kept her to himself for an hour before introducing her to everyone else. He might have driven farther, shown her more of the town. No one at home would know the difference.

He's not surprised that Glory leads them to the best rooms, the suite across from her mother's. He sets the valise inside the door. "We hope you'll be comfortable here."

"We would be comfortable with much less," May Rose says.

"Mrs. Banovic will have dinner ready when you are." His voice sounds too stiff, but he can't let it be anything else.

After he closes her door, he steps across the hall and looks into his sister's dark room. "She's here."

"Come closer," Hester says.

The nurse stands and offers her chair by the bed. He's no longer shocked by the bones that outline Hester's face.

Hester has little breath to talk, but her gaze is strong, and her smile is as always, tight-lipped. "May Rose. How does she seem?"

"Good. Worn down by travel, I think. Wanda's daughter is with her. She said something about Wanda being in Winkler."

"I believe... Wanda went to find her family. I told you."

He'd remember if she had.

She closes her eyes, as though the effort to keep them open is too great. "I'm sorry to leave you. With the house. And everything."

He doesn't say she's going to recover, for she insists on the truth. She's been his champion since he was a boy, and he's always valued her advice. Already he feels its loss. She may not know that Alice has closed the house to paying guests, but surely she understands they won't manage it without her.

"Glory will bring May Rose to see you in a few minutes," he says.

Hester gropes for his hand. When she has it, she turns up her most serious face. "I want you to have a good life."

"You've been the best part," he says.

She closes her eyes again. "I know the best part."

Going down the stairs, he thinks of that time. One year in Winkler. His heart rushes.

Banovic waits at the bottom. Hester hired him as their handyman, but Alice likes him to dress up and play butler. Because Banovic has a bit of flair and seems to enjoy this role, Hester for once conceded to Alice's wishes. Banovic and his wife have been part of the household nearly as long as Alice.

"Mrs. Townsend ask for tea and toast in her room," Banovic says. "You will eat there or with guests?"

"I'll have tea and toast with Mrs. Townsend, but I'll also eat with the guests."

Alice is in her reading chair, a newspaper spread before her face. She speaks without lowering it. "Will you go to the office tomorrow?"

"Is there a reason why I should not?"

"I thought you might want to entertain your guest."

He sits in the companion chair. "May Rose is Hester's guest, not mine, and she is not here to be entertained." His words will do nothing to change his wife's mood.

His current surge of vigor is inappropriate. Until this evening, he attributed it to a rallying of his body, a preparation for the loss of his sister. But his energy is not solely for performing the duties necessary in times like this. It's a heightening of feeling, an expansion that began the moment he heard May Rose was coming. And now she's under his roof, and though everything is more hopeless than before, he's happy, and that's not good. Alice misses nothing. She'll do her best to make everyone share her misery, especially May Rose.

If Hester is not worse, of course he'll go to work in the morning. He needs a distraction.

Today May Rose called him Barlow. The way his spirits leaped showed how confused his life has become.

3

MAY ROSE

Their suite includes a sitting room, a dressing room with a child's bed, and a door to their own bathroom. The bedroom has a bed so plump and high it has a pull-out set of steps.

May Rose shares Evie's awe of the velvet draperies, tasseled pillows, golden vanity table, and oriental rugs. Hester and Barlow have done well. In the old Townsend boardinghouse, she and Wanda felt pampered in a clean back bedroom with a view of the pig pen. Here she looks out on the river.

On the front lawn, a gas lamp burns above a wooden sign. It says "Townsend Guest House."

"We've accepted no guests since Mother got sick," Glory says. "Aunt Alice wants us to take the sign down or turn the lamp off, but Uncle Barlow says Mother will think we're hurrying her death. Mother knows she's not going to get well, but we all pretend. Except Aunt Alice, who I think is unhappy because she is no longer the sickest person in the house. You see why it would be wrong to take down the sign?"

"I see it's a problem." Alice does not look unwell, only thin and nervous.

"Aunt Alice hates having boarders, though they're the richest travelers, the ones who do not like to stay in public hotels. We never have more than one gentleman or family at a time, because while they're here, the house is theirs, and we become their servants. It's fun for me, but..."

"Not everyone is willing to play the role of a servant."

"Certainly not her. She says this business has ruined her standing in the town. Mother always said her standing is her own fault; she's done nothing to earn one. Unless a woman is very rich or well-connected when she arrives, nobody is going to reach out to include her in their circles. Aunt Alice keeps to her apartment when the house has guests. I think she and Mother settled that long ago. You know Mother."

She does. "Your mother is my oldest friend, but there was a time when she did not like or trust me." She feels some sympathy for Alice, yet the years should have reconciled Barlow's wife and sister, if only because they both care for him.

Glory grips her hand. "I'm so glad you're here." Her face turns solemn.

"I hope I can help."

"Mother says you're a sweet presence. And you are. We need that. So much." Glory's lips quiver.

If May Rose lets herself think of her friend's impending death, she'll be no use at all. "We'll help each other," she says.

Glory goes away and returns when May Rose and Evie have washed and changed into fresh dresses. She brings a doll with a white embroidered dress, a painted china face, and real hair.

Evie's face brightens.

"You may keep her," Glory says. "I was too old for dolls when Mother bought this one." She sits on the bed and motions Evie to climb up beside her.

"Thank you," Evie says. Wanda's quiet child.

Oh, Wanda, May Rose thinks. Where are you? But now she must see Hester. "Shall I go alone?" She's come east with only one certainty: to be with her friend when she dies. But knowing Hester, there's more to her request.

"I'll wait here with Evie," Glory says. "Mother's room is directly across the hall. You don't need to knock."

May Rose closes their door as Evie is saying, "Do you know my ma?"

Hester's room is dark and quiet and has a faint, familiar odor. It's sachet, the dried flowers and spices Hester kept in the boardinghouse laundry room between stacks of ironed sheets. Perhaps she's well enough to be assembling sachet packets. Perhaps by day they let the sun stream in, and Hester enjoys a bit of work.

As May Rose approaches the bed, a nurse in white cap and apron stands and lights a lamp.

Only Hester's eyes identify her, intense and slightly protruding from sockets that now seem too large. She stretches her hand over the bed cover. "May Rose. Still beautiful." Hester's voice no more than whispers, but her grip is strong. "Sit beside me." She lifts her eyes to the nurse. "Go along home. Take some of Mrs. Banovic's cookies to your children."

The nurse hesitates. "Are you sure? The night nurse won't come for another two hours."

May Rose kisses Hester's clammy forehead, then sits on the bed. "I'll stay until the nurse comes, and as long as you need me."

They gaze at each other, hands linked, until the woman leaves.

"How are you feeling today?"

Hester's eyes flick with impatience, but her speech is slow. "We should not waste time talking about me." There's a pause, and she begins again. "I suffer only from worry. It's difficult to stop. Especially when I can do nothing else."

May Rose waits while Hester catches her breath.

"You've seen Glory?"

"She's given us a warm welcome. Such a lovely girl. You have reason to be proud."

"Glory is full of ambitions. She wants to travel, study art, and meet her brothers. I will not... I will not leave her in the care of my sister-in-law, who wants to see her married and out of my house. You've met Alice?"

"When we arrived, yes." She sees something of what Hester wants her to do, but not how she'll do it.

"I think Barlow is grateful to have work that keeps him constantly traveling. But for Glory, you see..."

Hester's letters have said little about Barlow's wife, but noted his work as agent, securing freight, acquiring rights-of-way, and negotiating other agreements for the B&O Railroad. Convention might demand that she say Hester has years to guide and protect Glory, but in vital matters, they both prefer the truth.

Hester closes her eyes. Her grip relaxes and she slips into the quiet breathing of sleep.

May Rose adjusts herself on the bed in a more comfortable sitting position. Hester has called her to intervene on Glory's behalf. Does Barlow know? Except with squabbling children, she is not good at intervening. Tears wash her eyes as she holds Hester's limp, shrunken hand. It's a hand that loved to work. Even in a house as grand as this, she can imagine Hester scrubbing floors on her knees as they once did together in the boardinghouse.

Hester opens her eyes when a woman sweeps into the room with a tray and the aroma of beef and onions. "This...is Mrs. Banovic. We couldn't do without her."

May Rose rises from the bed. "How do you do?"

Mrs. Banovic sets the tray on Hester's desk. "Happy to meet."

May Rose helps set Hester up in the bed, careful not to tug on her thin frame. Mrs. Banovic arranges a bowl of stew, a thick slice of buttered bread and a cup of coffee on a lap tray. "You gonna eat all," she says.

Hester smiles. "All."

Mrs. Banovic moves a small table and chair to the bedside, sets a bowl of stew on it and nods to May Rose. "Be good you eat here. She do better when someone eat with."

May Rose takes her first bite. "It's wonderful." She has not eaten since the Wheeling depot, but she stops, watching Hester, who swallows with effort.

"I must see bowl empty when I come," Mrs. Banovic says.

When the woman leaves, Hester's spoon clatters on her lap tray. "I'll have the coffee." May Rose holds the cup while she sips, then Hester asks her to take the tray and fix the pillows so she can lie back.

The house is quiet. Outside, an automobile backfires, and farther away, a steam whistle blows. She pushes aside the table with her own dinner. The stew will be just as nourishing later, and just as tasty if it's cold.

"Please talk," Hester says. Her eyes open and close as May Rose recalls their Winkler days. She speaks only of the good times in the middle. Not the beginning, when Hester did not want her to stay because she was the subject of scandal. And not the end, when she embarrassed Hester and Barlow by telling their dining room guests first of his offer and then of his deceit.

Hester asks about the orphanage, and May Rose says the orphanage will get along fine in her absence. Between rasps of breath, Hester smiles.

May Rose says, "How can I help you?"

Hester reaches again for her hand. "Glory," she says. "And my brother. Barlow will need a friend." The same words he said about his sister.

Hester falls asleep without saying more. May Rose doesn't leave her until the night nurse comes.

~

Since the night of their arrival, Hester's communication has fallen to the barest shake of her head when they try to get her to eat. For three days, May Rose and Glory take turns relieving the nurse. May Rose reads aloud from a book found on the lower shelf of her bedside table, *Poems by Emily Dickinson*. The exposure of this woman's heart deepens her awareness of Hester, who like Dickinson, never married, but surely loved.

Early on the morning of the fourth day, the night nurse says Hester has passed away. They gather in her room, Barlow with his arm around Glory, May Rose beside Alice on the far side of the bed. The Banovics stand in the open door. Glory sobs. May Rose's head is thick with tears but she holds them until she reaches her room.

Throughout the day, May Rose, Barlow and Glory stiffen in grief and speak only of preparations.

She has brought a black dress, but Glory needs to find one ready-made. When she goes with Glory to a store that sells ladies' clothing, she hears Glory's first bitter words: "Aunt Alice had two new black dresses made weeks ago. I think she enjoyed that as much as if she were assembling a trousseau."

~

The embalmer took Hester away and brought her back in a coffin. She is now displayed in the larger of the two parlors. Visitors crowd the room and the large entryway.

Hester was not always easy to understand, so May Rose doesn't know if she'd like being the center of this tradition. She would approve the room's lighting, the quiet murmur, and the fine, somber suits and dresses of those who've come to express their sympathies. Business men, railroad officials and their wives. Every screened window is open, but full as it is, the room is insufferably hot.

May Rose and Evie sit on straight chairs in a far corner, strangers to the callers rotating past the coffin. At times the crowd parts, and she has a glimpse of Barlow, polite and composed between his wife and Glory, accepting condolences.

She doesn't know what she's supposed to do for Glory, or how she can support her against Alice Townsend, unless Barlow chooses to side with the girl. Already Alice has said May Rose no doubt wants to go home to Fargo as soon as possible.

At the end of three hours of visitation, two callers remain with the family at the coffin, a young man attentive to Glory, and another man with Barlow. Evie leans on May Rose's shoulder in sweaty sleep.

"This has been exhausting," Alice says. "Good night to all." She leaves the others at the coffin.

May Rose strokes Evie's damp hair from her forehead. If the young man is important to Glory, she will bring him for an introduction. But when she looks up, Barlow and the other gentleman stand before her, and no one else is in the room.

"May Rose, I'd like to present my cousin, Clarence Townsend. Clarence, this is Mrs. Long, Hester's dear friend. *Our* dear friend."

"Hello." She extends her hand. With Evie against her, she cannot easily rise.

"At long last, I meet May Rose," Clarence Townsend says. Were his cheeks and hands not plump, he'd be a younger version of Barlow. They're of even height and have the same shock of black hair, heavy eyebrows and dark eyes. She smiles. They have the same long ears.

Clarence Townsend's familiarity makes her wonder what's been said. She motions to empty chairs. "Would you like to sit down?"

"Thank you." Clarence sits beside her. "We've stood enough, haven't we?"

Barlow clasps his hands behind his back. "May Rose, I'm sorry I didn't introduce you to anyone, but I couldn't get away from the receiving line."

She shakes her head, glad she did not have to make polite talk. "It's fine."

Clarence angles his chair and loosens his collar. "I wish we'd met earlier. I'd rather have sat here with you."

Glory's return saves May Rose from the need to reply. The girl's cheeks are bright. From heat, or from something said by the young man? She sits and pulls Evie from May Rose's shoulder. "Shall I take Evie to bed?"

"Thank you. I'll be there in a moment."

Evie wakes and scoots from the chair.

"My dear," Barlow says to Glory, "our cousin is staying the night. Where shall we put him?"

"The suite in front would be nice," Clarence Townsend says. "Where I stayed for the funerals of Cousin Wilbur and Cousin Hobart. It has afternoon shade, and a nice cross-draft."

"I'm so sorry, the suite is not available," Glory says. She keeps her smile as she takes Evie's hand. "We have a room freshly made up in the back hall."

Clarence sighs. "I suppose the back hall will do. Make sure the windows are open, if you please."

"Of course." Glory leaves with Evie, and Clarence Townsend stands and offers his arm to May Rose. "It's stifling in here. Would you like to see if the air is cooler on the porch?"

"I was thinking of the porch, just now."

Barlow takes a step back to let them pass. "I'll see if Alice will join us."

On the porch, moths hover around the ceiling light. Clarence steps inside and turns it off. May Rose sits in a wicker rocker.

He moves to the other end of the porch and lights a cigar. "Do you mind? I'll try to stay downwind."

"I don't mind, and I'll be here only a moment. I have to see about my granddaughter."

He puffs a plume of smoke. "She's your grandchild? Beg pardon, but I thought you were the child's mother."

The screen door squeaks and Barlow appears, drops into the chair nearest May Rose, leans back and extends his legs. He's removed his suit coat, and in the dark, his white shirt is a ghostly glimmer.

"Alice has gone to bed."

"I'm sure she's tired, standing for so long," May Rose says. Everyone's attempts to make her feel welcome have not been strong enough to cancel the effect of Alice's disappearances. Hopefully Barlow's wife is kinder when there are no visitors in the house.

She lifts her chin to let her damp neck catch the breeze. She's eager to go home and worry no more about pleasing Barlow's wife, but first she must find a way to honor Hester's wishes. Hester did not want Alice to curtail Glory's ambitions.

Barlow clears his throat. "Clarence is an attorney, and the only son of my father's only brother. He's always taken care of our legal matters—Hester's estate, for example. You may remember, Clarence, that Hester named this lady in her will, a dollar amount." He turns back to May Rose. "It's not a major bequest. I see no reason not to tell you. Five hundred dollars, am I right, Clarence?"

Five hundred dollars. The amount seems like a fortune. She slides a paper fan from a fern stand and waves it to cool her face. She doesn't know what to say, or if any response is expected at a time like this.

Clarence removes his coat and lays it over the porch rail. "I haven't looked recently at Hester's will. I suppose you're right about the bequest, assuming other obligations of the estate can be met. We won't know final amounts for months."

She wishes she didn't know.

"Everything else to Glory," Barlow says, "including Hester's portion of this property."

The end of Clarence's cigar brightens. He turns his head and lets its smoke drift away from the porch. "We need to talk about that as well as the Hershman estate. Tomorrow will be soon enough."

"Let's talk about it now," Barlow says. "May Rose, you remember the cousins who lived with us in Winkler. Wilbur died this year, just after Christmas. His brother Hobart died the next month. Their mother was our grandmother's youngest sister."

She remembers them well, elderly gentlemen in loose suits who enjoyed mealtimes and slept in rockers every afternoon with newspapers over their faces. She thought they were dependent on Hester and Barlow. "Hester wrote of their passing."

"Cousin Hobart and Cousin Wilbur lived with us from the time of their retirement. When we moved to Grafton, they missed the comings and goings of our boardinghouse, so they bought this place for Hester to manage. In their last year, she wore herself out as their nursemaid. They always said the house would be ours."

Barlow's voice is tired, with an edge of disgust. "I should have bought it myself, or something I could afford, but they convinced Hester."

"We can talk about it tomorrow," Clarence says.

May Rose rises to escape what is beginning to sound like a private argument. "If you'll excuse me, I should see about Evie."

"Stay a moment," Barlow says. "Since the deaths of our cousins, Clarence has received information that affects the distribution of their estates. Two more heirs have come forward. I did not want to tell Hester, and have yet to share this with Glory."

Moments ago, she was suspended in awe of Hester's generosity. Now she worries for Glory and Barlow.

"I helped Hobart and Wilbur write the wills that benefitted each other," Clarence says. "In my presence, they never made another. Perhaps they had something done by an attorney here in Grafton?"

"Hester or I would have known about it. You didn't advise them to designate beneficiaries in addition to each other?"

"It was a little awkward, since I am as closely related as you," Clarence says. "They said they'd leave the final bequest to the one who lasted longer."

Barlow's chair rocks and stops. "Shrewd to the end! I suppose they held off in the event that Hester stopped taking care of them. Which she wouldn't have done, even if they were destitute. So now the estate is in probate, and we'll split five ways, Glory, Clarence, two distant cousins, and me. We'll have to sell the house."

Glowing ash drops from Clarence's cigar and dies in the air. "There are further developments. I'm sorry to say, in the past week others have been identified."

"Others?" Barlow sits forward, blocking her view of Clarence. "How many others?"

"Thirteen so far, people from Pennsylvania, cousins on the Hershman side. I know what you're thinking. Hobart and Wilbur never mentioned other cousins."

"They often said they had no one but us," Barlow says.

May Rose imagines Hester caring for them only months before her own death. Wearing herself out.

"I don't know how these claimants learned about the estate," Clarence says. "Someone local may have sent them the death notices. Anyway, they appear to be legitimate. So eighteen total, with you, myself, and Glory, as Hester's heir. I hope there will be no more."

"One-eighteenth, more or less, of the value of the property, minus probate costs. I don't suppose I'll receive compensation for the improvements I've made in the last ten years?"

"The only distinctions will be for nearness of relation," Clarence says.

Barlow leans back into his chair. "With an eighteenth share, I can't buy out the others."

They sit in silence, facing the quiet street. May Rose wonders how these changes will affect Glory, a girl accustomed to so much. Clarence takes a last puff and tosses his cigar to the grass.

Barlow's feet scrape the floor boards. "It may be for the best. Without Hester, we can't accept guests, and if the property earns no income, it will be too costly to maintain. At least Hester didn't know." His voice falters in outrage, as on a day she remembers well.

4

MAY ROSE

Just once, May Rose would like to be free of others' problems. Just once, she'd like to lean on someone else.

She thinks Barlow has not told Glory about the imminent loss of their home. He may not have told his wife, for when they sit together for lunch after the graveside services, Alice Townsend's mood seems bright.

Alice presides at the foot of the dining table, which to judge by the slight wrinkle in Glory's forehead may have been Hester's place. Clarence Townsend sits beside her, and Glory next to him. May Rose and Evie sit opposite. Barlow is at the table's head, in the only chair with arms. The master's chair. He had one like it in the boardinghouse.

"Glory," Alice begins, "did you not notice Joseph Treadway at the service? I think he was waiting to speak with you."

Joseph Treadway is possibly the young man who stood with Glory at the viewing last night. Banovic sets a bowl of chilled red soup in front of May Rose. "Thank you," she whispers. Hester would have approved her funeral service: short, impersonal, and well-attended.

"Aunt, I cannot tell you who was there." Glory sounds exhausted.

"Someone should tell Treadway it's not a proper time to be courting," Barlow says.

Banovic steps away from the table with his empty tray. May Rose folds her hands in her lap. Beside her, Evie does the same. Everyone waits for Alice to begin eating.

Alice suspends her spoon in air and peers at Glory. "Have you not given Joseph an answer?"

"I've made it clear I want to attend college." Glory glances from her uncle to May Rose. "Perhaps Broaddus, in Philippi. I could easily come home weekends on the train. Mother liked the idea."

May Rose twists her hands in her lap. Glory will not have her home much longer.

"College?" Alice purses her pretty lips. "Isn't that a waste, when you already have a marriage offer?"

"Some women go to college for reasons other than to find a husband," Glory says.

"Oh, for teaching. A low occupation. A woman can advance in knowledge and culture after marriage, especially if she has little else to do." She turns to Clarence Townsend. "Glory is at the most attractive age to secure a good marriage. She must not let this moment pass."

Glory's come-back is quick. "*Must not?*"

"Alice," Barlow says. "This is not the time."

"Why not? We're family here." Alice's eyes dart to May Rose. "Or mostly so. And I imagine May Rose knows the secrets of our closets."

May Rose pats Evie's clasped hands and smiles to reassure her. It's good that Evie's mother is not present. Wanda never lets an insult pass.

"Please." Barlow's voice is weary. "Let's eat. I should go to the office for part of the afternoon."

For a while there's no sound at the table but a polite clink of spoons and the hum of a fly. Banovic clears the bowls and brings in slaw and salmon patties.

Alice turns again to Clarence Townsend. "The Hershman estate. When should we expect it to be settled?"

Clarence clears his throat.

"It's a lengthy story," Barlow says. "Can we save it until evening?"

"Go to your office, if you must. Clarence can tell me."

Barlow presses his lips together and studies his plate. May Rose cuts a salmon patty in half and gives it to Evie, who never has much appetite.

"I'd like to eat first," Barlow says.

Alice dips her fork into slaw. "I only asked when we might expect the story to end."

"A month or two after the house is sold," Clarence says.

"Sold?" Alice straightens in her chair. "Barlow, why must it be sold? Doesn't it belong to you and...and to Hester's estate? I thought you planned to purchase Clarence's share."

May Rose glances at Glory, who has set down her fork and turned to her uncle.

"My dears, I hoped to tell you privately." He looks from Alice to Glory. "Hobart died, as you know, with no will except the one naming Wilbur, who died a few weeks before him. Now we've learned there are other heirs. I'm sorry, we'll have to sell the house."

"And we'll get...?"

"Not much," Clarence says.

Alice puts her fist to her mouth. "Those nasty old men! After all we did..."

Glory rises and throws her napkin on the table. "After all *Mother* did."

~

BARLOW

"You should have been more diligent," Alice says. She's followed him to their apartment, where he's changing his jacket for work. "To let Hobart die with a will that named only his dead brother?"

"I wasn't party to their wills."

"But Cousin Clarence was! Dear Clarence, how smart not to advise them otherwise, when he knew so well they intended the estate for us."

"That's all over. Can we look to the future, or do you intend to keep reminding me of my errors?"

She drops into a chair and fans herself. "I never wanted to live in the middle of your sister's business. Look to the future, then. Tell me where we're to live."

"I'll work on it."

"Today. Nothing is more important."

"I'll see what I can do."

"And no more guests. When will Mrs. Long be leaving?"

"Why don't you ask her?" His reaction is too sharp.

Alice exhales like she's blowing off steam. "I've never been in charge here. I won't start now."

"Then shall I find a house to rent or buy?"

"Ye gods," she says. "Not rent."

He walks to work, some ten blocks to his office in the B&O station. This gleaming structure and the Willard Hotel beside it proclaim the company's vision for Grafton: a metropolis created by the Baltimore and Ohio Railroad. Already the town is booming. Tracks, repair shops and the roundhouse fill the valley, and coal and lumber freight crowd the daily schedules. Not too long ago, he was proud to be part of it.

A dangerous idea—an impossible idea—inflames his thoughts. He might borrow enough to buy the house if he had someone as capable as Hester to manage the business. *Like May Rose*. Would she accept, for Glory's sake?

She would not. The idea is too similar to his old offer, the one that humiliates him still. And the house is no more than an excuse. It's not what he wants. Besides, Alice would give him endless trouble if he tried to continue Hester's business. When he thinks about it, he's relieved by the prospect of change. Years of treading a careful path between Hester and his wife have ended. Alice may not like the size of the house he can afford, but it will be hers to rule. Hester's portion of the Hershman estate will not be what she expected Glory to inherit, but it will be enough for the girl's education and a fine wedding, should she so choose. He will continue to travel for the company. The B&O Railroad has no customers west of Chicago, but no one has to know if he finds a reason to visit North Dakota. Another impossible idea.

Alice has every right to be angry—he should not have trusted his old cousins' promises.

That night he sits on the porch with May Rose and Glory. Wanda's child has gone to bed, and Alice has come out and gone in, claiming the air is buggy.

Sitting outside in the dark has always stirred him to reflect and confide. It's an expansive feeling, enhanced by quiet and perhaps by a primitive sense that the household is safe against the night and darkness hides him.

May Rose's rocking chair squeaks. "Your mother thought I could help you. I'm not sure how."

"I can't begin to think," Glory says, "but I wish you could stay."

He holds his breath. Today May Rose asked him for train schedules. "Don't go too soon," he says. "Stay as long as you can."

"I need to find out about Evie's mother."

"Of course." He wishes he hadn't stopped smoking. A pipe or cigar would give him something to do with his hands and cover the moments when he can't think of anything safe to say. The function of polite conversation, he believes, is to allow people to avoid what's in their minds. The orphanage seems an acceptable topic. "Do you miss the orphanage children?"

"Not as much as I expected. I startle every time I hear young voices, then I realize they're not in my charge. It's restful, being away."

Fireflies dot the dark, and crickets sing. For a moment, he's happy. "We could find work for you here. Where you'd be near Glory. Evie and her mother might like to resettle here."

"How I'd love that," Glory says.

Alice's parlor adjoins the porch, and its windows are up. He imagines her sitting in the dark, listening. "Are you attached to Fargo? And to the orphanage?"

"I think..." She pauses. "I think I'll have to be wherever Wanda and Evie are."

Wanda, the wild child of their Winkler days. Now May Rose has Wanda's girl, a quiet thing, not at all like her mother.

"Maybe before I go to school," Glory says, "I'll travel to meet my brothers. Mother promised we'd do that one day."

"I'm sorry we never did it," Barlow says. "You should know them." He remembers Will as a boy, but not Charlie, the one who ran away and later lived with May Rose and Wanda.

"We can find Will," May Rose says, "but I've stopped hoping to see or hear from Charlie. He was fifteen when he left us; he'd be twenty-four now. He wanted to be a cowboy, did you know that?"

"Hester told us." In case May Rose would not approve, he doesn't say that Hester sometimes let him read her letters.

"I love having an adventurous brother," Glory says. "But it's not nice to disappear like that. And he should care that you'd worry. You didn't hear from Charlie even once?"

Barlow thinks she did not, a circumstance that bothered Hester. It must hurt May Rose too.

"Not once," she says. "I believe your brothers are not much alike. You know Will is still in Winkler, and he writes to me every year. I sent a telegram saying we were coming here, so he could pass that information to Wanda if they happened to meet."

"I want to meet Wanda too," Glory says. "Mother told me what bits she knew about my brothers. Will was going to visit us one time, then he stayed home because a lot of people were sick with the flu, and he caught it himself."

"Will is always helping," May Rose says. "There's no doctor in a long way, so he reads medical books, and the hill people consider him their doctor. It worries him because he doesn't have real training."

Barlow has one strong memory of Will Herff. "Did your mother tell you about the wildfire that nearly took Winkler? Will was just a boy, yet he helped us save the mill. Men, women, and children, everyone helped." He waits for May Rose to add her account of that day, but she's quiet, and he thinks he knows why. It was the day Charlie ran away. The townspeople searched for the boy for months before giving him up for dead. He was the age Evie is now, nine years old. Later they learned he'd been found and sheltered all that time by May Rose's brother-in-law, Russell Long.

Glory stops her rocking chair. "Let's go to see Will! Winkler isn't that far, is it?"

"Half a day by train to Elkins," he says. "Then you travel for a day or two by road. I wouldn't want you to do that alone."

"Then Uncle, go with us!"

It's an exciting prospect, escorting Glory and May Rose, three days of close company. Also impossible, like most of his fancies. "This is not a good time...a new house..." His words stumble. "Other...arrangements. Besides, your Aunt Alice may need help with your mother's things...packing..."

Behind him, a window closes, Alice shutting them out. He hopes this time he's said the right thing.

~

MAY ROSE

When May Rose opens her eyes the next morning, Evie is sitting at the end of her bed, fully dressed. The house is quiet, also the street, for it's too early for traffic. Today she needs to decide about going home. She's talked with Glory about college. Glory says Alice no longer pesters her about Joseph Treadway, being preoccupied with decisions about a new house.

"I'm hungry," Evie says.

Because Evie seldom asks for anything, May Rose dresses and walks her to the kitchen. Mrs. Banovic is having her own breakfast, wiping tears as she chews. She jumps up and pulls two chairs from the table.

"This nice little girl." She hugs Evie. "I keep, teach to cook."

Evie looks like she wouldn't mind. The Banovics are a handsome, generous couple. From Glory she knows they live above the carriage house, are from Slovakia and have worked for Hester going on eight years.

"Evie would love to learn," May Rose says.

"If Ma lets me." Evie sits and folds her hands on the table.

May Rose stands behind Evie's chair. "Evie woke hungry. Maybe there's something I could prepare? I don't want to make extra work."

"Cooking never like work," Mrs. Banovic says. She ladles stewed apples into a small bowl for Evie. "Where you live is nice? Maybe we visit someday."

"It's nicer here," Evie says. "When we find Ma, we might live here."

When Evie makes one of her rare pronouncements, May Rose wonders if she eavesdrops or read minds, though it's more likely that adults forget she's present, aware and listening.

"Wouldn't that be nice? Of course we'd never have a house like this," May Rose says. "This is special."

For Evie's sake, she hides her fears. Without being told, Evie may know her mother left in an attempt to cure her recent fits of rage. Wanda told Evie she needed to help her grandmother, but she acknowledged to May Rose that she hoped money would solve her problems. Her husband's death had left her poor, exhausted, and sometimes frantic. In exchange for help, her grandmother had promised a reward.

Evie never says she's worried, but worry shows in her frequent small frown. Wanda may be lost forever.

"Miss Hester so good," Mrs. Banovic says. "We eat breakfast here together every day. Now we lose house too. Everything..." She throws up her hands. "In air."

May Rose hasn't considered the effects of Hester's death on the Banovics. "I'm sorry. If I hadn't come, I'd go on thinking of Hester as living, because I would not expect to see her every day. Being here, I feel her loss. When I go home I'll not notice it so much, but all of you will..." She stops, and says it again. "I'm sorry."

Mrs. Banovic is crying. "Very hard let go. Miss Hester never boss, always work with. Mr. Townsend too. They let my brother stay when he burn in mine. One year. He couldn't work, most time in bed. Miss Hester take turns with bandage, carry tray." She shakes her head. "The mine not care. If not us, no one. After year,

Mr. Townsend get him job in railroad shop. At start, I think Mr. Townsend hard man. But now... Best people."

She knows.

5

MAY ROSE

Because she's closer to the place where Wanda is supposed to be, May Rose is hesitant to go home, where they might wait forever for her return. She's tempted to go to Winkler and search, though the region around Winkler is a wilderness. With this in mind, she leaves Evie with Mrs. Banovic and goes to her room to compose a telegram asking Will's advice.

She stops at her door, for an argument is raging across the hall, women's voices, shrill. *Glory and Alice, in Hester's room.* Through Hester's open door, the cleaning girl sends May Rose a look of appeal.

May Rose responds as she would to a battle among children. In Hester's doorway she calls, "Good morning. Can I help with anything?"

The cleaning girl's arms are laden with Hester's dresses, and a mound of other clothing lies on the bed. Standing in a space among wooden crates, Glory and Alice acknowledge May Rose with irritated glances.

Glory clutches a ragged gardening hat to her chest. "I want to do it my way."

"That's no surprise," Alice says. "This time, you must listen to me. I'll dispose of your mother's things. If you want to do something, go to your room and pack what you want to take to that college. Everything else can be stored somewhere."

Alice brushes by May Rose. "I'll leave her to you. Perhaps you can explain this necessity." In the doorway, she turns back to the cleaning girl. "Please go on as I've instructed." Then she leaves.

"*Stored somewhere*," Glory says. "That means I'm not to expect a room in her new house."

May Rose transfers the clothing from the cleaning girl to the bed. She'd like to tell Glory she'll always have a place with her uncle, but who knows how Alice may direct him? What would Hester say? *Carry on my war with Alice?* Probably not. Hester wanted something better for Glory.

"Iris, you may go back to work," Glory says. "If my aunt inquires, tell her May Rose and I will pack Mother's things this morning, and you may finish what's left in the afternoon."

The girl hesitates. "Miss Alice asked if I would take Miss Hester's things."

"Take them?"

"To sell. Instead of pay."

"*What?*"

The cleaning girl looks at the floor. "I'd rather have the money, but I need a job, and she says she'll hire me for the new house."

Glory drops onto a chair and swipes her eyes. "Mother's things are not my aunt's to give away. Iris, I'll make sure you get your pay. And this afternoon you may do what you like with any clothing left in this room."

Hester's skirts and dresses are too short for either of them, but Glory selects a few broaches, a fur neckpiece with gold clips, two long aprons, and the gardening hat. They've buried Hester in her newest ensemble, a wool herringbone suit, over Alice's objections that it was wrong for summer.

For a keepsake, May Rose takes one of Hester's aprons and the volume of Emily Dickenson poems. She scans the room's ornate cherry bed, dresser, desk, and lounging chair, trying to think what Hester might advise.

"Ask your uncle if the furnishings of the house belong to the Hershman estate. If not, you should take your mother's portion."

"Take them? Where? To *storage*?"

"I don't know, but your mother would want you to be practical. In the future, you may need to be concerned about money."

"I'll ask." Glory looks around the room. "I'm going to be on my own, aren't I?"

"Eventually, we're all on our own. You may rely on your uncle, but in many ways you'll be free to make your own way."

"I used to tell Mother I wanted to make my own mistakes. She got so angry."

May Rose thinks of Wanda, ever heedless of instruction and determined to make her own mistakes. "You'll be cautious and remember your mother's words. Now I need to see if Evie is bothering Mrs. Banovic. Are you ready to go down for lunch?"

They carry Glory's keepsakes to her room and descend the stairs together. On the landing, May Rose halts. Alice stands in the open front door, speaking to a young man.

May Rose whispers. "Charlie?"

"We're no longer accepting guests," Alice says.

"It's my brother?" Glory runs ahead. "Charlie?"

May Rose cannot stop her tears. He's nine-years grown, taller and broader in the shoulders, but there's no mistaking his sharp chin and busy eyes.

Glory darts past Alice and seizes his hand. "Charlie! I'm Glory, your sister!"

"Hello, Glory." He lets her hang on his arm while he smiles at May Rose. "I'm not your brother Charlie. I'm your brother Will."

"Will! Just as wonderful!" When May Rose reaches him, he surprises her with a kiss on the cheek. Then they stand back, hands clasped, looking at each other.

Alice has stepped away from the door. "Pardon me," May Rose says. "Alice, this is Will Herff. Will, this is Mrs. Townsend, Barlow's wife."

Will offers his hand to Alice.

She surprises May Rose by accepting it with a graceful smile. "Shall I tell Mrs. Banovic to set another plate for lunch?"

"And dinner," Glory says, "and he'll stay overnight, days, weeks, as long as he wants."

Will has a smile for each of them. "I'm to go back on the evening train."

Glory slides her arm through his and pulls him toward the family parlor. "Absolutely not possible. I won't let you go."

"I have a ticket."

"Uncle Barlow will change it.'"

"I'll tell Mrs. Banovic we have a guest for dinner," Alice says.

May Rose follows Glory and Will into the parlor. His appearance in Grafton means he received the telegram she sent from Fargo. She's eager to know if he saw Wanda.

She sits, hands tightly clasped, as Will asks about Hester and expresses condolences for her passing. Glory asks about his travel and he asks May Rose about her brother-in-law, Russell Long, and if all is well in Fargo.

She makes the polite responses. As far as she knows, Russell and Fargo are fine. But Wanda. Anything could happen, and they might never know. When Glory leaves to tell the cleaning girl to ready his room, it's her turn to ask.

He anticipates her question. "If Wanda is not already in Fargo, she should be reaching there soon."

"So you met. Thank goodness. Did she have a good visit with her grandmother?"

"I suppose she did. There's a lot to tell, and she should be the one to tell it. She had an accident, not serious, but her face required stitches. The bruising will be gone by the time you see her. And her hair will have grown. She cut it off, nearly all."

"Cut her hair? Did she have a reason?"

"You know Wanda. Her hair was full of briars. She had some bad times, but she's fine, or will be soon."

Bad times. Since her husband's death, Wanda's had nothing but bad times. "I'm glad you met."

"I'll say this much. She made good friends."

"I'm relieved to hear it."

He nods, as though he knows what she's thinking. Wanda has always attracted trouble.

Now she and Evie can go home.

~

BARLOW

Barlow's dinner hour is happier than it's been in many years. He lifts his wine glass and smiles at his wife. Even she seems to like Will Herff, though he wears the clothes of a workman.

Alice smiles in return, then looks from Glory to Will and back to Barlow again. He gets her silent messages. If Glory doesn't marry, she can live with her brother.

At every dinner hour, he's careful to be polite to May Rose while devoting himself to his wife. Does this seem strange to Alice? His happiness is so obvious to himself he's certain everyone sees it.

The air is still and humid, and from time to time the ladies lift their napkins to blot their cheeks and foreheads. Wine makes him warmer. Beneath his coat, shirt and undershirt, sweat runs down his sides. He sobers, imagining dinners when they've all gone, dinners alone with Alice.

Will is a well-spoken young man, and already Glory loves him. May Rose's cheeks are flushed, and though Barlow knows her delight is due to the presence of Will Herff, it makes him glad. When she was new to Winkler, she took care of the motherless Herff children for a short time. But for his interference, she might have married their father, Morris Herff, an abusive man. If she knew he saved her from that fate, would she be grateful?

She has survived on her own. He admires that, and her silent grasp of essential things. He smiles again at his wife, but she is busy listening to Will.

Everyone lingers at the table after dessert. "Tell me about our father," Glory says.

Will hesitates while Banovic fills his wine glass from their last legal bottle. "What do you know?"

"That his name was Morris and he worked for Uncle Barlow, sharpening the mill's saws. That when your mother died, *our* mother, he had no one to take care of me."

"He was an artist, a carver," Will says. "He made beautiful furniture. Violins, too."

May Rose's smile fades. Barlow doubts Hester told Glory everything they knew about Morris Herff. That he beat his sons, was rumored to have beaten their mother, and neglected Glory to the point of abuse.

"Did you know my pa?" Evie's freckles stand out on her pale face. It's the first time she's spoken this evening.

"I'm sorry to say I did not," Will says. "I know his name. I know your pa had red hair and freckles, like you. I know he was a good man."

Barlow envies how Will brings back May Rose's smile. Will's face broadens each time he looks her way. He's years younger, of course, but he himself is many years her senior. The heart is not always sensible.

They adjourn to the cool of the porch, and this time Alice comes too. Glory and Alice take the rockers each side of Will, leaving a place on the loveseat beside May Rose. He avoids that danger by leaning against the porch rail. Evie sits with May Rose.

"I'm sure the ladies have questioned you all day," Barlow says, "but I'd like to hear what's happening in Winkler."

"You'd think," Alice says, "that Winkler was some seaside resort, the way Hester and Barlow spoke of it. A temporary mill town. In the mountains!"

"It was a fine town," Will says. "Your husband managed everything—the town, the mill and logging. The houses for mill families were well-built. Everyone admired Hester's boardinghouse. There were good people there—I wish we had some of them now."

"*People like May Rose,*" Alice says. Her voice teases.

Will lifts his wine glass. "*Exactly* like May Rose."

Exactly. And Barlow is going to lose her again. She and Evie are leaving tomorrow for Fargo.

Evie gets up and stands in front of Will, and he makes room for her to sit beside him. Will has an engaging manner with everyone, and evidently children too. Barlow would like to do something for him, help him along in business. Hester would approve, and Glory would like it.

"I'm sure it was quite the society," Alice says. "But I hope to goodness I never have to live in such a place."

No one adds a comment to her sentiments.

Barlow leaves the rail and sits on the steps where there's better movement of air. "We've heard, Will, that you bought all the Winkler holdings."

"Not everything on the other side of the river. Just the valley, the town, and some of the mountain on the town side. Everything was in ruin, but now I have three occupied houses, the store, and a new grist mill. I hold Trading Days every full moon. I hope the town will grow."

"I admire your work," Barlow says. "But I doubt the town will grow without a railroad. There can be no commercial industry without good transportation. I suspect your roads are passable only part of the year."

"There's some interest in coal," Will says, "so the railroad may return to Winkler."

Alice gives an audible yawn. She's always bored by business talk. After ten years, he still doesn't know how to please her.

A bicycle stops on the sidewalk, and a telegraph messenger walks to the steps.

"More business," Alice says.

"Telegram for Mrs. May Rose Long," the boy says.

May Rose takes it inside to read in the light. He hears her tear the seal. They're quiet until she comes back to the porch.

"It's from Wanda. She's coming here, to Grafton."

Evie jumps up and hugs May Rose. Barlow tightens his jaw to hold back a smile.

"Barlow, telegraph immediately," Alice says, "and tell this person there's no need to come. Hester has passed, and May Rose will be traveling west in the morning."

"Her name is Wanda," he says. "She's Evie's mother. May Rose, shall I do that? Or do you want to wait for her to arrive?"

"Evie and I should go," she says.

"Then I'll send the telegram. Will, would you like to walk to the train station with me?"

"Take the automobile," Alice says.

"Nonsense. A five-minute walk will make no difference." The walk will take twenty minutes, but his wife has no idea—she walks nowhere. She seldom goes out of the house.

Along the way, Will admires Grafton's street lights. "I'd like Winkler to be a good place to live. With electric and safe water to the houses. Inside plumbing that doesn't flush into the river. A school. A real doctor. It doesn't have to have industry."

Barlow seldom hears ambition like this, unrelated to personal gain. "Unless you can afford to fire a power plant, you won't have electric without industry. I doubt there will be commercial timber for another hundred years." When he managed the Winkler sawmill, the plant's sawdust fueled the town's electricity.

They wait at the railroad crossing for a long coal train to pass. It's empty, on its way to some coal camp. After they cross the tracks, he points to sidings where full cars stand ready for Baltimore markets.

"Grafton has grown because the B&O built branch lines to coal towns. Now with the war in Europe, we're in a coal boom; companies can't fill the demand, and the railroad can't find enough cars to carry it. Munitions manufacturers and shippers all burn coal. If America gets into the war, demand will only grow."

"Swelling the fortunes of the wealthy," Will says.

They're quiet for half a block. Barlow's work for the railroad has shown him the ugliness of enterprises built by wealthy men as well as by the penniless scoundrels who've invaded the region, pretending to know about coal. Still, he wishes that while he was attending to the needs of Winkler Logging and Lumber and the B&O Railroad, he'd paid more attention to the growth of his own finances. He's just offered to pay his entire savings for a new house.

"I own a coal seam," Will says. "You remember the coal bank uphill from the store? I'd like to find an honest man to evaluate it."

Barlow approves the lack of excitement in Will's description. Will is not dreaming of riches; he needs to know what he has, perhaps to protect his property.

"I'm sure you know that most mines are killers," Barlow says. "Even when an operator follows every safety regulation, disasters happen. There've been two this year, Layland and Carlisle. I suppose you heard of them."

"I did."

"Have you had offers to buy your mineral rights?"

"A couple of times."

"I can introduce you to a mining engineer or two. But you saw the end of Winkler's lumber industry. If you bring in a coal operator, Winkler will boom for a while, then the seams will play out. The town will have no lasting industry because it is not on a port or a road to anywhere. Which, incidentally, may also make it a good place to live for the few who can sustain themselves."

"I dig and sell a little coal for local use," Will says. "I don't want to let a mining company come in unless I can have some control. If I was rich, I'd have no trouble getting a loan to start my own company."

To Barlow, Will's life seems ideal. His town is remote and has no conveniences, but he answers to no boss and has no demanding customers.

"Before you decide whether or not to develop your mine, you might visit some coal camps. See if this is what you want in your valley."

"I'd have to be involved," Will says. "I've read about strikes and killings. Surely a business can be operated for the benefit of all."

"You would think so," Barlow says. He knows no industry that cares about benefitting workers. "But the problems of running a dangerous business aren't all about safety. At a Farmington mine near here, management decided miners were pulverizing coal because they used too much blasting powder. To make them use powder more prudently, the company started charging for it. I guess there was some other compensation, but the miners said it wasn't enough to make up for their new costs. Most of the miners were immigrants, and they led the strikes. Some said they were socialists."

"Developing a coal business is just an idea," Will says. "I've about made up my mind to study medicine."

"Medicine!" Barlow stops. "No money in that, especially not if you stay in Winkler. But you've said you're not interested in money."

"I'm interested in money if it can do some good."

"Then you'll be wise to strive for the best mine or none at all. One with electric cars and tools and a good ventilation system. You want an operator who exceeds the safety regulations instead of looking the other way."

"Sure to be rare and expensive," Will says.

"You don't have to do anything now. The coal has waited millions of years—it will be there when you're ready."

"I think I'm never satisfied," Will says.

"Then you may do well." Barlow says no more. Satisfaction is a perilous topic.

At the telegraph office, he copies and sends May Rose's message to Wanda, advising her not to come and asking for a reply. He hopes his telegram will arrive too late. He's not ready to say goodbye.

6

MAY ROSE

It seems Wanda is on her way, for they've received no response to Barlow's telegram. May Rose is caught between Evie's excitement and Alice Townsend's aversion to more guests.

"This is a difficult time for Mrs. Townsend," she says to Barlow. "And I don't want to add my family to her burden. When Wanda comes, we'll move to a hotel or another guest house."

They're walking to the train station to see Will off, she and Barlow following Glory and Will, who stroll arm in arm.

"Glory will be disappointed if you move," he says. "As for Alice, she's never let herself be burdened by our guests. She's not totally well, and has always let others run the house."

May Rose can't think why Wanda is making this return trip, unless she hopes to see Hester. "I'm sure we won't stay much longer," she says.

"Then please remain as you are."

She stumbles on the walk's uneven bricks, and he pulls her arm through his. "Rough going here. Lean on me."

They've walked like this on Winkler's gritty street, times when she was grateful for the sturdiness of his arm, and in winter, when he blocked the wind. She's grateful now, and can't help wondering as they walk in step if they might have been suited after all, or if it's only that they're more comfortable as friends.

"Is there some way I might help Mrs. Townsend?"

"Don't worry yourself," he says. "Hester stopped trying to please Alice long ago. She rests morning and afternoon, and spends her time reading. Her opinions always clashed with Hester's, but she's quite intelligent. She likes her life, such as it is."

Alice Townsend does not seem like a woman who likes her life, but May Rose doesn't want to say anything that could not be said in her presence. One thing she can say. "She's beautiful."

"Yes. I don't think she's aged a day since I married her. While I..."

"Look no older than the last time I saw you." She means only to reassure, because he sounds gloomy. But her comment may have embarrassed him, for as Will and Glory stop and look back, he releases her arm.

She doubts he's told his wife everything.

~

It's afternoon, and with Will gone and Wanda on her way, the atmosphere in the house is less hospitable. May Rose is helping Glory sort her clothes, some for a college trunk, some for storage, and some to be made over for Evie. The open windows bring only blasts of heat, and they stop from time to time to sip icy glasses of water.

Glory tosses a dress toward a pile on her bed, the clothes for make-over. They're of strong material, well-stitched and un-faded. May Rose thinks Glory will not mind if she alters a dress or two for herself.

"I loved having Will here," Glory says. "Now I'm eager to see Wanda. I feel like she's my long-lost sister."

May Rose folds a coat and lays it in a hand-embroidered laundry bag. "Wanda calls me 'Ma,' but she acts more like a sister." She smiles. "A bossy sister."

"Mother said she's not much younger than you."

"Seven years. When I married her father, I didn't know he had another woman and a little girl."

Glory presses a folded dress to her chest. "I thought Wanda's mother was dead. Was her father a bigamist? Or were they divorced?"

"They never married. My husband abandoned Wanda and her mother, and later he left me."

May Rose sits on the bed. She has no idea what Hester has told Glory about men. Such a talk is important to give grown-up girls in the orphanage, soon to face the world alone, and she is often the one to give it. She thinks she has more experience than the other matrons, though she has never shared it. This may be the time.

"A girl or woman alone is always at risk," she says. "But I was not alone when I married my husband. I had a good family, my uncle's family. I was young and foolish, and I fell in love and married too soon. My husband brought me to Winkler, far from my family."

"And left you there?"

"Not immediately. We had a cabin a few hours from town."

"Mother said you lived on a mountain."

"It was very remote. I had no neighbors, and he was there only on weekends. He worked in a lumber camp, higher on the mountain. Then he stopped coming home. He may have been seeing Wanda's mother, or other women."

"I'm sorry," Glory says. "He must have been a fool."

This is the first advice she gives the orphanage girls. *A man may be handsome and charming, full of promises and even well-regarded by others, but you must know him well before sealing your life to his.*

"I was a fool, too, and not just in choosing my husband. My uncle was a decent man, and I didn't know all men weren't like him. I didn't know how men like to brag and how cruel they can be."

"Mother told me about some of her boardinghouse customers," Glory says.

"I'm glad she did. It's not safe to be sheltered from such knowledge. A woman must also understand that even her innocent, well-meant acts can bring trouble. Like waving to strangers."

Glory's arms are still crossed over the folded dress. "You did that?"

"It sounds terrible, doesn't it? A railroad track ran past our cabin and trains went back and forth to the logging camps. Most days, the train operators were the only people I saw. The engineer, the fireman and brakeman. They always waved, and I waved back. They seemed to be kind men, and I got to know their faces. But loggers rode the trains too, going down to Winkler for Saturday night. I suppose that's how the talk started."

"I think I can guess. They called you a loose woman."

"Something like that. My husband fought a man in his camp and knifed him to death. He blamed me, said it was because of what I'd done. Not my waving, he said there were worse things. Then he ran from the law, and I was truly alone."

Glory's eyes are wide. "Mother said your husband was killed in a train accident."

"That was later."

"Did Mother know the rest of it?"

"All of Winkler knew the gossip and what my husband did. They knew about him and Wanda's mother too. Your mother and uncle believed I'd done no wrong, and in many ways they saved me. Wanda saved me too, coming to my cabin after her father left me. I loved her from the start. Later I got to know her mother, a sweet woman. She was ill, then she died."

There's no need to tell Glory how Wanda's mother made her living and that Wanda's experiences with men were worse than her own. Wanda is no longer frank about such things because she doesn't want Evie to know. But someday they must tell Evie that all men aren't as good as her father.

Glory drops the dress into her trunk. "What a story! But I'm sorry it happened to you."

"I no longer think about it. I've been fortunate to have good friends." Her face is hot and her mouth and throat are dry; she sips from the water glass.

Glory picks a paper from the floor, presses the paper on a tabletop and begins to make narrow accordion folds. "I was lucky to have Mother and Uncle Barlow. I'm sure Wanda knows she's lucky to have you. I do want to get to know her. We're all orphans, aren't we?" She pinches the folds at the narrow end and spreads the rest to make a fan. "You absolutely cannot leave as soon as she arrives."

Too much depends on Wanda. "I know she would like to know you too. But it's awkward, being here, because Alice doesn't want us. You see, your uncle once offered to marry me. I suspect Alice knows."

Glory hands her the folded fan. "Mother told me about that."

May Rose flutters it in front of her face. *Surely not all.* Not how Hester warned Barlow against her. Not details of Barlow's first proposal and how it ended. Not how she humiliated him and Hester too, revealing everything in front of the dining room guests.

"If Aunt Alice doesn't want you here," Glory says, "it's because Mother liked you. She didn't like Mother and she doesn't like me."

May Rose wonders if Alice likes her husband. "I think she liked Will."

"She did, didn't she? But he's a young, handsome man. Please don't go too soon. Having you here makes me happy, and Uncle Barlow too. Stay until I'm settled; I don't want to be alone with her."

"I'll try to stay as long as you need me. I'm surprised Wanda is making the trip east again so soon. I left a message about your mother at her house. It's possible she decided to visit your mother before..."

"Yes. Mother would have been happy to see Wanda. But I hope she won't be hurt when Aunt Alice slights her."

May Rose chuckles. "Wanda has never been bothered by slights. We may have to protect your aunt."

"Better and better," Glory says. "Believe it or not, Aunt Alice has been agreeable lately. We haven't squabbled over the furnishings, I guess because she and Mother never liked what the other chose. Uncle Barlow is arranging to store everything from my bedroom and Mother's. He'll keep what's in his apartment, and we'll sell and divide the proceeds from the rest. So everything is working out, except where I'm to perch when I'm not at college."

Glory pauses. "You're going to say that will work out too."

"I have every confidence." May Rose threads a needle to reattach a button. It's impossible not to have confidence in Glory, who is young and resilient, who will receive an inheritance from Hester, and who will have Barlow and perhaps Will to look out for her. She has no confidence in herself, almost no money, no close family but Wanda and Evie, and no home but an orphanage. Perhaps by the end of the year she'll receive Hester's bequest, but that must be put aside for the time when she can no longer work.

Now Wanda is traveling to meet her. And how bad was her bad time?

~

BARLOW

They've not heard from Wanda, and now Barlow must travel on railroad business. He may never see May Rose again.

He's distressed by one other fact. May Rose may be rich in spirit, but she's poor in the world's goods. He doesn't care that the heels of her shoes are run down or that the straw is breaking at the edges of her hat. He worries that someday she may be cold and alone. He thinks Glory shares his concern, for she's asked him to confer privately in her room.

"You've made progress," he says. As in Hester's suite, every surface has been cleared. Glory's easel is folded against the wall, her paint box is shut, no brushes soak in thinner, and her sewing machine is folded into its table.

She motions him to sit beside her in one of the chairs she upholstered in shining green and pink-flowered cloth.

"Did you show your chairs and your paintings to your brother?"

"No, would he be interested?"

"'I think so. You're artistic, like your father."

"Mother never mentioned that. Do you know, many people think I'm her natural child. I think she enjoyed the sensation of people thinking she gave birth to me without being married."

He believes it; he's done his share of explaining how Hester acquired her daughter. "Does that bother you?"

"Why should I care?"

Memory catches him, and he smiles. "You should have seen her back then, how fierce she was, claiming you. May Rose wanted you too. You changed our life." He's close to tears.

"Lucky for me. How did they decide who got me?"

"You decided for them."

She laughs. "I'd have been all right with May Rose."

"Even though she's poor."

"I know," Glory says. "It's why I want to talk here, where we can plot in secret."

He leans back in the flowered chair and crosses his legs. "Oh, my. Plots and secrets."

"We should do something for May Rose," she says. "You mentioned you might find work for her."

"And you heard her say her plans will depend on Wanda."

"Money, then."

"She has a small bequest from your mother."

"If other claims don't absorb it."

Like his cousin's fees. He pulls from his wallet all the cash he's put by for the week's travel. "I'll think about it while I'm gone. This is for emergencies."

"For May Rose?"

"For anything you need. Your mother always kept ready cash. I don't want to leave you with nothing. You're good to think about helping May Rose. Let's watch for an opportunity."

Glory folds the bills into a leather drawstring purse. It looks like the one Hester kept tied at her waist. She asks, "Where are you going this time?"

"I'll be convincing coal operators along the Ohio River to sell to Baltimore markets."

Glory kisses his cheek. "So they'll ship their coal on the B&O. I forecast late dinners and smoke-filled rooms. Best carry your bicarbonate. Take heart, Uncle. Maybe she'll be here when you return. Maybe she'll never leave."

He has no expectations.

~

MAY ROSE

May Rose expects that she and Evie will be gone when Barlow returns from his trip.

He comes to the kitchen at breakfast time, carrying a suitcase. "I've come to say goodbye."

Rising from the table to give him her hand, she focuses on his forehead. Back then, she needed months to recognize his feeling, but she sees it readily now. She dare not look into his eyes.

"Safe travel, and thank you for our stay." She has stopped addressing him by name.

"You were good to come," he says. "Give Wanda my best." He hurries away.

~

Changes are rapidly unfurling in the house. In the past two days, the Banovics and the cleaning girl have crowded everything to be sold into the formal parlor and dining room downstairs and in four guest bedrooms upstairs. Glory says her aunt has agreed to a smaller house on the same avenue, one with a library, a rose garden, and a servant's room over the carriage house. Alice seems happy issuing orders.

At noon, May Rose receives another telegram from Wanda, sent during a Wheeling layover, saying to expect her on the 7:35 passenger. That evening, she huddles with Evie and Glory under the eaves of the depot. A storm has broken the heat, and though they hold umbrellas, their skirts are heavy with rain. The 7:35 has arrived, but among all who hurry from the cars they see no one who matches Wanda's form and face.

Evie tugs on her arm. "Maybe she can't walk. Maybe she's waiting for us to help her off the train."

"We'll see her any minute now," May Rose says.

Evie's voice rises. "Maybe she got left somewhere."

"I'm sure that didn't happen." But like Evie, May Rose always fears Wanda may be in trouble.

Then they see her farther down the track, standing in the rain among packing crates. Evie breaks loose and splashes through the puddles, and Wanda turns and holds out her arms. May Rose and Glory hurry under their umbrellas.

For Evie's sake, she hides her shock at the pink puckered stripes of new skin on Wanda's face. Short rust-colored curls straggle beneath her hat. She gives them her lopsided grin. "I made it."

May Rose struggles not to cry. "Do you remember our Glory?"

"Not like this." Wanda shakes her dripping hat and plops it back on her curls. "You've sure grown up pretty." She waves a hand over the crates. "I didn't take time to sell my stuff."

Sell? She is never prepared for Wanda. "If I'd telegraphed our news, you could have taken your time. Hester has passed away."

"Oh, I'm sorry," Wanda says. "I did want to meet her again." She winks at Glory. "And see her eyes pop when she gave me the once-over."

Glory laughs. "I know what you mean. I'm sorry I missed that too."

"Let's get out of the rain," May Rose says. She looks at the crates. "What did you bring?"

"Just about everything. I'm gonna try Winkler again. It feels like home."

Home?

Glory motions for a porter. "I so want to see Winkler. My brother told us about it when he was here."

There's no missing Wanda's reaction, a stretch of eyebrows and slight opening of her lips. "Will Herff?"

"He left a few days ago," Glory says.

The rain ends. They shake and fold their umbrellas as a porter loads Wanda's crates and luggage on a cart. May Rose's thoughts are tangled. "You want to live in Winkler?"

"You're welcome to come along," Wanda says. "Will said he'd like to have you in his town."

Will. He barely spoke of her, but there's decision in Wanda's voice when she says his name.

"I'll have to think," May Rose says. But maybe she doesn't.

Evie tugs her mother's arm. "Will there be lots of children?"

"Almost none," Wanda says. "Is that all right?"

"I might like it."

"McGraw Avenue," Glory says, laying a coin in the porter's hand. "The Townsend Guesthouse. You may leave everything on the porch."

On the porch. Alice will not like this.

7

Wanda's crates have remained on the Townsend's porch all night without objection from Alice, who did not appear when they returned from the station. May Rose sat there with Wanda, Evie and Glory past midnight, listening for signs that Wanda's troubles are over. Wanda made light of her accident and spoke only briefly of finding her granny and two aunts. Mostly she entertained Glory with stories of Charlie, funny stories of boyish pranks in Fargo. She didn't mention his terrible childhood in Winkler, for Evie is a rapt listener.

The morning is humid again, and Alice does not come to breakfast. "Mrs. Townsend never eat here," Mrs. Banovic says. She serves them gravy and biscuits at the kitchen's enamel-top table, because the dining room is laden with dinner china, house linens and ornaments to be sold.

May Rose watches Wanda take second helpings. She's too thin. Her face is scarred and her nose is crooked. A fall from her horse, she told them, prompting Evie to say she would never ride a horse and Wanda to say it wasn't the horse's fault.

"Granny has a plow horse they call Old Henry," Wanda says. "Old Henry's best friend is a dog that follows him everywhere. They call him *Old Henry's Dog*."

In Wanda's nervous chatter, May Rose senses something untold that's neither nice nor funny. Yet Wanda is eager to go back.

Evie asks, "Is this the day we're going to Winkler?"

"It could be." Wanda turns to May Rose. "I'll wait until you're ready. If you've decided to come with us."

She's thought about it all night. "Russell might send my things." Few as they are.

Wanda's mouth is full, and she holds up a finger while she finishes chewing. "I forgot to say. Uncle Russell has gone looking for Charlie again. Left a note nailed to my door."

Glory stops her teacup halfway to her lips. "Russell the wild man?"

Wanda laughs. "Wild man—I guess some would say he is. He's brother to my pa. He's forever going to stock sales and packing houses, asking cowboys if they know Charlie. Then he rides out every summer to search."

The excitement on Glory's face embraces them all. "I always wanted to see the wild man. And Charlie."

"Russell found Charlie the first time he run off," Wanda says. "That was back in Winkler. You might as well come with us, Ma. Uncle Russell will find us."

Wanda is like a strong current, whirling her along. "I want to see Glory settled in college. And I'll need work. Will I find that in Winkler?"

"Plenty of work, nobody to pay. I got enough to get us through winter. Then we'll plant a garden, raise pigs and chickens, sell ginseng. We'll make things to trade."

"It sounds like fun," Glory says. "The college term doesn't start for a month. May I go too?"

Wanda tilts her head and appraises Glory. "You might not like it. First..." she looks at May Rose. "The train takes us only to Elkins. Then we go two days by road."

"We can take Uncle Barlow's auto. He taught me to drive."

Wanda laughs. "An auto wouldn't get over that road. Horse and wagon."

"Even better," Glory says. "Won't Will be surprised!"

May Rose's thoughts are jumbled. She's unwilling to let them go without her and reluctant to leave children who must be wondering where she is.

Mrs. Banovic bursts into the kitchen with Alice's tray. "Mrs. Townsend on floor, not get up!"

She leads them to Alice's bedroom. "I try help up." She flicks her hand. "She all floppy."

Alice lies on a woven carpet of green foliage and white birds. Glory stoops and touches her arm. "Aunt Alice. Are you all right? Can you sit up?"

Alice's eyes shift to Glory. "Gili," she says. Saliva drools from the side of her mouth.

Mrs. Banovic wraps her arms around Alice's chest, and with Glory and May Rose each holding a leg, they lift her onto the bed.

Alice blinks from one to the other. "Why are you handling me?"

"Aunt Alice, thank goodness." Glory takes her hand. "You had a spell. I think you fainted on the floor."

"Do I know you?"

May Rose whispers to Glory. "You should call a doctor."

Alice tries to lift her head. "Why am I not dressed? I was going to church." Her summer nightdress reveals bony shoulders and a thin chest.

"Call your uncle, too," May Rose says.

"No, don't call Barlow," Alice waves like she's brushing away a fly. "He's traveling. Important business. Always."

"But the doctor," Glory says. "Just as a precaution." She hurries out.

Alice directs her stare to Mrs. Banovic. "A few sips of my tonic." Mrs. Banovic follows Glory. Alice grips May Rose's hand. "Don't leave me."

"Do you know who I am?"

"What a question," Alice says. "You're the woman everyone loves. I'll think of your name in a minute. Would you find my bed jacket? I'm feeling naked, with the church so full of people."

Is it heat stroke? Already, hot sun fills the room, and there's not a breath of air. "May I pull down the blinds?"

"I like the sun to shine in," Alice says. "And I'm cold."

Mrs. Banovic comes back with a small glass of red liquid. Alice's hand is shaky, so May Rose tips the glass to her lips while Mrs. Banovic finds the bed jacket, pale silk with satin ties. Mrs. Banovic puts the jacket over Alice's shoulders, makes a bow at her neck and helps her lie back on the pillow.

The doctor arrives, listens to Alice's heart and pulse, then sits by the bed and asks questions about ordinary things. *Where's Barlow? How did your cherry trees do this year? Your mother and father, when did they pass away? Do you know what took them?*

"My baby died," Alice says.

Glory and May Rose watch from the door. Glory whispers, "If she's not better tomorrow, I'm calling Uncle Barlow."

May Rose goes to find Wanda. Glory will not be able to leave with them until her uncle returns.

"We can wait until then," Wanda says. "I'll walk Evie uptown so she can look in the store windows."

After the doctor leaves, Glory comes to the kitchen where May Rose is sitting with Mr. and Mrs. Banovic. "The doctor says she's had a seizure or a light stroke. He's prescribed rest. May Rose, she's asking for you."

"For me?"

Glory shrugs.

When May Rose enters the bedroom, Alice motions to a chest of drawers. "Top, on the right. A handkerchief, if you please."

She finds two embroidered handkerchiefs trimmed in lace.

"I've thought of your name. *May Rose.*" Alice wipes her tears. "A sentimental name. Do you like it?"

"It's my given name. I have no choice."

"You could call yourself something else. Whatever you like."

"It's not important. People are used to this one."

Alice gives her the damp handkerchief and tucks the clean one up her sleeve. "Hester doesn't like me, but she loves you. So I think you might tell me how to please her."

"Alice?"

"What? Oh, I see. Hester is dead, I know that. But it's true, she never liked me."

May Rose lays the damp handkerchief on the night stand. "Hester didn't always like me. We grew closer because of our letters, mostly about Glory."

"Yes, Glory, a spoiled, indulged child. She's yet to discover the real world."

May Rose bristles at this rude appraisal, and is tempted to ask which real world Alice knows. But Alice is not well, and she does not want to create more grief for Glory and Barlow. "I'm sure Hester appreciated you, because she loved her brother, and he loves you."

"I should have refused him," Alice says. "Remained single, like you."

"I was married," May Rose says.

"So you were. Mrs. Long, May Rose Long. Was Mr. Long important in some way?"

Hester never wrote anything critical about Alice, but it's not difficult to imagine their interactions. May Rose takes a long breath before she replies. "He was important to his mother, I'm sure. For a while he was important to me."

"So he was nobody." Alice moves her head on the pillow from side to side. "Hester thought I was lazy. Barlow thinks I read too much, but I know who put that idea in his head. It doesn't matter. I worry about more important things than what others think of me. The liner Lusitania, sunk by those Germans. Did you hear of that in the West?"

"Of course. Everyone talked of it."

"No one in this house cares what I think," Alice says. "It's Europe's war, but we will profit from it. Even if German U-boats sink half our merchant ships, our coal barons and munitions manufacturers will send what Europe needs to keep the war alive.

Possibly to both sides. Now those awful Zeppelins are bombing London. We'll get into that war, no matter what President Wilson says. It may come here. Do you worry about that?"

"I'm not as well informed as I might be," May Rose says. "As for the problems of the world, I'm afraid I've always been distracted by problems closer to hand."

"I'm warm now." Alice turns back her sheet, pulls her handkerchief from her sleeve and blots her face. Her thin gown has pulled up, revealing stick-thin legs. "I suppose you think I have no problems."

For the good of the household, Hester must have learned to avoid open combat with Alice, but May Rose's patience is frayed. Silently she counts to ten. "I don't pretend to understand anyone's problems, but I should be better informed about world events. Now I have time, but I'm so far behind. Names and places in the news confuse me. I envy your knowledge."

"You understand me," Alice says, "and you've made yourself useful. You have no clothes, but you have the air of needing nothing. As if you could have anything you want."

May Rose grips her hands behind her back. "I'll be leaving soon. My stepdaughter arrived last night from Fargo. Evie's mother."

"Hand me my newspaper."

May Rose gives her a *Pittsburgh Press* from the top of a stack of papers.

"I know who Evie's mother is," Alice says. "I haven't lost all my wits. Just a little sketchy today. It's the heat. But you. You watch and say nothing, like Barlow. Don't you know how silence disturbs people? I suppose you think I'm lazy too."

"Of course not. We don't know each other."

"They've talked behind my back."

"Not to me."

"You feel sorry for me."

"I'm only sorry you don't feel well."

Alice reaches for May Rose's hand. "Don't let her call Barlow home, not yet. And that girl of yours, she can't stay. We're moving, my husband and I."

May Rose goes to the door. "I'll tell them you're feeling better."

"May Rose?"

She stops. "Yes?"

"You can't have what's mine," Alice says.

~

The next morning, Alice comes to the kitchen and stops by the table where May Rose and Wanda are finishing breakfast. "Banovic has hired movers for today. So if you people have somewhere else to go, perhaps you should go there."

"Suits me," Wanda says.

May Rose stands. "We were to leave yesterday, but did not think we should go while you were ill."

"I'm fine," Alice says. She gives Wanda an accusing look. "Please do something with those crates on my porch. I don't want the movers taking them to my new house."

Wanda twitches her eyebrows. "*Yes, ma'am!*"

May Rose stifles a smile.

~

They oblige Glory by staying one more day. Wanda ships her crates ahead to Elkins, and Glory directs the movers to store her furnishings in the carriage house of her aunt and uncle's new home. May Rose and Evie spend the morning walking through town and watching trains come and go. At noon, they join Glory and Wanda in the dining room of the Willard Hotel, where Glory treats them to lunch.

May Rose is not sure Glory should go with them. "Your uncle might prefer that you stay with your aunt until he returns," she says.

Glory waves aside her concern. "Oh, Aunt Alice is her old self again. She doesn't need to move to the new house so soon; she's doing it so we'll have nowhere to sleep."

Wanda looks around at the hotel's pillars and high ceilings, the chandeliers, linen-covered tables and fine china. "Winkler's rough, like no place you've been, I betcha."

"I'm tired of places I've been," Glory says. "It's my brother's town, so I'll like it."

For Evie's sake, May Rose pretends there are good things ahead for all. Separating her life from the orphanage will be difficult. Like a husband, it has been her provider, and the orphans her children. But like Glory, she's tired of places she's been, and she's eager to leave Alice's house.

They go with Glory to her uncle's office, three floors up in the B&O station, where Glory gives a letter to a woman to put on his desk.

Glory has a railroad pass. May Rose gets a refund on her return ticket to Fargo and purchases one to Elkins. She adds the bills to the coin purse in her skirt pocket and clips its chain to her belt.

For the evening meal, a haggard Mrs. Banovic brings sandwiches to the porch. All day she's moved kitchen and pantry items into crates to be carried down the street to Alice's new house. Her husband brings a tray of water glasses.

Alice takes a glass from the tray. She wears a pretty white cleaning cap, and her dress is covered by an apron without smudge or wrinkle.

Glory turns to Banovic. "I know my uncle would not like us to travel with a chaperone. Could you ride with us to Winkler? We're leaving tomorrow."

Alice, whose posture is always rigid, seems to grow taller in her chair. "Absolutely not. I need Banovic to arrange things in the new house. You uncle will want to see everything in place."

With apologetic smiles for Glory, Mr. and Mrs. Banovic pass quietly into the house.

"Well, Aunt Alice," Glory says, "should we stay here another week? In your new house? We can help—many hands make light work."

Alice wraps a handkerchief around the sweaty glass. "You should not delay on my account."

"Then please explain to my uncle why we left without a chaperone."

Alice does not respond. Wanda hugs Evie. "We don't need a chaperone. Four big girls, what can happen?"

8

Since settling beside May Rose in the passenger car, Wanda has been describing how Winkler has grown: a new grist mill and a total of nine residents, counting children. Gone are the smoky trains and screaming saws of the old days. Wanda speaks of birds in a clear sky, the sound of water rushing over rocks in the river. Goats and dogs. And sprinkled through every description, his name. *Will.*

Glory and Evie sit across from them. Glory, who is just as eager to talk about Will, may not notice Wanda's obsession. But Evie does. She steals glances at her mother and May Rose.

For Evie, May Rose maintains a smile of assurance. The smile has soothed others, seldom herself.

"Will lives in his store," Wanda says. "He cooks, digs coal, does all kinds of work. People call him Doc, have I told you? He sewed my lip."

May Rose nods. Wanda has said all this before; the retelling betrays her. She's had no private time to ask Wanda about her scars or the more worrisome topic, her fits. Perhaps the trip has cured her, or she's been cured by her new interest in Will Herff.

Evie lays the doll on Glory's lap and unbuttons its white christening dress. "Did he cut your hair?"

Wanda touches her hair like she's forgotten about it. "Your granny cut it. Granny Lucie. When I fell off my horse into all those brambles, my hair got too tangled to comb. But it's growing, see?"

Apparently satisfied, Evie pulls off the doll's dress and takes another from a bag of doll clothes.

Wanda lies easily, and May Rose has known her too long to be fooled. She's said nothing about her grandmother's request for help, and she's had more than a fall from a horse. She may never tell.

Glory, whose lips rise easily in a smile and whose eyebrows seem always lifted in anticipation, listens to Wanda like she's Annie Oakley.

"The house won't have inside plumbing, just a hand pump on the porch," Wanda says. "No electric, no telephone, no daily mail or newspaper. No shops, just Will's store, and not much in it."

But a house, May Rose thinks. Not a two-room cottage that belongs to the orphanage, not a back room in a boardinghouse or a richly-furnished suite in the house now being emptied by Alice.

Walls of her own, after Wanda marries Will. He may not have caught up with her affection, but Wanda is unstoppable. May Rose feels hopeful. Wanda's spells of rage may have ended.

"Everything sounds fresh and unspoiled," Glory says.

"Oh, no, it's plenty spoiled. Wait till you see the burned trees. But the land is coming back."

"Uncle Barlow would like to see it."

Barlow. Someday, when time has reduced everything to insignificance, May Rose will let herself reflect on that awkward interval with his wife. Glory did not share what she wrote in the letter left in her uncle's office. Perhaps details about her stored furniture, where she's gone and when he might expect her to return. Perhaps a complaint about Alice turning them out.

Until her few possessions find their way from Fargo, May Rose has not even a wash rag to contribute to their new house. She regrets the pride that kept her from asking for the mended sheets and dented cookware Alice directed to the trash heap.

Looking back, she regrets her unintended role in Alice Townsend's unhappiness. Looking ahead, she wonders if in the Winkler house they'll start by sleeping on the floor.

There's a three-hour layover at a crossroads called Belington while they wait for another passenger train to Elkins. A few minutes' walk takes them the length and breadth of the town's business district, smaller than Grafton's, but with a bricked street and a few two- and three-story brick buildings. Coal cars wait on a siding here, as in every settlement they've passed. Tracks along their way have taken them by more coal tipples and shanty towns than fields of corn. They've glimpsed flat land only in strips by creeks and rivers.

Seeking shade, they follow Wanda into Shinn's General Store. While Glory takes Evie to look at children's boots, Wanda speaks quietly to the clerk. "A handgun, medium size, a holster, and bullets."

May Rose moves closer, spurred by a new concern. A handgun is not for shooting squirrels and rabbits.

The clerk glances at Wanda's scars. "Just a moment."

As he walks toward the back of the store, May Rose whispers. "If you need a gun, perhaps we should go home."

"I am going home, to my new home. And I'm not going to shoot anyone. The gun's for show. A dog don't have to bite, long as it can growl and show its teeth."

The clerk lays two revolvers on the counter. "I don't know anything about these," Wanda says. "Which would you say, for me?"

"Neither," May Rose whispers.

"These are Colts, Army issue." The clerk demonstrates the bigger gun's swing-out cylinder and how to load the bullets. "Give a heft, see what feels good to you. This here's a seven-inch barrel. The little one is a five-inch, 38 caliber."

Wanda likes the five-inch. She tries the holster in her skirt pocket, but it sticks out above the top. Alone, the gun lies hidden. When Wanda replaces it on the counter, May Rose opens the cylinder to make sure it's empty.

"We can shoot it out back, if you'd like," the clerk says.

"Ma, want to try?"

"No. And I'll carry the bullets."

Wanda pays and gives May Rose the box of bullets. "When did you get so bossy?"

May Rose glances with emphasis at Wanda's pocket, now weighed down by the gun.

~

Elkins sits in a valley that's wider and flatter than Grafton. It's higher too, Glory tells them, nearly twice the elevation, and the air is said to be cooler. In the distance, tree-covered mountains fade from green to slate gray.

May Rose must have traveled through here before, but aside from the depot that looks like every other red brick depot and sidings crowded with coal cars and flatcars of sawed lumber, nothing in Elkins looks familiar.

As they wait for Wanda to collect her crates, Glory points to mansions on a nearby hill. "Uncle Barlow had a meeting up there with coal and railroad people, and Mother and I came along. That was before he married Aunt Alice. She never went with him on his trips, but he stopped taking us."

Wanda checks her crates with the station master and leads the way across the street to the Delmonte Hotel where she haggles for a room with two beds. Then she asks them to stay while she goes to arrange the next part of their trip.

"Let me go with you," May Rose says, half afraid they'll lose her.

"Stay with Evie and find something to eat," Wanda says. "This may take some time."

They wash and try to rest. Evie seems to read May Rose's darkest thoughts. "If we leave the hotel, Ma won't know where to find us."

"We'll find her," she promises.

They have no idea where she's gone. In a drug store with a soda fountain, they sit at a table with wire legs and eat egg-salad on bread. Night is falling when they return to the hotel with egg salad for Wanda, and there she is. She smells like horses.

She hugs Evie. "You're going to love what I bought." She'll say no more. May Rose is relieved, and Evie is excited again.

Wanda's late husband left her with no money, but somehow she's buying things and plans to set them up in a house. If her new wealth has come from Granny Lucie, why doesn't she say?

~

BARLOW

Barlow carries no new shipping agreements for the B&O, but his mood lightens as his train nears home.

Either the coal operators were genuinely distracted by the coroner's report of the Chicago River disaster, or they were using it to avoid business. Recently an excursion boat capsized, drowning nearly eight hundred passengers, mostly Western Electric Company employees bound for a picnic. Many were women. The coal men in his meetings shook their heads and blew smoke. Tipped right over at the dock, top-heavy, one said. Top heavy with the installation of new lifeboats, mandated by the government, another said, wouldn't you know? Yet the ship's owner, captain, and engineer were blamed. Inevitably, the coal men's discourse stuck on the stupidity of government restrictions and government inspectors. Then they complained about Germany's sinking the Lusitania, nearly three months ago, followed by Britain's blockade of shipping from neutral European ports. President Wilson wants peace without victory; they want to sell coal to both sides.

Alice, who spends her days reading newspapers, will know about the ruling in the Chicago River disaster, and be even more fixed against all means of modern transportation. He refuses, in this age, to keep a horse and buggy, and she refuses to ride on a train or in their automobile. But she also seldom ventures from the porch, never visits neighboring houses, won't walk to town or to church. Has she been like this from the beginning? Among his other failings, he's not been the most observant of men.

Coal will boom, whether the country enters the war or not. It's booming already. Still, he's brought home no contracts. Maybe he was not as alert as usual, distracted by events at home. *May Rose.* Possibly she's still there, as Glory suggested. He's tried not to think of her, and struggles to conceal his fancies. Either Glory is too perceptive, or his sentiments are plain to all.

He walks from the station. His house is uncommonly dark, but someone rises from the steps. Banovic.

"Mr. Townsend."

"What's happening here?" The porch furniture is gone.

"Mrs. Townsend sick. And we move."

He stares at his door, needing his room, his bed. "She got sick, and you moved?"

"We move first, then she get sick. Have nurse since yesterday." Banovic takes his travel case and motions him down the street, hurrying, as though his presence will make her well.

A nurse. Alice has always claimed to be unwell, but the doctor could never produce a diagnosis.

The new house is too quiet. A lamp burns on a table in the entry. Mrs. Banovic comes to meet him.

"My niece?"

"She go with others on train."

Gone. All gone.

"Mrs. Townsend is first door top of stairs."

The stairs are as yet uncarpeted. Alice didn't need to move so soon.

9

BARLOW

Alice has wet the bed. While the nurse changes her sheets and nightgown, Barlow escapes the room. For years she did not allow him to sleep in her bed, but on his arrival last night, she seized his hand and would not let go. He slept on her left; she can't move her right arm or leg. Her few words were garbled, but the message of her left hand was clear. She needs him.

He slept in his clothes, now damp. Banovic, who always anticipates where he'll be wanted, follows him to his room and opens a closet door. "Dress for work now?"

He nods. Unshaded, the new house is already sweltering. He must plant trees that will grow rapidly. Alice was always afraid the trees outside her window would fall on her in a storm. Hester refused to let them be cut down.

His wet trousers and shirt reek of urine. He drops them into a laundry basket and finds the bathroom. Banovic is there, drawing water into the claw-foot tub. The sink is low and built against a corner. The bathroom faces the street, a tall window that has no blind. Someone has draped it with a sheet.

"Good man," Barlow says. What would he do without the Banovics? Yet with a new mortgage, how can he keep them? And a nurse?

Downstairs, the Banovics have arranged Alice's parlor furniture, but there's nothing but his desk and chair in the dining room, and no draperies anywhere. His anger builds.

The nurse, a woman with shoulders like a man, comes to the kitchen while he's drinking coffee.

"Will there be a day nurse? Your wife is very restless, moaning and crying. Someone needs to sit with her. I'll come back at dark."

A day nurse? He looks at Mrs. Banovic for suggestions. He should go to the office and see what business he can stir up.

"I take care Mrs. Townsend," Mrs. Banovic says.

"Good." He hasn't discussed the new burdens on his finances, but the Banovics manage to know everything. "Can you advise your husband about bringing blinds and curtains from the other house? Surely some will fit?"

He misses talking with Hester. Perhaps, when Alice recovers, having a house to themselves will make her care more about his troubles and opinions. If that happens, he may no longer be burdened by thoughts he should not have.

~

MAY ROSE

Wanda's surprise is a rolled-up canvas tent and a two-seated wagon hitched to a pair of stout gray horses. To May Rose, the greater surprise is that she has not hired this rig, she's bought it.

Glory swings Evie's hand. "A tent! What an adventure!"

Evie pats the nose of one of the horses and springs back with a giggle when it bobs its head. She climbs to the front seat.

"I doubt we'll need the tent," Wanda says. "But I can always sell it at Trading Days."

As their elder, May Rose should be able to provide guidance, but Wanda has always been better at getting from place to place. Now she must trust her to deliver them safely to Winkler.

At the depot, Wanda claims her crates and Glory buys loaves of bread and summer apples from a vendor on the platform. Wanda has hard tack and deer jerky, scant rations for a two-day trip.

"We'll have a meal and stay overnight at Jennie Town," Wanda promises.

In the months since they parted in Fargo, Wanda has become skillful in handling horses. May Rose is glad the bench seats have springs and that the horses don't shy or bolt when a nearby locomotive blasts its whistle.

The trip starts smoothly with the horses at a walk. She and Glory sit in the second bench, for though Evie is shy of horses, she fancies that Wanda might let her hold the reins. For the first hours, they're entertained by the scenery, which changes from rolling farmland to a road that winds through a wide valley.

When they make the turn that's supposed to take them to Winkler by the next day, Wanda twists in her seat. "Look, they've scraped the road." Their shady new road has a wooded mountain slope on one side and a shallow river on the other. Its flattened, dusty surface is tracked by shoes of horses and humans.

May Rose feels better, seeing bare prints of children's feet among the other marks. For some time they've passed no houses, but those prints make the route seem less wild. According to Wanda, Winkler has nine residents. Their party will enlarge that number to twelve. When May Rose came to the mountains as a bride, she lived in an isolated cabin. She wants never to live like that again.

"Here's something else." Wanda directs their view to a railroad grade between the road and river. "New stone, new ties and rails. Last time I passed this way, the grade was grassed over."

"Someone is opening a mine," Glory says. She grins at May Rose. "I don't know, but that's what Uncle Barlow would say."

They sit straighter, warned by snorts of an engine. Directly the horses stop behind a steam roller packing the road's dirt surface. A man with a whistle motions their wagon to the grassy berm, and they ride past the roller and through the dust cloud of a horse-drawn grader. Ahead of the grader, men with picks and shovels are cutting and throwing sod to the bank.

Encouraged as she is by these signs of progress, May Rose is glad when they emerge from dust to cleaner, quieter air. They continue on a weedy road pocked with holes and wet crossings.

Construction sounds fade, and once again only bird calls
accompany the sounds of the wagon's turning wheels.

Later Wanda stops the team in a wide place by the road. They
step over the new railroad tracks and push through brush to the
shallow, rocky river. Stooping at the river's edge, they splash cool
water on their arms, rinse their handkerchiefs and wipe grit from
their necks and faces. All but May Rose pull off their shoes and
stockings and wade in. Evie cups her hand and lifts water to her
mouth.

"Not here," May Rose says. "Evie, don't drink that."

Evie opens her hand and lets the water drop.

No one has thought to bring drinking water. "I'll find a
spring," Wanda says.

"I've never done anything like this," Glory says, drying her feet
on her skirt. "Thank you so much for letting me come!"

Farther along the road, Wanda stops and they take turns
drinking from a thin stream that drips between rocks. Wanda fills
one of her cook pots, and they go on.

Glory takes old garments from her bag of discards, and she
and May Rose snip threads from seams while they listen to Wanda
and Evie sing. A pile of disassembled dresses and coats grows on
the bench between them. May Rose admires Glory's swift, tireless
fingers. Spoiled and indulged, Alice said of Glory. Unaware of the
real world. *"You can't have what's mine,"* Alice said.

Glory will have a new life in college. May Rose will have a new
life in Winkler. She'll no longer worry about Alice or think of
Barlow.

Late in the afternoon, they come upon men walking, and
behind them, one woman and a pack of barefoot children, all but
the smallest with bundles tied on sticks.

When one of the men hails, Wanda stops the team. "We're
looking for the Jennie Town mine works," he says. "Is this the
right road?"

"I figger it is," Wanda says. "You might get there by nightfall."

The woman, who holds a crying infant, clutches the curved arm of the bench where May Rose sits. "Could I ride awhile? I'm awful tired."

Wanda pulls Evie close. "Sit up here," she says. The workmen trudge ahead.

When the woman climbs beside Evie, the children press at the wagon sides, calling "Me too, me too!" The tallest boy grabs a harness and tries to pull himself onto one of the horses. The horse shies, lurching the wagon.

The woman switches the infant to her other shoulder and swats in the direction of the nearest child. "Get back! You'll get a turn."

May Rose counts eight children. "Are these all yours?"

"They'll be all right." The woman gasps for breath. The children run beside the wagon a few steps, then resume a discouraged walk. The wagon moves slowly, but distance between them grows.

May Rose asks again. "Those children, are they yours?" Far back, a toddler sits in the road. The infant on the woman's shoulder has not stopped whimpering.

"I'm looking for their pa," the woman says, "and I can't walk another step. Some are them are mine, some are his. He better be at Jennie Town."

Wanda stops the horses. "Let your biggest boy carry the baby. You've a kid back there can barely walk."

The taller children catch up, climb over the tail gate and sit on the crates. Two small ones lift their arms and howl.

"You big kids get down," Wanda says. "We can't carry everybody. Ma'am, why don't you rest your kids by the road for a while, then walk on together?"

"We been resting off and on," the woman says. "And it don't help. I ain't gonna make it lest I can ride, and if I can't make it, who's to look after them?"

The children hold tight to the edges of the crates. Glory gets out of the wagon and goes back for the toddler, a girl who look like she's rolled in mud.

May Rose stretches out her arms. "I'll hold her." Glory sets her on May Rose's lap. Immediately, the child pushes her dirty fingers into May Rose's mouth.

May Rose pulls the fingers away. "Don't do that." She wipes slobber, snot and grit from her tongue, then holds the child's wrists.

The two who can't climb into the wagon are clamoring around Glory, and she lifts them to the bench beside May Rose. On the front bench, the mother slumps as though in a faint.

"I'll walk for a while," Glory says.

Evie steps over Wanda and jumps down from the wagon to walk with Glory. A boy crawls past May Rose to Evie's seat and picks up her doll.

Wanda snatches the doll away and stows it under the bench. "You can't hold this with filthy hands."

The woman seems to wake. "I'm Luzanna Hale. We've not ate since yesterday. Have you got anything?"

In the back, the bigger children are warring over Glory's bag of bread and apples. "Stop it," Mrs. Hale says, "and give that there to me."

The children whine and struggle with the bag but one of them raises it in the air and passes it forward. Wanda reaches out and tucks the bag between her feet. "You can eat when we do."

Warily, Glory, Wanda, and May Rose give their names. They're surrounded with fumes of dirty underwear. "This ain't gonna work," Wanda says.

May Rose stands and sets the toddler on the wagon floor. "Baths in the river, everybody. You can eat when you're clean. Mrs. Hale, you too."

Mrs. Hale does not get down when the others jump from the wagon. "Me and my kids can't swim."

"You can't ride with us unless you bathe," May Rose says. "Most places, the water isn't high enough for drowning, 'less you lie down and put your nose in it. Take your little girl and I'll wash the baby."

Half the children follow Wanda across the tracks to the river while the others huddle near their mother.

Glory leads a resisting boy to the water's edge. "It's shallow here, don't you see?"

It's shallow but swift-flowing, splashing over rocks. Wanda and Evie hitch up their skirts and stand mid-stream, where water reaches no higher than Evie's knees. "Stay between us and the shore," Wanda calls. "Sit down and let the water rinse over your clothes. You'll soon dry. Mrs. Hale, show them how cool and nice it is."

May Rose lays the infant in a patch of sand and unwraps its sodden rags. "This filth will never wash," Glory says. The infant, a boy, is skinny as a newborn. May Rose is proud of Glory, who hides her shock at his bony chest. Glory holds the infant's head while May Rose lays him in the water. Then Glory fetches pieces of cloth they've cut for Evie. They pat him dry with one and wrap his bottom in another.

Mrs. Hale carries the toddler, but does not step into the water until the children begin to laugh, squeal and splash. One by one, Wanda pronounces them clean enough to leave the river. At the wagon, she holds them back with threats while Glory cuts the apples and May Rose breaks off chunks of bread.

Evie whispers, "Ma said not to do it, but I saw the kids drink in the river."

May Rose saw too. "Maybe they'll be all right."

"We can walk," May Rose says. "Let the Hales ride." The tallest girl gets down and walks beside her.

Later, Wanda stops the wagon. "Mrs. Hale, time for you-all to walk awhile."

Mrs. Hale looks like she's being turned from her home. "Is it far to the place where the mine is?"

"With all these delays, we won't get there till after dark." Wanda peers through the treetops to the sky. "Maybe five hours more."

Mrs. Hale hesitates. "You'll let me ride again?"

"I expect we will."

"Here, Alma, you hold Davis." Mrs. Hale hands the infant to the tallest girl, who has climbed to the bench beside May Rose and the toddler. Mrs. Hale tugs Wanda's sleeve. "Don't go so fast we can't keep up."

May Rose gives Alma a pad of cloth to lay under the infant. "I hope we'll find your pa."

"My pa is dead," Alma says. "A mine fell on him. I'm not a Hale, I'm a Donnelly."

Wanda twists with a sharp look, first to the girl, then to May Rose and back to the girl. "What was your pa's name?"

"John."

John Donnelly may be a common name, but May Rose has good reason to dislike it. During her time in Winkler, two Donnelly boys performed acts that still give her nightmares. One was named John.

"Ma called the baby Davis for the place we was when he was born," Alma says. "She said it would bring him luck, 'cause it's a rich man's name."

"And this one?" The toddler has slipped from the bench and lies curled at their feet. May Rose touches the toddler's forehead, then her own. "She's fevered."

"That's Dakota," Alma says. "She come with our new pa."

Dakota sits up and tries to climb over the infant lying on Alma's knees. May Rose pulls her to her own lap. When Dakota twists and whimpers, May Rose dips a cloth in water and presses it on her hot arms and face.

This family's story is too common. She glances back, sees them straggling along, none together. Soon she'll have to give the mother her seat in the wagon.

The road grass is well trampled by other wheels and might be a good surface if not for dips, rocks, and fallen branches. May Rose shifts Dakota in her arms. Nothing soothes or settles her.

"Sing for us, Wanda," she says.

"What do you want to hear?"

"Redwing," Evie says. "Pa's favorite."

"Not that one. How about this?" Wanda hums a few notes, then sings. "The sun shines bright, on the old Kentucky home..."

Evie puts one arm around her mother's waist, and the other around Glory. Dakota relaxes in May Rose's arms, and the infant stops crying. Behind them, the straggling Hales cease their complaints. The song blends with the clop of the horses' hooves as if they are matching their stride to the rhythm of the song.

Wanda stops singing in the middle of a phrase. On the road ahead, a walker comes their way. Like other workmen, his shirt and trousers are faded to gray. He wears a smudged felt hat and carries a bundle over his shoulder.

One of the children calls, "Pa!" Wanda halts the horses while the family overtake him. On the bench beside May Rose, Alma hunches over the infant.

Mr. Hale pushes his children away and takes three quick strides to the wagon. May Rose gasps as he drops his pack and snatches the reins from Wanda's hands.

"Missus, me and my family needs this here."

Rising, Wanda swats and grabs at the reins, jostling the wagon. He wrenches her arm and drags her to the ground. When Wanda falls, May Rose jumps to her feet, letting Dakota slide to the floor.

She climbs over the driver's seat and reaches for the reins. "Mr. Hale, we've fed and carried your family. Go along and leave us be."

Her request is too reasonable, and Mr. Hale answers by shoving her backward onto Alma and the infant. The wagon erupts in a babble of confusion, Glory protesting, May Rose righting herself, and Dakota and the infant wailing again.

She is about to jump from the wagon to see if Wanda is hurt when Mr. Hale reaches into the wagon and seizes Evie's arm. "The rest of you—out!"

Close behind him, Wanda rises from the ground, Colt in hand. When he tugs at Evie, she pushes the barrel against his back. "Let go of my girl!"

May Rose grips the edge of her seat. Released, Evie crawls to the back seat and huddles between her and Alma.

The Hale children rush to the wagon. "You kids, get back," Wanda says. "I'll be shooting your pa if he don't let go them reins." Her face is red.

Mrs. Hale calls the children to the side of the road. Her husband tries to sidestep Wanda's revolver, but Wanda moves with him, trapping him against the side rails.

He wraps the reins over his fist. "I ain't afraid of no woman. Come on, you kids, get in the wagon. She ain't gonna shoot."

She can't. The bullets are still in their box, and the box is in May Rose's pocket.

"I will," Glory says.

May Rose stops breathing. Glory's jaws are pressed tight, and she's pointing a gun no bigger than her hand. "It'll be best, Mr. Hale, if you drop those reins and go over there to your wife and children."

Mr. Hale squints at the small gun like he's trying to decide what it is.

Wanda pushes the Colt's barrel against his back. "We got you both ways. Time to give up."

May Rose exhales as Mr. Hale opens his hand and lets the reins unwind. Wanda steps aside to let him walk away, but keeps the Colt aimed.

On the back bench, May Rose pulls Dakota into her lap. Holding a child usually brings some comfort, but not when the child is hot and squirming, and not in the presence of guns.

Wanda passes the Colt to Glory and climbs to her seat. "Keep that on him. We're moving on." She looks at Alma. "Girl, you can get down now. Mrs. Hale, come get your little ones."

Alma reaches for May Rose's hand and mumbles toward the wagon floor. "Don't make me go with him."

Wanda looks back and forth from Alma to Mr. Hale, crouched in the shade of a tree, stuffing tobacco under his lip. "Alma can come along," she says.

Mrs. Hale clings to the wagon. "Please, take them all, find them a home."

Wanda shakes her head. "Folks who need extra children are few and far between."

Glory drops the smaller gun into a pouch at her waist. "There's a children's home north of here a couple of days, run by the Methodists. Go back to Elkins, find a church and ask directions."

Alma lays the infant in her mother's arms.

"Please, at least take Dakota," the woman says.

"Ma, Dakota's sick."

"Honey, I know. I can't do nothing about it. She might have a chance with you."

Alma bends from the wagon and lays her head on her mother's shoulder. The other children huddle a few feet from the wagon, listening like their lives depend on it.

"We'll take Dakota and Alma," Wanda says. "That's all we can do." She empties her pockets of hard tack and jerky and throws the pieces across the road. Mr. Hale and the children scramble to find them in the grass. Mrs. Hale stands crying in the road as the wagon pulls away.

Alma cries too. May Rose's throat thickens.

Glory sniffs. "Leaving those children is the worst experience of my life."

"Let's hope that turns out to be true," Wanda says.

10

BARLOW

A tremor in Barlow's hand spatters ink before he touches his pen to the ledger page. He blots the spill and returns the pen to the inkwell, clasps his hands and squeezes his fingers until they hurt. The remorse in his chest makes him take short, shallow breaths. It's useless to try to work. He's losing everyone.

He returns to the house and finds Banovic hanging blinds in Alice's room. They leave the windows open for the morning breeze, but close them as day heats up. Alice gives no sign that she knows he's there. Because she cannot close her right eye, the doctor has placed a patch over it. He says if a patient does not die in the first twenty-four hours, there is hope of recovery.

With her mouth awry, Alice cannot chew well. They feed her a few spoonsful of soft food--applesauce, pudding. Sometimes she chokes. She's had one convulsion, and passed her bowels in the bed. She would be mortified if she knew. Maybe she does.

He picks up one of her well-worn books, *Wuthering Heights*, and as he begins to read aloud, is surprised to discover a name she called him in their early days: Heathcliff. His interest is quickly disappointed. Didn't she say "Heathcliff" with loving overtones? This Heathcliff is a disagreeable sort, passionate and harsh. One description might be true of himself. Heathcliff's "reserve springs from an aversion to showy displays of feeling." Can one be both passionate and reserved? Yes. He knows the struggle.

The story seems highly exaggerated. Why has Alice loved it? How little he knows her.

When she appears to sleep, he goes through mail brought from his office, largely memos, but there's a letter from Glory. He reads between the lines: Alice moved the household early so she and May Rose would have to go. Poor Alice.

He goes to the office after lunch, walks through the train yard and passes the time of day with conductors, who always have the most current news about the lumber industry, glass manufacturing, and new seams of coal, lifeblood of the B&O. As yet, no one knows his trouble, so no one murmurs sympathy as he picks up rumors in the barbershop. There's a lot of talk about Europe's war. Coal operators already are holding back on shipping, waiting for the price of coal to go up. He needs to plant the idea that everything is relative: shipping may be cheaper now than later.

Most of his earnings are based on commission. One new contract can justify a month of travel and cultivation. Today he hears of no regional expansion that's not already owned by the B&O or its rivals.

A good railroad agent does not wait for the boss to direct him, nor does he rely on routine calls to current customers. It is up to him to dig up new business. In the old days, all he had to do was show up. Now he must bring something better—deals on rates, empty cars at their sidings the minute they want them, schedules that make their lives easier, and maybe lunch, because he's not a jolly fellow, like some of his colleagues, who make customers happy with their outlook.

With the exception of his sister, who seemed satisfied with their years together, he's made no one happy. He can't even tell a joke, though no doubt customers would find his personal life humorous. His former personal life. No one will think this one is funny.

The owner of the new house told Alice they could rent until their purchase was final, so he's not committed. He's certain he can't afford a nurse for both day and night. He's also not sure he can employ the Banovics—Hester paid them from guesthouse income. He can't ask Glory to return, a girl eager for her future. May Rose might come if he asked, but what a scandal her presence would create, if only in his own mind. And how could he ask her to take care of his wife?

Near day's end, he receives a telephone call from Franklin Coal and Coke. Among other operations, the company is opening a mine at Jennie Town. The location gets his attention. But Franklin Coal and Coke has not telephoned to arrange freight. Is he interested in a position? Yes, it would mean travel. Then, no, he says, but perhaps in the future. He thanks the company for thinking of him.

It's unlikely he'll find a position with the B&O that will keep him in the office. He's been envying Will Herff, dabbling in this and that, living in his store building and working for himself. If he were to buy a little grocery with rooms above, would Alice sense the difference?

On his way home, he stops at a hardware store and selects three electric pedestal fans to be delivered before evening. Unshaded by day, the upstairs bedrooms are fiercely hot at night.

~

MAY ROSE

The western sun glints on the river and throws thin tree shadows on their road. Dakota's whimpers merge with sounds of plodding horses' feet, jingling tackle, and creaking wagon springs.

May Rose shifts the child on her lap, watching white-tipped sprays of water that fall and swirl around rocks, drift into pools and flow on. She's stopped caring about anything beyond the moment. She sees in drooping shoulders how they're all wearing down. Food would help. Only Evie and Alma have eaten since morning.

"I judge three hours till dark," Wanda says, breaking their silence.

Glory gives the Colt back to Wanda. They've not sighted Alma's family for a long time.

Dakota is satisfied nowhere. She reaches her arms to Alma, then to May Rose, and they pass her back and forth. They've been squeezing water between her parched lips.

"She liked Ma's song," Evie says. "Sing for her, Ma."

Wanda shakes her head. "Might be better for that child if we find a place to set up the tent."

It might be better for them all. May Rose begins to watch for a level spot along the river. The newly-laid rails have ceased to be the cause of wonder, but now she sits forward and stretches her neck, hearing a pump of pistons. An engine chugs toward them, smothering every other sound. It pulls a short train of empty flatcars. They turn to watch the caboose disappear. Smoke flattens over the rails.

"Maybe the tracks go all the way to Winkler," Wanda says.

It's something to distract their thoughts. Evie has clutched her doll since Mr. Hale tried to take their wagon. She shrinks at the sight of burned trees along the road and says they're scary. Wanda says the fire was long ago. Glory tells Evie there's nothing to worry about.

There's everything to worry about. Evie keeps glancing back at May Rose as if she'll find a place of safety by her side.

They come to a wide place by the river, but it's stacked with rails and ties. Ahead, two boxcars sit on the track, one with a stovepipe on top.

"We could stop and stretch our legs," Glory says.

A man with an apron tied over his chest eyes them from a boxcar's open door.

Wanda slows the wagon. "Meat's cooking. What do you think, Ma? Suppose we can bum a meal?"

The odor of sizzling fat arouses her hunger. Ahead on the old railroad grade, workmen chip sod; others dump wheelbarrows of gravel in its place. They stop, lean on their picks and stare. One lifts a hand and calls hello. Another blurts a string of words that bring laughter and more taunts.

"We should go on," May Rose says. "Look straight ahead." Like bullies on the playground, men love to astonish their fellows by seeing who can be most rude. She tolerates them better if she can liken them to children.

In response to the taunts, Wanda lifts her arm and waves. "Three women traveling alone, you know what they think we are."

Evie looks from the shouting, leering men to her mother's crooked grin. "What do they think?"

Glory shakes her head.

Alma's face has been solemn since they met her, and it's wary now. May Rose smiles to reassure her. "They think we're three women and three children, that's all. Wanda, don't stop, we'll rest ourselves and the horses farther on, even if we don't find a place for the tent."

She'd like Wanda to hurry the horses, but the wagon rolls on at a steady pace, and soon they leave the noise and sights of railroad construction behind.

May Rose and Alma continue to cool Dakota with wet cloths. "She ain't gonna make it," Alma says.

May Rose brushes a fly from Dakota's eyelid. "We'll fix her a nice bed in the tent. A good rest may make all the difference."

A sudden foul odor strikes them, and Alma gasps. "Her bowels has let loose."

Wanda stops the wagon, and May Rose gets out and takes the child, holding her at arms' length. Dakota's dress, the cloth padding on Alma's lap and Alma's dress beneath it are stained brown. They cross the railroad grade to the river, where she lays Dakota in a pool and tries to rinse her off. Glory finds a dress for Alma in her bag of discards. They tie it up at her waist, but cannot fix how it droops from her shoulders. Alma rolls up the sleeves. She might be pretty with her hair clean and her cheeks and arms filled out. If she's the child of the John Donnelly they hated, it's not her fault.

They rest on the grass while Wanda lets the horses graze and drink from a stream at the roadside. Before they leave, Dakota has another watery discharge and seems weaker for the effort. There's nothing to do but clean and swaddle her as they did her infant brother, make thicker piles of cloth to lay beneath her, and ride on.

"Maybe Will can help her," Wanda says. "If we don't stop at Jennie Town, we can be in Winkler by dawn."

But when they reach Jennie Town, they're too weary to go on. Wanda hitches their horse team near others at a public house, an old depot run by a man who greets her like a lost friend. "Miss Bosell!"

Wanda doesn't correct him, and May Rose whispers to Glory. "Bosells are her mother's family."

The man motions. "Get down, get down, and come in! I figger I've got enough corn bread and beans to fill six little women. Sorry I can't offer beds. The mine bosses has got 'em till some of our houses is fixed up." He grins at Wanda. "Things is hopping here. We're getting a coal mine, and the railroad's on its way!"

Inside, workmen at plank tables look up from their drinks. The tavern keeper, whose name is Roy, clears a table of dirty glasses and brings a pot of beans and a platter of cornbread. May Rose lays Dakota on a bench between herself and Alma.

"I'd like to trade my horses," Wanda says to Roy.

"Someone might trade, Miss Bosell, but you'll get nothing fresh. Every horse and mule here works sunup to sundown, hauling timbers and dragging out dirt and coal at the mine works."

May Rose spoons brown beans into their bowls. "Maybe you know a private spot we can set our tent?"

Roy pushes back his hat. He seems eager to please Wanda. "I'm thinking of a place by a stream the miners mightn't of found. I'll show you directly."

The beans are lukewarm and the cornbread is hard, but Glory pronounces their meal one of the best she's had. Alice would be horrified. Faced with the real world, Glory is doing just fine. Hester would be proud.

~

BARLOW

When the night nurse comes, Barlow leaves Alice's bedside for the cooler air of the porch. Mrs. Banovic said she rested well through the afternoon, but from the moment he entered her room, she thrashed and moaned. He imagines he hears her still.

11

MAY ROSE

In their final hours on the road, Wanda sings their favorite songs, like *Oh, Susannah* and *Church in the Wildwood*. May Rose and Glory do their best to cheer the girls with fairy tales. Evie gets to hold the reins, then it's Alma's turn. Dakota lies in the wagon between crates, wrapped in the quilt in which she died last night.

The old rhymes and tales sink into May Rose with new meaning: despair and hope, mothers faced with bare cupboards, the magic growth of a few bean seeds, *Hansel and Gretel*. Dark stories with happy endings, the kind people have always needed.

Though Wanda has prepared her for the ruined and restored aspects of Winkler, the first sight fills her with dread, particularly the high stand of thick, burned timber across the valley. A scattering of houses on the hillside. Piles of rubble and circles of burned ground along the road and river. No hotel, no boardinghouse, no boardwalk. The store's tan stucco is crumbling and the church's paint has peeled away. What remains is the feeling she doesn't belong. But the town was also not kind to Wanda, and this is where she wants to be.

There's a babble of greetings when they step down at the old company store. May Rose leans against the wagon, waiting her turn, taking in Will's surprise, Glory's delight, and Wanda's happy introduction of Evie to one of her aunts, Piney, who lives here.

"We're going to live here too," Evie says. "Is this our house?"

Piney bends and kisses her cheek. "This is the store, sweet thing. We'll find you a house." Wanda's Aunt Piney is a plump, pretty woman whose cheeks wrinkle in pleasure and concern. May Rose tries to recall what Wanda has said about the infant in Piney's arms and the two small children, a boy she grips by the hand and a girl who clutches her skirt. Her thinking is fuzzy, but the sun is terribly hot, and she's stiff from the ride, or bruised from sleeping on last night's hard ground.

Alma stands apart, but Evie takes her to Piney. "This is my friend Alma."

Piney beams. "Ain't we lucky? Another pretty girl."

Something may be made of life anywhere. If Wanda is determined to live here, what can May Rose do? When greetings settle down, she reminds them about the small body in the wagon. "We have a sad duty, and should take care of it soon."

Neither Will nor Wanda's Aunt Piney seem surprised that they've acquired a dying child along their way, but Will has questions. "How long was she sick? Were there others?"

She understands; in the orphanage, a child who arrives in sick condition is quarantined. She puts her arm around Alma's shoulders. "As far as we know, Dakota was the only one in her family who was sick. Alma was with her, and she's been fine."

Will says he'll find a box for burial. They tell her name, Dakota Hale, to be chiseled later on her stone. Alma does not know her birthdate.

Sweltering in the sun, May Rose fans herself with her hat. "Shade," she says finally, holding tight to the iron railing in the center of the steps. "May we go inside?"

"Are you sick?" Alma runs ahead and opens the door.

"Tired," she says. "So thirsty."

~

BARLOW

On his way home for lunch, Barlow takes a round-about walk and stops in three neighborhood grocery stores. Each occupies the main level of a house and dominates a corner where streets cross.

Each appears to be operated by a husband and wife, the man behind the meat counter, the wife at the cash register. Outside, he gazes at the buildings, judges them half the cost of his new home. It's something to take his mind off Alice.

At home, he sits at her bedside while Mrs. Banovic goes down for lunch. Alice's stare seems to want something. When he holds a glass at her lips, she tightens them and closes her eyes. He replaces the glass and sits back. When she opens her eyes again, he says, "Would you like me to read? *Wuthering Heights*, or something else?" She turns her head away. According to Mrs. Banovic, Alice has spoken a few words. Not to him. As though all of this is his fault.

"The house looks good," he says.

He tries again. "Please tell Mrs. Banovic or the nurse if there's anything I can get for you." Last evening he brought her papers from the newsstand. Someone has been through the stack of newspapers on her favorite reading chair, for they are folded inside-out. The night nurse, he suspects. He's not sure Mrs. Banovic reads much English.

"Do you like the nurse?" The two women who cared for Hester are busy with new assignments. He doesn't like this one, though he can't say why. "Does she read to you?"

Alice makes no sign of hearing. At last she's ruling her house.

~

MAY ROSE

May Rose remembers collapsing inside the store, remembers being carried to this room. Its walls and ceiling look to be made of siding from old houses. It has no window. An oil lamp glows from a table between two half beds.

Alma rises from the other bed. "You're awake." She sounds relieved. She goes out and comes back with Will.

He sits beside her, touches her forehead, slips his arm beneath her back. "Can you sit up? You should drink something."

When he lifts, the room seems to dip and spin.

"You're fevered," he says.

"I'm sorry."

He pulls down the thin blanket. Except for shoes and stockings, she's fully dressed. He speaks to Alma. "Can you undress her or do you want me to call Wanda?"

"I can do it," Alma says.

"May Rose, have you drunk from the river?"

She hurts all over, and now she's cold.

"She told us not to do it," Alma says.

The springs creak and the mattress rises when he stands up. "You're a good girl, Alma. Are you sure you want to stay with her?"

"If it's okay."

"You know where to call me." He bends over May Rose. "Wanda and Evie are with their Aunt Piney. Our friend Virgie has taken Glory for the night. I'm sorry you've had a rough trip, but you'll be better in the morning."

~

BARLOW

The idea of owning a corner grocery has fired Barlow's thoughts. It would be a tiny operation, compared with managing the Winkler Lumber Company, but it would have its challenges. In Winkler, he liked making diverse and remote components work together—laborers and their talents, camps and supplies, a steady flow of logs to the saws, shipping, markets. What soured him was the incessant barrage of interactions, the wants, the holdups and complaints. But he knows when work began to wear him down. The day she left.

Come what may, the grocery business is stable, vital as coal, no need for travel as long as wholesalers make regular calls. He couldn't serve as a butcher, for he knows nothing about cutting meat. And he sees another problem. In the stores he visited both yesterday and today, the proprietors maintained a jolly, welcoming tone. Customers need to like their tradesmen. Alice has taught him what boredom looks like. He sees how he bores his freight customers.

Banovic, however, worked in a slaughter house, and Banovic has a manner that pleases everyone. Customers would love Banovic.

12

MAY ROSE

Amid all the comings and goings, May Rose hears the word, "Typhoid." She has no strength to worry.

She doesn't know this place, a small dark room, a narrow bed. The bed hurts her back, her arms, her legs, but she can't get up. *Somewhere, Wanda is singing, much too loud, and running up and down the back stairs. She needs to stop her before Hester turns them out.*

Any time she opens her eyes, there's someone watching from a bed against the other wall. Her hands feel thick. Other hands lay cool cloths on her face and arms, pull her shift over her head, put a fresh pad between her and the rubber sheet. She aches everywhere, can't keep her eyes open for long. There's something she's supposed to do, but she can't remember what it is.

"I'm a lot of trouble," she says.

She hears voices beyond the door, Wanda and a man. Is it Homer, Wanda's husband? She thought he died of blood poisoning. *But here he is, a red-headed boy, begging at the boardinghouse for food.*

Wanda comes into the room, and the girl on the half bed goes out.

"Who was that girl?"

"It's Alma, Ma. The girl we picked up on the road."

"Alma, that's right. Did I hear Homer just now?"

Wanda touches May Rose's forehead. "It was Will, Ma."

"I'm mixed up."

"Fever does that. Homer died more'n a year ago."

"Have I been sick for a year?"

"Twelve days." Wanda sits on the other bed. "It's going to be noisy tomorrow, so we're thinking of moving you to our new house."

A house. "Where am I now?"

"This is Will's store. We're in Winkler."

That's right. They're in Winkler, and Hester is dead. Her chest heaves in sorrow, but her eyes are too dry for tears.

"People will be coming for Trading Days," Wanda says. "It's a market, folks bring goods to sell, food, things they've made. They camp and stay a couple of days. It gets noisy."

"Your tent."

"Yes, I'll try to sell the tent. See, you're remembering. A lot has happened, but we'll catch you up."

~

BARLOW

The B&O doesn't appreciate Barlow's need for a steady salary. He might find a position in the Baltimore office, his manager says, or Wheeling. But he doesn't want to move so far from...

He travels to Elkins to see if Franklin Coal and Coke or the Western Maryland Railroad has a salaried position for a man experienced in rail and lumber. He learns there might be something for him at the Jennie Town mine. So many mines are opening, and this one is short of workers who know anything.

A Franklin official suggests he visit the mine and tell the boss what he has to offer. The pay would be atrocious, but with the new branch line, he could go back and forth by train. And from Jennie Town, it's half a day to...

In his walk through Elkins, he passes a corner grocery for sale, a house with a six-room apartment upstairs. When he returns to Grafton, he sends Banovic to Elkins for his opinion. Does the business seem prosperous, and is it the kind of place he and Mrs. Banovic might like to work?"

~

MAY ROSE

They tell her she's been in Wanda's house several days, but she's seen only this room. It has a double bed, a chair, a coatrack, and a rag rug.

"I'm glad to see you sitting up," Glory says.

They've stopped staying with her around the clock. Will says she needs to take care she doesn't relapse.

Glory is carrying an armful of muslin. She pulls the chair close to the window, steps on it and hangs a curtain above the paper shade.

"Pretty," May Rose says. She woke this morning with a feeling of peace and overwhelming love. She doesn't know why, but the feeling remains. She sits very still so it won't leave.

Glory steps down and pulls the chair close to the bed. "I've a letter from Uncle Barlow. Shall I read or do you want me to tell you about it?"

"Read, please."

Glory draws a folded paper from her apron pocket. "*Glory, dear, I've been eager to hear from you since I learned you were traveling to Winkler. I hope your journey was pleasant and uneventful.*" She stops. "Pleasant and uneventful? Shall I tell him?"

May Rose pictures the snub-nosed gun in Glory's hand. "Wait a few years."

"Very good." Glory smiles. "I can tell you're feeling better." She looks again at the letter. "*I was quite surprised to discover you had left so suddenly, but I perfectly understand your reasons.*"

Glory looks up. "*My* reasons?"

"What did Alice tell him?"

"Not a word. Listen to this: *I have bad news. In my absence, Alice had our furnishings removed to the new house. I suppose this needed to happen, but her haste may have caused a stroke of apoplexy. She needs constant care, and seems not to know me.*"

Glory lowers the letter. "What do you think of that?"

"A stroke." They sit a moment in silence. May Rose murmurs, "Poor Barlow. Poor Alice."

Glory agrees. "Very sad. And difficult for all."

"Did he ask you to come home?"

"To take care of Aunt Alice? He'd never do that. She wouldn't so much as sit and read to Mother. Here's the rest: *Please write with your news, and give my kind regards to May Rose and Wanda. It eases me to know you are with friends, and with your brother.*"

"Well." Glory adjusts May Rose's pillows. "I'll have another surprise for Uncle Barlow. I hope he won't be angry. I'm not going home, and I'm not going to school at Broaddus. I've asked him to send my college trunk to Richmond."

"Virginia? Isn't that farther away?"

"I'll be with Will. He's enrolled in medical college. I'll stay with him and go to school there."

May Rose opens her mouth, but cannot find words to match her thoughts. She shouldn't say them anyway. She's heard Wanda, the past two mornings, throwing up in the slop jar. Wanda says not to worry, she's not sick.

Like fog, her serenity dissolves.

~

BARLOW

"The store is good, apartment good," Banovic says.

They speak on the porch, which is dimly lit by the waning moon. "What would you think of working there?"

"Maybe fine, but we like job with you."

"I'm thinking of a partnership—I buy the property and give you a share. For the present, we live in the rooms upstairs. You take a salary from the business and I'll pay Mrs. Banovic to take care of Alice."

Banovic is smoking a stogie. "You're quitting B&O?"

"It's my hope."

"We should move while you have railroad pass," Banovic says.

He agrees, proud of his choice. Banovic is a practical man.

A letter from Glory comes to his office the next morning. She's received his news of Alice. He stops at the second paragraph. May Rose has typhoid fever. His chest tightens, and he reads on, scanning past their speculations about how she acquired the disease to the words he's desperate to find. Will believes she will recover. *She will recover.*

He lays the paper on his desk, searches his pocket for a cigar, and finding none, remembers he doesn't smoke anymore. *May Rose.* Hester is gone, Alice sick. They're all beyond his help. They can't console him, and work is no longer his friend.

The third paragraph of Glory's letter concerns her own plans.

That evening, he tells Alice a portion of Glory's news while he waits for the night nurse. "Glory wants me to send her college trunk to Richmond. She intends to go to school there with her brother."

Alice keeps her stare. He imagines what she would say. Talking to Alice is one way to think aloud, but he chooses no disturbing subjects. "I don't know what to do about the furniture she's stored in our carriage house. I may have to visit her in Winkler, make arrangements." He can't get there soon enough. He looks to see if Alice registers anything. Her mouth is permanently twisted, but did her lip move?

"Our real estate broker says there's a prospect who would like to buy the furnishings Glory and I own jointly. I'd planned an auction, but a direct sale may be just as profitable." A direct sale will please Alice, if she cares for anything now. If there's no auction, no neighbors will witness their possessions set out on the lawn.

He's given Banovic an estimate of what he and Hester paid for those items and asked him to negotiate with the prospect. Banovic is a born dealer. Perhaps Glory will agree to sell her things also, when she learns he'll have no place to store them.

He touches the hand Alice cannot move. "We're starting over, dear." She no longer thrashes when he enters the room. Perhaps when they move, she'll not know she's in a new place.

Glory's letter said it's possible May Rose caught the disease from a child who died. But she's strong; certainly she'll come through this.

Nothing is certain.

13

MAY ROSE

Wanda's Aunt Ruth and her granny, Lucie Bosell, have made a three-hour trip to see Wanda and meet Evie and May Rose. May Rose sits on the chair in her room and lets Wanda help her dress.

"Don't let Granny upset you," Wanda says. "She talks rude, but means nothing by it."

"I'll be fine." One of the orphanage matrons has a sharp tongue. The orphanage seems years away. It could be time and distance, or being immersed in a different setting that makes the old one seem unreal.

Wanda holds her arm to help her walk. May Rose holds on to the stair railing. It's good to be clean, dressed, and standing up.

This is her first view of the rooms below, but she remembers the layout; the house where she took care of Will, Glory, and Charlie was exactly like this. Board walls, plank floors, a pot-bellied stove. Gratings in the ceilings so heat can pass to the two bedrooms upstairs. She wonders if this could be that place, though all company houses were the same. Will should know. Wanda said he has six houses that were not destroyed by flood or fire.

The aunts and granny look up as she comes down the stairs. They're sitting on three of the room's four unmatched straight chairs. Curtains of yellowed muslin hang at the windows, and multicolored rag rugs are scattered on the floor. Wanda's Aunt Piney holds an infant on her lap, youngest of her husband's three grandchildren.

Wanda directs May Rose to the empty chair.

"You're a strong woman," the old woman shouts as May Rose sits down. "Or you wouldn't of come through it."

"I'm happy to meet you," May Rose says.

Granny Lucie's gray hair is pulled tightly from her face and hangs down her back in a thick braid. She thrusts her head side to side and peers at May Rose from the outside corners of her eyes. Hard of hearing, Wanda warned. And nearly blind.

Wanda's Aunt Ruth sits with her ankles crossed and a twist to her mouth that suggests she can't wait to hear what Lucie will say next. Ruth has high cheekbones, long arms and large hands like her mother and Wanda. Piney doesn't look like them; her cheeks and smile are plump and rosy.

Piney jiggles the infant and peeks shyly at May Rose.

Ruth says, "Wanda told us you was pretty."

Lucie frowns. "Maybe someday, with fattening." She gestures to baskets of potatoes, corn, cabbages, and onions along the wall. "Them's from my garden."

"Your garden," Wanda says, "planted and tended by Aunt Piney and harvested by Aunt Ruth."

Her illness has left May Rose wondering if she'll ever work again. "Thank you," she says, teary with gratitude. "You're kind to think of us."

The women bob their heads. Wanda, who is standing by the stairs, leans toward Lucie. "Glory bought us a heifer and three hens at Trading Days."

Lucie turns her head to Wanda. "That's the other one that come with you? Doc's sister? I'd like to get a look at her."

"She's not at home this afternoon," Wanda says. "There's a baby coming, and Glory went with Will to help." There's a trace of discouragement in her tone. Glory seems to be always at her brother's side. Wanda has not said, but she must know that Will and Glory are leaving soon for Richmond.

"A baby," Lucie shouts. "Next one should be yours."

Wanda lifts her chin and gives Lucie a sullen look. "Wouldn't you like that."

Wanda's granny and aunts seem short on words, and following this exchange, the room is quiet. May Rose is shocked by the way Wanda speaks to her grandmother, almost a snarl. She keeps forgetting that Wanda spent most of the summer with these women. There must be stories she hasn't heard.

Piney passes the infant to Wanda and hands around a plate of sugar cookies.

"With them kids hanging on you, it beats me how you find time to make these things," Ruth says.

Piney says nothing, but continues to offer cookies.

Lucie lifts a cookie to her mouth with a quivering hand. "We hear them children's ma has run off again."

"Good riddance," Ruth says.

Piney looks happy. Wanda says she hasn't been married very long. Her husband, Simpson Wainwright, runs the new grist mill.

It's clear that Wanda admires her aunts, who may be part of the reason she's decided to settle here. It's the other, unspoken reason for Wanda's return to Winkler that has given May Rose new concern.

There's another spell of silence while they chew the crisp, sugary cookies. Too sweet for her taste. May Rose is suddenly hungry for fresh-baked bread.

The visitors watch like it's her duty to carry the conversation. When she tries to think of an agreeable topic, what comes to mind is the yeasty aroma of rising bread in the boardinghouse kitchen. That was years ago, right here in Winkler, when she sat at breakfast with Barlow Townsend.

~

BARLOW

The Banovics accept Barlow's choice of the Elkins grocery as though it's a move up in the world.

Mrs. Banovic thinks practically. "What furniture we take?"

He's caught short of a reply. He supposes he will reside for a time in the apartment with the Banovics and Alice, yet he has not once imagined himself there. "What do you suggest?"

"Rooms are small," Banovic says.

With Barlow's permission, Banovic trades Alice's delicate parlor furniture for a few of Hester's pieces deemed more suitable for the apartment. He thinks two, maybe three freight wagons will carry what they need to Elkins at a rate cheaper than rail freight. He's not sure how they will transport Alice. She can't sit up unless propped by many pillows.

First he has to complete the transaction and ask Glory what to do with her furniture. He's already shipped her college trunk to Richmond, and hopes to go to Winkler before she leaves. As Banovic suggested, he's not yet given notice to the B&O. No need to burn his bridges.

In Elkins he sees a Ford panel delivery truck, the kind of vehicle that would be good for the grocery. They could make a bed in it for Alice's journey.

Energized by new horizons, he tells himself this uplift has nothing to do with May Rose. When he's not in her presence, he's not sure who she is. The intervening years have altered or reaffirmed his habits and opinions. That time must have done the same for her. He dare not follow his imagination. It will be better if he believes she detests him still. Better still, that she does. *Yet.* Midlife, he's desperate for a new start.

He signs the purchase agreement for the grocery, then visits the office of Franklin Coal and Coke, where he's given a rail pass to meet the superintendent of the Jennie Town mine. There's no passenger service. The engine pulls flatcars of mining equipment—drills, coal carts, large ventilator fans, sheets of metal, strapped-down crates. He rides in the caboose.

Jennie Town is a has-been that's sprung to life. He sits in the depot's tavern and eavesdrops on conversations of men who hope to be hired. There's no love lost for the mine boss, an attitude which could signify he has a mean streak, is likely to be careless of danger, or is a good disciplinarian.

To reach Glory before she departs Winkler, he'll delay meeting the mine boss until the return trip. He hangs onto Glory's statement that May Rose will recover.

~

MAY ROSE

Wanda and Piney are cutting two bushels of cabbage for sauerkraut and won't let her help. It's just as well, for she exhausts her strength just lacing her shoes. She's come outside to sit in the shade and watch the fence-building. Will and Simpson, Piney's husband, are stretching barbed wire on the slope between this house and Piney's.

Inside that wire, Will's hired man is building a hay shed that will also shelter their animals together—Simpson's mule and cow, Wanda's riding horse, and the young cow Glory bought. She doesn't know where they'll find hay, for it's late to be harvesting, and most everyone's corn was killed by a June frost. Their cow, a pretty brown heifer, will come fresh when her calf is born in the spring. If they can feed her through the winter. If they can feed themselves. Glory's gift, meant to be helpful, feels like an extra burden.

She loves to watch Will, who walks backwards, unrolling the wheel of wire while Simpson pounds staples on fence posts. Three strands should discourage the animals from straying, unless they get hungry or thirsty. In that event, no barbs will stop them.

In a few days, Will and Glory are to leave for Richmond, and Simpson will be the only man in Winkler. One man, four women, five children against the winter. She'd worry less if she felt stronger, had a scythe, and at this moment could be cutting and raking hay for the shed.

The hired man, Ebert Watson, will help in the store whenever weather allows him to reach Winkler. Will, she knows, is uneasy about leaving, but he's passionate about his chance to study medicine. He sold his goats, Wanda said, at the last Trading Days, and his dogs with them. Wanda sold the tent, the wagon, and the horses that brought them from Elkins.

One of the five women is Virgie White, a pretty widow near Wanda's age, now lounging beside May Rose in the dry leaves. Every day, Virgie wears a different dress and matching ribbons in her brown curls. Wanda says Virgie is more capable than she looks. While Will is away, Virgie will manage the store.

Virgie chatters away. "I love to watch men work, don't you? Do you think Piney is growing her own baby yet? I hope so, she wants one more than anything. Well, she's got Simpson's grandkids, sure, but you never know about the kids' ma. She might steal them away some day. Them kids is lucky to have Piney. She might be too old for a baby of her own. Has she said?"

May Rose answers with a shake of her head. In the distance they see Alma helping Piney with the children. Alma helps everywhere.

"That Alma is like Will," Virgie says. "Ready to work at whatever's to hand. Lord, we're going to miss him." Virgie gives her a sideways look. "Has Wanda said anything?"

"About?"

"Her and Will. I thought for sure she'd got him. I'd say she thought so too. But way back, I thought I'd got him." Virgie giggles. "Never set your sights on a dedicated man. Will's more honest than a preacher, but didn't we have some high old times? I know for a fact him and Wanda did too. He ain't the most handsome of men, but I don't want one who's prettier than me."

May Rose doesn't want to think of Wanda's high old times or the trouble that scarred her face, but if there's a baby, she hopes it did not start in trouble.

"I want a man who wants me for myself," Virgie says. "Take Ebert over there, a regular-looking man, busy day and night, got a farm, a nice old ma, and a boy about the age of Alma. Ebert asked me to marry him, said he needed a mother for his boy. I said I don't want to be mother to nobody. Don't be surprised if he comes calling."

"Evie needs a father," May Rose says. *If she's right, the other one will need a father too.* "Is Ebert a good man?"

"Good as any. I suppose he might call on Wanda, but I figger he knows about her and Will. I mean he'll be calling on you."

For the first time in what seems like years, May Rose fills with laughter. It leaves her exhausted but refreshed. She wipes her eyes. "Me? I'm past all that."

"Go on," Virgie says. "You don't look no older than me and Wanda. She says you married her pa. Was he a good husband?"

"A good husband?"

She watches Will and Simpson stretch the third strand of wire. Ebert Watson climbs a ladder with a sheet of tin for the shed's roof.

"He wasn't even a good human being." She didn't intend to say it aloud.

14

To get to Winkler, Barlow will have to walk, for every horse and mule in Jennie Town is committed to the mine. If he walks briskly, he'll get there in half a day.

At the start, he hangs his coat over his arm. Not long after, he unbuttons the neck of his shirt and rolls up his sleeves. After an hour on the road, he wishes his shoes had thicker soles. Wet with sweat, he rinses his shirt in the river. It cools him for a while. He's desperate for water, but thinks of May Rose, who may have acquired the typhoid bacteria in this river, though Glory said there was a sick child who traveled with them, one May Rose held most of the way.

He never quite stops thinking of her. In her presence, he felt forgiven; away from her, he feels guilty about Alice. He's never been unfaithful to his wife, but he's also never been entirely true.

Along the road, the burned-over sections are only partly disguised by vines tipped now with red. The prospect of seeing Winkler again is as appealing as digging up a corpse. He was there before the town's birth and left before its final destruction. No one blamed him except perhaps Cousin Wilbur and Cousin Hobart; it was boom and bust, the regular cycle of lumber, like coal. But Will Herff was enthusiastic about his town and Glory was eager to see it. And now May Rose is there.

He's cooling his feet in the river when he hears the approach of a wagon team. Coat over his arm, shoes in hand, Barlow waits at the roadside. The driver stops his mules and pushes back his hat. "Awful warm day for a walk," the driver says.

The driver's name is Loughrie, and he's hauling store goods to Winkler. "I hope you're a good talker," Loughrie says. "These mules don't entertain me much."

Loughrie says he's been everything, but thinks he's only good as a fiddler of music. Barlow is pleased to learn they have people in common to talk about. Loughrie knows Will, who ordered most of what's in the wagon. He also knows Wanda, and hopes to be her uncle someday. He names Ruth Bosell, the woman he intends to marry, and others in Wanda's family. Loughrie doesn't mention Wanda's mother, who worked in the Winkler brothel. Perhaps no one in the family has told him about her.

"My niece is in Winkler with Wanda," Barlow says, "and another old friend, a sick woman."

When Loughrie says he prayed recently over the sick woman, worry strips Barlow's desire to talk.

Polite and soft-spoken, Loughrie asks no questions, but reminisces about Winkler as it was and is and as Will Herff would like it to be. Market days once a month; Will calls them Trading Days. In the future, a railroad and a paved road for trucks and automobiles.

To be honest, Barlow must admit he knew Winkler in its past and share something about himself. "I managed the lumber mill. Now I work for the B&O."

"Did you now," Loughrie says. "Folks will be glad to see you."

He hopes it's so.

When at last they arrive, the valley floor looks much as it did at the time of his first acquaintance, when it was no more than a farm and a trading post. The space seems too narrow to have held mill buildings, lumber docks and railroad tracks, and he can't imagine how so many houses once fit on the hillside.

Burned swaths along the road mark what he thinks must have been sites of the tannery, bar, hotel and boardinghouse. There's no gain in looking back.

Loughrie stops the mules in front of the old company store. A boy on the steps gets up and helps them unload the crates, all but one Loughrie says belongs to Wanda's stepma. May Rose.

Will is not at the store. The boy points to the hillside. He's up there, building fence.

To deliver May Rose's crate, Loughrie drives the wagon to the house. She and another woman are sitting outside, and Will isn't building fence—he's sprawled on the grass beside her. The afternoon sun glints on her yellow hair. She lifts her hand to shade her eyes.

Will rises when Loughrie stops the wagon. "Mr. Townsend! Will turns to the women. "Here's a surprise!"

She'll think he's breathing hard from the effort of climbing the slope—an old man, she'll think. But it's relief that hammers his chest. Her hands are crossed in her lap, her cheeks touched by sun. She's better, and he thinks the pleasure on her face reflects his own.

It's necessary to look away and acknowledge everyone. May Rose introduces the woman beside her, Virgie, a brown-eyed beauty. Will is in his undershirt. He looks young, tanned, sweaty and fit.

Virgie hurries inside to tell Glory and Wanda of their arrival. Loughrie and Will carry May Rose's crate up the slope and into the house. They're alone.

He hunches to the ground. "I think you're better. I'm relieved. She lets him hold her hand. "I've been a lot of trouble."

"You've given your share of aid."

She asks about Alice.

"No change." He lowers his head, overcome, though not about his wife.

~

MAY ROSE

There's an air of desperate excitement about Barlow, though May Rose could be reading too much. She's never seen him unshaved like this, wearing a rumpled shirt and no tie. Never seen him

108

CAROL ERVIN

crouch down, like now. He has a smudge of dirt on his forehead. Alice would not approve.

"Glory will be glad to see you." She'll wait for Glory to ask why he's made such a long trip.

"It's good to be among friends." His eyes stare, like he's lost in some other thought.

To break the connection, she motions to the valley. "Can you believe how everything has changed?" She does not ask how he feels about the changes. Feelings are too personal.

He releases her hand and turns to look. "Given what I heard of the destruction, I'm surprised Will has accomplished so much."

She's relieved when Will and Price Loughrie come from the house and Barlow rises to meet them.

"I'll be on my way," Loughrie says, "but I hope to see you again."

Barlow and Loughrie exchange a hearty handshake. Loughrie's manner is as formal as Barlow's, and he's nearly as solemn. From Wanda, she knows Loughrie has been both a marshal and a bootlegger and would like to be a preacher, though he has a hard time staying sober. He'd also like to marry Wanda's Aunt Ruth, who has her own trouble with strong drink.

"Thank you for the ride," Barlow says.

"Anytime. You're good company." Loughrie tips his hat to May Rose and strides away.

"I'll be back," Will says. "Gotta lock up the store."

May Rose and Barlow are alone on the lawn for another second, then Glory opens the screen door and hops down the steps.

"Uncle!" Her forehead wrinkles. She gives Barlow a quick hug, then stands back and inspects his face. "Aunt Alice?"

"Your aunt is just the same. I'm here because I have business at Jennie Town, and you and I have some decisions to make. I'm giving up the new house, and need to know what to do about your furniture."

"Giving up? Are you moving back to our house?"

"We're not moving back—we're moving on. To Elkins—I've bought a grocery."

May Rose smiles, thinking how Hester would approve. And now he won't have to travel. She doesn't know if he'll miss that or not.

"You're leaving Grafton?" Glory shakes her head. "And quitting the B&O? I can't imagine. But look at us—Wanda and May Rose moved here, and now I'm moving to Richmond. With my brother!"

Virgie comes from the house and links her arm through Glory's. May Rose would like to join them, but she's too weak to rise. Looking toward the doorway, she sees Wanda. Her scarred face is white with misery.

Virgie angles her head and gives Barlow a full smile. "I also moved recently, Mr. Townsend. Just after I was widowed."

"I'm sorry for your loss." He looks back to May Rose. "And I wish everyone happiness in your new homes."

She's been outside too long, and the shadows have moved, leaving her in full sun. She fans her face with a folded paper. "I think I should go in now."

"Let's all get out of the heat," Wanda says. "I'll bet, Mr. Townsend, you'd like a drink of something. Piney has given us buttermilk, and we have cool water from the well."

"Thank you. Either buttermilk or water would be wonderful."

"I'll help," Virgie says. She and Glory follow Wanda into the house.

May Rose pushes her palms against the ground to rise, but she has no strength in her arms.

Barlow reaches both his hands and pulls her to her feet.

Inside, he helps her to a chair, then sits between her and Glory, hands on his knees and bristling with uncommon excitement. "The Banovics are coming with us. We'll operate the business together."

"That's a relief," Glory says. "I mean, I'm glad you'll be with Mr. and Mrs. Banovic."

"You're right, my dear. I would not want to do this alone."

"What does Aunt Alice think?"

He shakes his head. "It's impossible to know if your aunt thinks anything."

Murmurs of sympathy go around.

Wanda brings glasses of buttermilk, then Will returns and Wanda finds another chair for their circle. May Rose would like to lie down, but she sips buttermilk and listens to Barlow discuss the grocery trade with Will and Glory. From time to time, he glances to include her, but she can think of nothing to add to the conversation.

Barlow and Will talk together like old friends. "Banovic is a clever man," Barlow says. "Together, I think we'll do well."

She smiles at his excitement, and when he catches her in the smile, his face takes on a shadow of remorse. He looks around the circle. "You see, I have to go on."

~

MAY ROSE

She tells them she is well enough to walk down to the celebration. Barlow has come to walk with her. Wanda, who was sick again this morning, says she does not care to go.

Word has circulated that Will is leaving, and the valley is full of wagons and tents. It's an unplanned gathering to say goodbye and tell Will how much they need him to return.

She likes to think he'd change his plans if he knew Wanda's condition, assuming he's its cause.

"You need a railing here," Barlow says. He holds her hand and helps her down the three stone steps from the lawn to the street.

When they turn to walk on, he offers his arm. She needs it more than she thought. He's leaving tomorrow, riding as far as Jennie Town with Will and Glory.

Since yesterday, they've spoken only in the presence of others. She hopes he will not say anything he should not, which might lead her to say something she should not. "Did you rest well in the mill?"

"Very well. It was cooler than my house in Grafton."

"I'm sorry a dusty grist mill is all we could offer. Wanda would like to fix up one of Will's empty houses for travelers. I'm told they stop here on occasion, drummers and coal speculators."

They walk in silence a few more steps. Then Barlow says, "Is Wanda all right? She looks tired."

"I think she's had a hard month, getting our house set up and taking care of me." With him she might share her new worries, if telling did not feel like a betrayal.

Near Piney's house, they turn downhill. At the next terraced street, she stops to rest. "This is Virgie's street. The houses on either side of hers are vacant. I think Wanda is interested in one of those." She leans on his arm. "I'm sorry to be so slow. This is the first time I've gone anywhere."

"I could bring a wagon to take you the rest of the way, or we can go back if you've changed your mind."

"The walk should do me good."

On the street below, men carry pews from the church. Others are setting up a long table, boards on sawhorses. Clouds in the sky bring periods of relief from a sun that feels too bright.

Barlow stands perfectly still, with his head turned toward the valley. "Good for Wanda. The boardinghouse, I mean. Doing something about her future."

"As you are. I feel odd, being so unoccupied."

"Don't be in a hurry. You're still getting well."

"I'll find something to do. Wanda says the store basement is full of furniture that might be repaired, bed frames and such left behind. She's not afraid of work. I'll help all I can."

They walk on. The weedy street is rough, and May Rose watches her steps. Barlow's boots, caked with mud when he arrived, are shiny again.

They meet Virgie, who takes her other arm and walks with them. "Will is going to be busy all day treating infected toenails and stomach complaints," Virgie says. "Whatever will we do without him? He's leaving me his doctor books. Nobody better get sick." She releases May Rose's arm. "I best hurry on, I'm supposed to help in the store."

Virgie gets a few steps ahead, looks back and smiles at Barlow. May Rose resists looking to see if Barlow is smiling too.

When they reach the main street, they walk slowly, allowing time to study the foundation stones, all that's left of mill buildings. High on the slope across the river, the ancient trees remain, black and skeletal. She thinks of the old trail to the cabin where she lived with her husband, Jamie Long. The cabin must have burned too.

"I'd like to see the boardinghouse," she says. "I mean where it was."

He turns her toward the lower end of the valley and stops at a mound of brush and vines. "This is it."

"Are you sure?" She tries to imagine the railroad track that ran between the boardinghouse and the river. The house was surrounded by an iron fence. There's no sign of the fence, no outbuildings, nothing familiar.

He pulls away vines, revealing a pit of fallen timbers. "Here's the basement. Does Will own this property?"

"I haven't heard anyone say."

"I know he bought the Winkler Company's land at auction, but I don't know if he bought the privately-owned real estate too. My Hershman cousins owned all the private businesses—the tannery, hotel and bar, and upriver, most of Italian Town. Everything was lost in the fires and floods, of course. Cousin Clarence must know if they kept up the taxes on the land or forfeited everything at a sheriff's sale."

"This pit should be filled in," she says. "Think of the children."

~

She hurts for Wanda's sadness, though Wanda talks as though all is well. She's also sorry for Barlow. Three family deaths this year, and now his wife is stricken. Yesterday he and Will blocked off the boardinghouse basement with a barbed-wire fence, not as safe as filling it in, but better than nothing. At the end of the day, Barlow carried a bag of cornmeal from the mill to their house, a gift, he said. She could not refuse it. He seemed happy then. Of the three now leaving Winkler, she thinks he is the only one reluctant to go.

She and Wanda stand at the door and watch Will's wagon take them from view. They'll see Will and Glory next summer. She doesn't know when or if she'll see Barlow again.

"We'll be fine, Ma," Wanda says. She sounds lost.

15

BARLOW

Barlow likes Randolph, the young superintendent of the Jennie Town Mine, maybe because he seems uncomfortable sitting down. Randolph's desk is in a tent with the sides pinned up, allowing shade, a breeze, and a view. He reminds Barlow of himself, twenty-five years ago, trying to keep his eye on everything at the startup of the Winkler Sawmill.

It's a drift mine, presently with two horizontal entries. Randolph says he's fought the mine owners for two more plus a separate ventilation shaft. Ideally each underground work space should have its own air flow, not air that carries dust and methane from other working sections.

Barlow is not surprised that the mine's investors don't worry about the law. The state has few inspectors, regulations aren't well enforced, and fines for infractions aren't as costly as doing what's legal. On the other hand, human life is abundant and cheap.

He confesses at the start that he's not worked in a mine. He's picked up the language of mining, knows the work from hearsay. He has skills to offer, not with shovel, blasting powder, or engineering, but in management.

"I need two of me," Randolph says, "but so far the company won't hire a second. I don't suppose you'd be a fire boss. I don't like the one I've got."

Underground, the fire boss checks the air with a safety lamp, one that burns blue in the presence of explosive gasses and extinguishes in the presence of blackdamp, oxygen-poor air that can kill instantly.

"I've a fear of going underground," he confesses.

"You're claustrophobic?"

"Just afraid."

Randolph likes his answer. "I'll tell the company I want you to help me aboveground. They'll say no, but check with me in a few weeks. If they can't send me better bosses, I may have to go underground myself."

Three trains and twelve hours later, Barlow reaches Grafton. He hopes Banovic is awake, because he has forgotten his key to the new house. He is, however, carrying keys to the Elkins grocery.

~

MAY ROSE

It's September. Today May Rose has taken Piney's place, caring for Simpson's grandchildren while Piney and Wanda spend the day in the woods, digging ginseng. May Rose doesn't feel strong enough to manage the little ones alone, but Alma and Evie are there to help, especially with the middle child, a toddler who tends to run off when he tires of getting into things. Alma and Evie take turns pulling him away from trouble and letting him help push the youngest in a baby carriage.

It's her favorite kind of weather, a fine fall day, and after a lunch of bread and cottage cheese, they take the children outside to play in the leaves. She's blinking back the need for a nap and wondering if she dare lie down in the leaves when Alma jumps up and shades her eyes. "Ma! It's Ma!"

Alma takes off at a run, followed by the toddler. Evie catches him and sets him in the carriage with the baby. They watch Alma run downhill and stop short. The woman in the distance is trailed by two children. May Rose worries, because if this is Mrs. Hale, there should be more children.

Alma runs again, reaches the woman and catches her in a hug. No other children appear, and no Mr. Hale.

"I've worried about them," May Rose says to Evie. Now she fears the worst, that like Dakota, the others have died. "They'll want something to eat and drink." She hustles everyone inside and applies a smear of butter to the remaining slices of Piney's bread.

On the back porch, Evie holds a pitcher under the water spout and lets the boy work the pump handle. The water trickles slowly and has a brown cast—in dry weather, their shallow well dries up every day.

Since their parting, Alma has been as silent about her family as though they never existed, but when she brings her mother to the house, she can't stop crying. If possible, Mrs. Hale looks worse, her graying hair thin and her sun-browned skin hard and wrinkled. She does not cry, perhaps too dried out for tears.

"Come," May Rose says, "come and rest. This way." She leads them to the table with its glasses of water and platter of fresh bread.

Alma encourages her family to sit down. "This is Emmy and Tim." She kisses each dusty cheek. "Emmy is seven; Tim is six. Isn't that right?" The children nod.

Evie pushes the buggy into the kitchen, and Piney's children lean against the table and watch the two new ones, who drink and look steadily at the bread.

"You gained some kids, and I lost some," Mrs. Hale says.

May Rose nods, a spot of worry in her chest for the absent Hale children. "We're watching these little ones today for a neighbor."

Evie takes Piney's children outside. Alma pumps and pours more water, and her mother drinks the second glass, then sits with her hand pressed on her ribs, as though she's consumed too much.

Mrs. Hale doesn't speak again until they've finished the bread. "That was good, thank you." She covers her eyes with one hand. "My baby died a while back. Davis, you recall. I almost died myself. I don't guess Dakota is somewhere?"

"She's buried here, Ma," Alma says. "It was typhoid. May Rose got it too."

"I feared that's what it was." Mrs. Hale bows her head. "May Rose. I forgot your name, so sweet. We been all over. Mr. Hale put his kids with some o'his family, all but the oldest boy. Then him and the boy lit out somewhere. I got nobody else, so I brought my kids here."

Alma's sister and brother leave the table and sit with Evie and the others on the back porch.

"My first husband was from here," Mrs. Hale says. "Donnellys. I thought his family might take us in."

She needs no reminder of that name. "They may have been at one time; there are none here now."

Alma lifts her wet eyes to May Rose. "Can they stay?"

"Fetch Virgie," May Rose says. "We'll need another house."

One man, five women, seven children.

~

"Just as we're wondering how to feed ourselves," Wanda says, "we get John Donnelly's wife and kids!"

May Rose sits on the edge of the back porch, brushing dirt from ginseng roots the size of a man's thumb. They're mature roots, but even so, it takes a lot to make a pound.

She sets a root on the brushed pile and picks up the last one. "We have to forget about John Donnelly. And never tell."

"Some things you can't forget," Wanda says. "Like how him and his brother beat up on Will, what they did to me and would've done to you if Charlie hadn't found you. Charlie never would say, but I'm sure he run away so they couldn't kill him. A nine-year-old boy!"

"I don't mean forget. Just don't connect Alma and her family with the Donnellys we knew. Her pa is dead. And she was so happy to see her ma. I almost cried too."

Wanda washes dust from her face and arms in a basin of water. "I wouldn't tell. Alma's a good girl, and her ma seems all right, just knocked about."

"She has bad luck with men, doesn't she? I'd rather be on my own than tied to a man like hers." May Rose sets aside the last root. "What should I do with this ginseng?"

"Put it somewhere shady," Wanda says. "The roots have to dry, like potatoes. That house Virgie is showing Mrs. Hale has no water and no outhouse. No wood stove, nothing."

May Rose gathers the precious roots in her apron. "It's a roof, and I don't think she's had one in a long while. Will wouldn't refuse them."

"I'm just thinking out loud, Ma. I can't turn them away, neither. We'll cobble something together from the store basement."

"Maybe they won't stay."

"Maybe I'm not growing a baby."

May Rose halts in the doorway, holding the ginseng roots in her apron.

Wanda rubs a towel to dry her arms, then pats it on her face. She doesn't look at May Rose. "I'll just run to the store and see what I can find for the Hales."

One man, five women, eight children.

~

BARLOW

Barlow sent Glory's sewing machine by railroad freight to Richmond, and found cheap, dry storage for the rest of her furniture. His wagon drivers have tied down their canvas covers and are ready for the road to Elkins. He and the Banovics lead in the new delivery van, which they've tried to make comfortable for Alice. The van has a split seat, so the driver can reach delivery items without getting out and opening the back doors. The gap allows Mrs. Banovic to sit between Barlow and her husband and extend a reassuring hand to the woman cushioned on the floor behind.

The trip is miserable from the start—for Alice, who moans half the time, and for himself, equally jolted by the bumpy road and unnerved by her cries. When she sleeps, he relaxes and talks with the Banovics about plans for their grocery. When she wakes and moans again, he hangs onto the steering wheel and hopes he's not killing her. They stop frequently to let the horse-drawn wagons catch up; at other times they pull off the road to let vehicles pass.

"Sweetheart," he says, fanning her. "Just a little farther. We'll be there soon."

He's surprised that his resignation was no surprise for his boss at the B&O. It was the right time to go—he and the railroad were tired of each other. There's a bank draft in his pocket that will stock the grocery and leave a cushion for emergencies.

The widow who sold the grocery business had substantial receipts and only a small number of credit customers, which he takes as a positive sign. She also furnished him with a box of invoices from wholesalers. The invoices will help them know products and quantities to stock. He's been too busy to study them.

His only goal is to get Alice safely to her new room. After that, everything will seem easy.

~

MAY ROSE

May Rose has been wondering how they will repay Ebert Watson, who brought a wagonload of hay for their shed. She supposes he and Simpson have payments and arrangements between them, for Simpson's animals will also eat the hay, but she doesn't like to be a freeloader. When she asked what she owed him, Ebert said, "We all help as we can."

Still not fully recovered, she's the only one who spends most of her time at rest. In the days since her arrival, Mrs. Hale has been swinging a pick at the hard ground, trying to dig an outhouse. Virgie will not dig, May Rose cannot, and tells Wanda she must not. Because Wanda also wants a privy for the house she's fixing up for travelers, Virgie has promised to find someone to dig when people come for Trading Days. The fall market will be the last one until spring, sure to be big, with a good mix of buyers, sellers, and folks who come to socialize.

Wanda says, "The hay won't last through winter. I should sell Glory's heifer."

They haven't enough of anything. May Rose has a small stack of bills and coins, but can think of no way to multiply them.

The same day that Ebert brings the hay, she finds Mrs. Hale in the store, fingering softened deer hides. "Someday I'll make gloves for all of you," Mrs. Hale says. "But it will never be thanks enough. You've saved us, me and the kids."

Mrs. Hale's hands are hardened from digging and stained by walnut shells. She and her children have been living on walnuts, plus daily portions of whatever is cooked in the other three homes.

The hides are cheap. "If I buy the leather," May Rose says, "do you think we could sell gloves at Trading Days?"

Mrs. Hale's eyes spill over. "Everyone says I make nice gloves."

Virgie supplies scissors and stout thread. For patterns, Mrs. Hale traces the fingers and palms of every adult in Winkler. Piney and Simpson think gloves are a good idea. May Rose worries they'll do all this work for something no one will buy.

Every day and most nights of the following week, she cuts while Mrs. Hale assembles smooth leather gloves with outside stitching. When they've used all the deer hides, they make gloves of cloth from one of Glory's old jackets. Alma, her sister and her brother continue to hull walnuts.

People drift into Winkler a few days before the full moon and set up tents along the river. The children cannot contain themselves, and beg to run free. Forever wary of strangers, Wanda orders them to stay together.

Trading Days are always held during the full moon. At the last one, May Rose was sick and unaware, and now she's as eager as the children. If nothing more, she hopes to earn back at least as much as she invested in the deer hides. Mrs. Hale has grander ideas, a whole cured ham. Wanda hopes to meet a ginseng buyer.

May Rose and Mrs. Hale have their own table, squeezed among others that line the street. Wanda roams the crowd, carrying the ginseng root in a sling against her body, because the root is too precious to lay on a table where a hand might snatch. Piney, who has stayed home with the children, has sent a few rag rugs to sell. Mrs. Hale spreads out her gloves and mittens and looks hopefully at hill farmers and their wives wandering by. She wears one of Glory's old dresses and a pair of her own cloth gloves to hide her stained hands.

People glance, stop and look, wander away. But some return, and soon their business seems as brisk as at any. "Don't worry if you don't sell every pair," Virgie says. "Your gloves are nice. I'll buy them for the store." She glances at Wanda. "Ginseng too."

At the end of the first day, Mrs. Hale carries home a ham, and the next day, a bushel of potatoes. By the end of the third day, only a few pairs of gloves are unsold. Wanda has sold the ginseng and May Rose has doubled her money. With no market until spring, she can think of no way to earn more.

~

May Rose keeps her ears open for clues to the unspoken topics in their house. Will Herff, now studying medicine in Richmond. Wanda's bad time. The baby.

Repairing and furnishing her boardinghouse has kept Wanda busy and moderated her temper. She and Virgie have an arrangement. When travelers come to Winkler, Virgie will send them to Wanda, for without Will in residence, the store no longer accepts overnight guests. Wanda will collect their quarters in advance, provide clean sheets and wood for the stove. If they need meals, Virgie will feed them at the store.

Except for her one offhand reference, Wanda has not said anything about the baby to May Rose. Soon others will notice. Maybe they'll all pretend it's not there, and when it comes, pretend it's not new.

16

As Virgie predicted, Ebert Watson has come to call. It's Sunday, their day of rest—a necessary time, but hard for men and women anxious about the winter to come, having to sit when they could be stacking wood or remaking old coats for growing children.

Ebert's cheeks are cleanly shaved but his upper lip hides under a thick moustache. He speaks louder than necessary and in awkward spurts. May Rose smiles as she would to reassure a shy child. Ebert's boy has gone with Evie and Alma to carry water from a spring upriver, an allowable Sunday task. Dry weather has nearly stopped the river's flow, and neither Mrs. Hale's house nor the one Wanda is fixing for travelers has a functioning well. But both places have new outhouses, the last boards hammered this week by the women.

May Rose has inquired about Ebert's mother and asked if his harvest was satisfactory. Wanda, who usually has little to say, wants to talk about squirrel hunting. She's traded her revolver for a shotgun.

"Sit under a nut tree and wait," Ebert blurts. "Hours, if you got to. Don't move."

His advice amuses May Rose, for Wanda is not patient in any way.

Wanda jumps up to make coffee, and Ebert begins a topic of his own. "Ma gives my boy lessons at home like she did me, but I'd like him to know more. Will said you're smart. He thought you might get the school started."

She's been preparing lessons in her head, her solution for repaying Simpson, Piney, and Ebert for much kind assistance. "I've thought of holding school in this room." The school building has no doors, its windows are broken out, and Wanda has moved its stove to her boardinghouse. Desks remain, a cracked chalkboard, and a box of moldy books.

The way Ebert is watching gives him away, a silent study unrelated to the topic of school. But they talk of possibilities, what she can teach, books Ebert can donate, what he might pay.

"I'll take no money," she says. "It's my way to help."

"Then I'll bring coal, time to time." His farm is an hour distant, rough travel for his boy in winter. "I've thought, when the weather turns, I could board him somewhere."

"Perhaps at Virgie's," she says. "Virgie is the only one with an extra room."

"Virgie don't care much for kids."

"Then Mrs. Hale's house. He could sleep with her boy. Even a small payment would be a help."

Wanda returns with Ebert's coffee. He holds the cup and stares into it like he's reading tea leaves. "I've seen that woman. She's dirty."

"So would you be," Wanda says, "if you wandered weeks with little food, never mind soap. The Hales carry every bit of water from the river."

May Rose winces at Wanda's tone. "Mrs. Hale has put herself and her house in good condition. As you said, we help each other."

When he leaves, Wanda says, "Ebert's wasting his time. He's all right, but you'll not marry him."

"He hasn't asked." For which she's grateful.

"Don't worry, I'll tell Virgie about the ones you've refused. He'll hear about it. Though that might be encouraging to men who think a lot of themselves."

"I'll worry about lessons and wood for the firebox," May Rose says. It's not easy to keep a man on friendly terms when he wants something more.

"You've toughened up."

It's true. Work has strengthened her body, but her spirit is weakening, and she doesn't know why, unless it's memories of winter in her mountain cabin, a terrible time to be alone.

~

Holding school for the children helps everyone, and the teacher most of all. Starting in November, the daily arrival of her six students gives May Rose something to work for. She teaches reading and arithmetic half the day, then the girls go to Luzanna for sewing instruction, while the boys go to Simpson for whatever task he's set for them.

Today when the children leave the house, Wanda picks up her shotgun. "I can't afford a freeloader. That Johnson has been in my boardinghouse a week and hasn't paid for anything but the first night. He says he's flat broke. It'd be nice if someone settled here who wasn't so needy."

"What are you going to do with the gun?"

"Turn him out, what do you think?"

"Leave the gun," May Rose says. "I'll go with you."

"You think you'll say *go* and that'll do it?"

"Think ahead," May Rose says. "If the gun doesn't scare him off, will you shoot?"

Wanda's mouth turns down, wrinkling its scar. "I wouldn't like to."

"Please, leave the gun. We'll get Virgie to go along. Or we could wait and take Simpson."

"Would you feel safer if we take along some of the little kids?"

May Rose doesn't say *"What's got into you?"* Soon everyone will know, though perhaps never the father. "Let's talk with Virgie."

Virgie says there's a simple solution, and she proposes it when together they confront Johnson on the steps of Wanda's boardinghouse.

"No money, no food. And no store credit," Virgie says.

Johnson limps and one foot turns out, like something was broken and not set right. He holds an armful of wood that's been chopped, split and stacked by Wanda. Smoke drifts from his chimney. Except for necessary cooking, everyone else in town is hoarding their wood for colder weather.

Wanda pulls loose a chunk of kindling, and he lets the rest drop to the ground.

"I'm not against work," he says, "but I've run out of places to go. If you lend me that there shotgun, I'll pay in squirrel and deer."

May Rose thinks he might be trusted.

"Not on your life," Wanda says.

He sits on the step. "Then shoot. Makes no difference to me."

A gust of wind blows chimney smoke into their eyes. May Rose takes a step forward. "How did you hurt your foot?"

"Coal cart run over it. Was never set right and took months to heal. 'Course I lost my job. I complained to high heaven about that and fell in with some unionizers for a while. Got so no company would have me."

Virgie says, "Do you have anything against digging coal?" At the last Trading Days, she sold off the pile left by Will.

"I'm not quick no more, but I can dig and load. You got a mine?"

Wanda sighs and lowers the gun. "Nickel a night, if you chop your own wood and carry your water. And keep others from letting their friends in free."

"Come winter, there'll be no others," he says.

"All right. But dirty my house and out you go," Wanda says. *Two* men.

~

BARLOW

Barlow peels limp leaves from unsold cabbages and puts them in a bucket with shriveled carrots. Upstairs, the Banovics are canning the grocery's fresh meat before it spoils.

"We'll carry no more milk and cream," he told Banovic, who didn't need to be told. He should have known—most people have milk and butter delivered to their doorsteps. Coffee too.

He's afraid he's frightened customers with his false, hearty greetings, for everyone who comes into the store looks startled when he speaks. But in truth, there haven't been many. He looks again at the widow's deposit records. The business was doing well. Most groceries serve a neighborhood. When she left, did she direct her customers elsewhere?

He opens the box of wholesaler invoices and compares the new to old. He ordered the same products in the same quantities. But laying the invoices side by side shows something he should have noticed before. The widow's invoices are three years old. He shuffles through the box, looking for a recent date. Nothing. It's possible she neglected to give him the newest ones.

It hardly matters. For the sake of continuity, they didn't change the store's name, but now, after four dismal weeks, he thinks changing the name can't hurt. So he's hired a painter to put "Banovic's Grocery" on the side and front of the building. Not his name, because he feels stupid and useless in this business.

Banovic says he's been talking to people and has a new strategy in mind.

"I'll leave it to you," Barlow says. In the interim, he needs an income, and the store doesn't need two proprietors. He still has the rail pass to Jennie Town.

After he locks the store, he sits by Alice's bed and reads another chapter of *Wuthering Heights*. Often the story exceeds his patience. He wishes he and Alice had talked about this book, but maybe it's better they did not.

Alice is not improved, yet she's easier to care for and they no longer watch her through the night. She doesn't struggle when he holds her good hand. Perhaps she understands his trouble and feels sorry for him. Perhaps she's glad.

"If I don't get a job at the mine," he tells Banovic, "I'll be back tonight or tomorrow. If I'm hired, you won't see me for a week or more. I'll send a note by mail. And my pay."

17

May Rose holds the ladder for Wanda, who is nailing gutter supports on the eaves of their house. They've not had rain for a month, but when it comes, she wants to collect the runoff in a rain barrel. Like most of their treasures, the iron gutter and pipe have come from the store basement, a damp and crowded place that fascinates even the children.

Piney has come with her little ones to collect the oldest from school. She's stayed to worry over Wanda on the ladder, for wind is blowing in gusts. Wanda's skirt whips around her legs. May Rose leans against the ladder to hold it in place.

"Better save this for another day," Piney says.

May Rose agrees. Black clouds threaten the sky. "Wanda, please stop. It's too late to collect this rain."

When Wanda sets her feet on the ground, wind flattens her skirt over her front. Catching Piney's stare, she lays both hands on her rounded belly and grins. "Yep. Something there, all right." Raindrops strike the roof.

Piney's mouth opens and closes. Her eyelids flutter.

Wanda lowers the ladder and lays it against the house.

Thunder breaks Piney's stillness. "Ruby," she says to the girl, "take your brother's hand. We'll run for it."

"I'll carry him." May Rose lifts the boy and runs toward Piney's house. For once, he doesn't struggle. Lightning flashes from cloud to cloud, and as soon as they're inside, rain pours down.

The water on Piney's face is not rain, but does not seem to be tears of joy. She lifts her apron and blots her eyes and cheeks. "I'm sure this is good. Leastways it'll make Ma happy." She sets the baby in his crib, fumbles in the cookie jar and splits a cookie between the girl and boy, who've climbed onto chairs at the table. "I don't like them to spoil their supper, but they're always hungry this time of day," she says.

"I'll go in a minute." May Rose watches at the window for the rain to stop. There's relief in having Wanda's secret exposed, though she never worried that anyone in Winkler would condemn her. Thunder shakes the house. "Rain. Thank goodness."

"You might as well sit," Piney says. She pulls out a chair. "A baby is always good."

Time and again, May Rose has said the same thing, though it never seemed to console her listeners, women overburdened with children, women alone.

"It's God's child, no matter who got it," Piney says. "What does she say?"

May Rose comes to the table. "Not a word."

Piney bows her head. "I hope it wasn't..."

May Rose waits.

"Is she happy?"

"No. But she's been sick. And touchy."

"I'm afraid it was them..." She stops and sets the boy down from his chair. "Ruby, take your brother into the room and roll the ball." When they leave, Piney says, "You know, the trouble."

She doesn't know.

Piney whispers, "These kids' pa. And his brother. I'm afraid it might of been them, when they kidnapped her."

Kidnapped? Kidnapped? The word wraps her in terror. Wanda's scars. On the train, how she laughed. Her silence about the baby.

Piney drops potatoes in a pot and begins to peel.

"Does everyone know—the trouble?"

Piney nods.

"Virgie too, and Will?"

"Them too, me and Simpson and Ma and Ruth and Mr. Loughrie. And the sheriff."

May Rose paces to the window and watches rain run down the glass. *Kidnapped.* She returns to the table and braces her hands on a chair back. "I haven't heard the whole story." She's not heard any of it.

"It was due to the whiskey," Piney says. "And Ma's homeplace. Not where Ma and Ruth live now. Our old burned-out place west of the mountain." Piney points her paring knife toward the river. "Ma's family made whiskey way back, bootleg whiskey because they paid no tax on it, but it was known all over as a fine product. There was barrels of it stored in a cave on the old place. Ma wanted Wanda to help her get it out, but then..." Piney whispers again. "These kids' pa and his brother kidnapped Wanda and made her take them to the cave. They held her two or three days and left her tied up to die, but she got away. That's how she messed up her face. Kept rolling and falling in briars. It was ripped to shreds."

May Rose has to sit down. Piney moves her potatoes to the table and sits too. "Awful, ain't it?"

"I hope the kidnappers went to jail."

"Not that we heard of. These kids' pa fell and killed hisself on the store steps a couple of days later when him and his brother was trying to steal some guns. His brother got away. And federal men busted up the whiskey barrels, so Ma got nothing."

Piney bends her head over her potatoes and peels off a long curling strip.

May Rose feels sick. "Is there a chance the baby could belong to someone else?"

"Maybe. I don't know. Lots about people's doings is secret, ain't they?" Piney turns pink.

It's not possible to change the father of Wanda's baby. Even so, she has a new prayer. *Let it belong to Will.*

~

Holding school in their house has made everyone feel free to open the door and come in, even on days when they're not having lessons. So May Rose is surprised, on a Saturday afternoon with rain loud on the roof, to distinguish knocking at the door.

She's been sitting in the kitchen with Wanda and Evie as they write cursive letter m's and n's, v's and w's. Wanda, who missed more years of school than she attended, is eager to keep up with her daughter.

"My goodness," she says at the door. Four men stand there in dripping oilcloth. The one in front is Barlow Townsend.

"May Rose." He takes off his broad-brimmed hat, which has not been enough to shield his face from the driving rain. He swipes water from his forehead. "The woman at the store—Virgie—directed us here."

"Please, come out of the weather." Wanda joins her as the men gather inside the door.

"We're surveying for Franklin Coal and Coke," Barlow says. "We need lodging until Monday."

He's a surveyor? Glory's latest letter said her uncle and the Banovics were operating a grocery in Elkins.

Wanda gathers an armload of sheets and blankets newly hemmed by Mrs. Hale. "It's a quarter the first night," Wanda says, "and fifteen cents the next. You make up your own beds. John Johnson will fill your wash pitchers. There's only one spittoon and no slop jars--use the outhouse, if you please."

Smiling at her no-nonsense tone, May Rose touches Barlow's arm as the men turn to follow Wanda to the boardinghouse. "Come back when you're settled. Virgie will feed the others, but we owe you many suppers, and we'd like to hear your news."

While they're gone, she makes pancake batter with Piney's buttermilk and sends Evie to the store for maple syrup and a pound of side meat. Barlow returns before Wanda and Evie. He shakes his hat, slides off the oilcloth coat, folds it inside-out, and steps into the schoolroom.

"Let me." She lays his hat and coat over a desk.

He stands on the entry rug. She follows his gaze over the six student desks, a chalkboard and a desk and chair like the ones she had when she worked for the Winkler Company. "This is interesting," he says.

She loves this room. "You've become a surveyor, and I've become a teacher."

"Good for you." He wears a knitted sweater, canvas trousers, and the hook-and-eye boots of an outdoorsman. His hands are white with cold, and new wrinkles line his forehead. Alice, she thinks, or some other worry.

She invites him to the kitchen and puts fresh beans in the coffee grinder. "I thought you were operating a grocery."

"I'm working for Franklin Coal and Coke, presently at the Jennie Town mine."

"A surveyor and a miner?"

He moves to the stove to warm his hands. She pours boiling water to drip through the ground coffee and into the pot.

"Trying new things." He has a resolute look, like he's trying to make the best of whatever those things are.

Politeness demands that she ask about his wife, though she's afraid to hear. "And Alice?"

"No better. Mrs. Banovic cares for her." He pauses. "There will be no good end to this."

She sets the coffee pot on the stove. No one is free of sickness and loss. "I'm so sorry."

"Thank you. We're adjusting."

Evie brings her purchases from the store, and May Rose slices three strips of meat and lays them in the frying pan. Evie moves her writing practice to a student desk.

Barlow blinks and covers a yawn. "A branch line is coming to Winkler. It will stop at the lower end of the valley and follow the creek west. We're here to find the most economical terrain for it, a route that avoids the need for tunnels but does not create grades that are too steep. Tunnels are expensive, but sharp curves and grades are dangerous and require greater locomotive power. I'm sure we'll often have to decide between two bad options."

The meat begins to sizzle, and she turns the pieces with a fork.

He sits when she carries his coffee to the table. He lifts the cup. "Thank you. Ours is just the first survey; there'll be more in the spring. Possibly as early as next summer, you'll have two new mines a few miles away."

She transfers the meat to a platter and pours circles of pancake batter into the skillet. "And a railroad."

"A coal railroad. But there may be an occasional passenger car. I think Winkler could have a mail hook by the track where it turns west."

"Regular mail—wouldn't that be wonderful?" She brings the meat platter to the table. "Tell me about Alice. Does she speak? Does she know you?"

"Alice no longer tries to say anything, and we don't know how much she understands. Mrs. Banovic feeds her. She opens her mouth but never eats or drinks enough. She has trouble swallowing."

May Rose counts twenty-one bubbles on the pancakes, flips them and waits until twenty-one appear on the top side. Satisfied they're done, she carries them to the table.

"You know," he says, "for years Alice was unwilling to leave our house. I never understood, was never sympathetic." He pours syrup over the pancakes.

She's quiet, sensing his burden.

"Very good," he says, after his first taste. "You're kind to feed me."

While he eats, she washes the skillet and utensils, wondering if he deliberated long before leaving the B&O, or if it's possible that leaving was not his choice.

He brings his empty plate to the sink and refills his coffee cup. She slides the plate into the wash water and pours a cup of coffee for herself. Then they sit together at the table.

"We have rooms over the grocery," he says. "I'm afraid Alice knows we've taken her from her sanctuary."

May Rose can think of nothing to comfort or help. "Sometimes I feel like Alice, afraid to go anywhere."

He sets down his coffee cup in a studied way that reminds her of another time. "That can't be true. Look where you've been and what you've done."

"I never had a choice." She's been both pushed out and pulled along by the needs of others.

"Alice envied you," he says.

"Poor Alice. Nobody should envy me."

His arms lie crossed on the table within easy reach of a consoling hand, were there not so much to hold her back. He is not a child and he is not free, so she can give him nothing but the words of a friend. "I'm glad to see you," she says.

~

BARLOW

Snow continues to fall, nearly eighteen inches since Sunday evening. The boardinghouse has a coal shovel, and after John Johnson digs a path to the store, Barlow shovels his way to the promised breakfast in May Rose's kitchen.

She stands above his place at the table, slides a spatula under corn fritters and sets them before him. He thinks she loves to make others happy. Moved by her smile, he imagines she loves having him at her table. He waits to eat until she sits down with her own plate.

"You can't think of starting today," she says. "And surely it's late in the year to be surveying."

"Everything in this company runs late. We won't be able to start today, but there's a warm wind. John Johnson predicts the snow will be gone tomorrow."

They're quiet, eating. He doesn't remember ever being so hungry, or corn fritters being so satisfying. "That was wonderful," he says, at the end. He hates the thought of leaving. "While I'm here, I'd like to do something for you."

It sounds foolish, but he's pleased when she looks intrigued.

"You have something in mind?"

"Not yet. I'd like you to tell me what you need. Something within my capacity, of course." The brightening of her eyes makes him vow to try anything.

"I have six students," she says, "and one is ready for algebra. Jonah Watson, Ebert's son. He has a book, but I can't instruct him. Though perhaps, with the snow, he won't come today."

"I happen to love algebra," he says.

When Wanda and Evie come into the kitchen, he lights a lamp and sits at the teacher's desk to look through the algebra book. The children begin to arrive shortly after daylight, but not Jonah, who as she predicted, does not make the trip from home.

Barlow stays anyway. She has five other students from three families, each on a different level. He dictates spelling words to Alma, listens to a younger girl read, and stoops beside Evie's desk and points to a wrong number in her addition. May Rose seats a small boy beside her, holds a girl on her lap and traces their fingers over letters of the alphabet.

Being enclosed with her half a day in this room fills him with wonder and despair. Now and then her eyes meet his, and he sees pleasure in her face.

~

By Tuesday morning, rain has washed away most of the snow. Barlow gathers his gear and ties his horse and pack mule near her house. A man and boy are in her kitchen. She introduces Ebert Watson and his son Jonah, and tells Ebert about the survey for the railroad branch.

"Mr. Townsend," Ebert says. "I worked for you. On the lumber docks."

He tries to remember, but there were many men. "Did you like the work?"

"Not especially. And the money was slim. But when my wife died, you came to the funeral."

There were many funerals, and he always attended. He remembers the service for his purchasing agent, and the one for Donnelly, the logger killed in a camp by May Rose's husband. He remembers the day of Donnelly's funeral, the first day he spoke to her. That day he walked her home from church.

Ebert turns to May Rose. "I hear you have some gutter needs put up. I can take care of that before I start home."

He sees how the man aims to please her.

She comes outside as Barlow is mounting his horse. "Please stop here before you return to Jennie Town."

"I'm not sure I'll be able. It will depend on our time and what the others want to do." He has nothing to offer, not even total devotion.

"Then send a letter, so we know you arrived safely."

He smiles. "Yes, Sister."

He's made her laugh.

18

BARLOW

Barlow sends most of his pay to Banovic, along with a note that he's working overtime. At the end of the survey, Franklin Coal and Coke said he could have his pick of mines, or he could travel for them as he did for the B&O. He has chosen to work at the Jennie Town mine because he likes the boss. And because it's only a few hours from Elkins and...

When he's bone-tired, he cares less about his reasons and what anyone might think.

Jennie Town miners work six days a week, but he and Randolph, the boss, have been working seven, for the enterprise has one problem after another. There's currently an influx of Slovakian immigrants brought by an agent who says they know mining. Not one of the immigrants speaks English, and Randolph says these agents always exaggerate the immigrants' experience. To start, Barlow needs to pair them with experienced miners, who will grumble about losing time and money helping men who can't understand directions. His clerk has given each immigrant a numbered tag to wear on a neck chain. He wishes Banovic were here to interpret.

He and Randolph take the immigrants into the store, see the ones who go directly to the carbide lamps, augers and fuses, and the ones less certain, who watch and imitate. Inexperienced men in a mine endanger everyone. It's not all drill, blast and load—they need to know about dust, open flames, carbide safety, ventilation doors, hidey holes and escape routes. They need to know how to make the undercut and how the coal will fall. They need the instinct that comes with experience.

He knows the pressures inflicted by men who have money but no flesh invested in this industry. They're rushing into production, eager for profits in the coming war. The company has not fully supplied the store nor fixed up more than a few houses. Jennie Town miners leave every day for better jobs somewhere else.

He's not the only man in camp who's left his wife behind. Most certainly, the Slovaks left wives and sweethearts in their homeland, and may not see them for a long time. The agent said immigration has slowed because of German U-boats. He and Randolph need to keep all of them content and productive.

Most miners want to bring their families, but as yet there are few houses. The few who've come with wives and children are still living in tents, though the weather is colder every day. The company has installed cots in the town's former school and church, and the mine carpenters are building bunk houses. He doesn't know where he's to put the immigrants. Perhaps the company expects them to sleep underground with the ponies and mules.

"Let me go for an interpreter," he says. Banovic can teach the words they need.

Randolph agrees. Barlow looks forward to Mrs. Banovic's cooking, a good bed and a warm bath. Banovic has not described his new strategy for the grocery, and has sent only one message: *Business good, Mrs. Townsend not change.*

Barlow tells himself he hasn't deserted his wife. Still, he's not eager to see her in that wretched state.

~

MAY ROSE

"Mine," Wanda says. "It's mine."

Virgie has asked the question May Rose would not. *Whose baby you got there?"* They're in the kitchen, Wanda sitting and Virgie behind her, trimming Wanda's shaggy hair.

Virgie slices a razor through the end of a curl. "Does Will know? We got no midwife close that I know of. Maybe you should get him home, delivery-time."

Wanda keeps her head bent.

Virgie holds out another strand of hair. "Maybe you're not sure. Is that it? Not sure? You rascal, worse'n me."

Wanda smiles. "Not possible."

Not possible to be worse than Virgie? Not possible for Will to be responsible or to be told? Not possible for him to come home? As usual, Wanda doesn't explain.

When Virgie leaves, May Rose sweeps red-brown twists from the floor. "I know it's not my business, but if it's Will's baby, he deserves to know. You'll have to explain, sometime. What name will it have?"

"I won't explain if I don't want to," Wanda says. "It'll be a Bosell. Granny will like that. She won't nag about where it come from."

"Have I nagged? I've said nothing. You're like my daughter, yet I'm the only one here who doesn't know everything about your accident. *The kidnapping.*"

"That?" Wanda snorts. "You wouldn't like knowing. Besides, I can't talk about it. I never want Evie to know."

"It's all right," May Rose says. "I don't need to know everything, though I might help you if I did. If it was one of those men... It just doesn't matter. We'll all love your child, no matter what."

Wanda sighs. "It wasn't them. There's been nobody but Will. He was gonna marry me, said he'd come to Fargo and do it for you and Evie to see. Then I did some dumb things. He doesn't want me anymore. I won't tell him about this baby."

May Rose closes her eyes in relief. "Whatever you want."

Wanda bends over the coal bucket and brushes her hair with her hands. "I'm not the only one doesn't tell everything. You and Mr. Townsend? I'm thinking you're more than friendly. You've got a secret."

"Not one I'm proud of," May Rose says.

"Huh. I'm not proud of a lot of what I've done, but I told you about Will. It's your turn."

"I suppose it is." For this, she needs to sit down. "It was when your ma was sick, and you went to Russell's to be with her."

"You worked for the Winkler Company, in Mr. Townsend's office."

"Several months. We became close. Then...we hurt each other. I can't tell you what I did without explaining his part."

Wanda shows her wicked grin. "He must not be hurting anymore."

"We've not spoken of that time. I think he's forgiven me. It's a relief, but I'm still ashamed."

"You shame too easy," Wanda says. "And I know—I'm shameless. I don't need a father for my baby. But you can bet Mr. Townsend will keep coming around. Then what about poor old Ebert?"

"Ebert? Wanda, stop."

"Ma, latch on to somebody, whoever you want. Don't let things just happen."

"You're a good one to talk. But don't worry, nothing is happening to me."

"That's what I'm afraid of," Wanda says.

~

BARLOW

If anything, the grocery has less merchandise than before. There's no fresh or salt-cured meat, no milk or vegetables. Barlow studies the store's newest deposit slips. They show a rising income, nearly what they'd hoped. He doesn't understand why the shelves are bare.

Last night he started to ask about Banovic's new strategy, but Alice had an accident in her bed, and in a rush of shame, he insisted on cleaning the mess himself. He wasn't good at that, either. Mrs. Banovic hovered in the doorway, wanting to take over when he asked what to do with the mound of sheets, her gown, the smeared wash cloths. She brought clean linen, offered to apply cream to Alice's withered buttocks, but he insisted on doing it. While Barlow was taking care of Alice, Banovic went out to meet someone. Friends, his wife said. This morning Banovic took the early train to help the Slovaks in Jennie Town. Barlow slept late and missed him.

Waiting for a customer is so useless and exhausting that midafternoon he turns the door sign to "Closed" and goes to sit with Alice. It hurts to see her beautiful face reduced to a tracing of skin over bones.

Her unblocked eye shifts to the table with *Wuthering Heights*, and he opens it to the bookmark. He does not work underground, but coal dust penetrates everything in Jennie Town, and in spite of last night's tub soak, his thumbnails against the white paper are ringed in gray.

"I'm working at a coal mine, dear," he says, to see if she reacts. When he begins to read, her eye shifts again to the table. Does she want him to put the book down? Or does she mean anything at all?

Wuthering Heights is a story of passionate love. The characters seem unreal and foolish, but the story makes him curious about his wife and her preferences. He's never fully understood either. He's ashamed that she must be insensible before he dares to wonder.

Banovic returns the next morning with a notebook he's filled on the train, pages of Slovak words and phrases. "Gift for miners," he says. As Banovic points to each phrase and tells what it means, Barlow writes an English translation.

"Simple words only," Banovic says.

"Good man." Barlow returns the store's newest deposit slips. "Now tell me about your strategy. What are you doing different?" He's been imagining exotic foods, something new on the market or rare and costly with a high profit margin.

Banovic takes him to the dungeon-like room below the store and opens a crate that says "Sunshine Dairy." Instead of milk and cream, the crate holds mason jars filled with a clear liquid. "Shine," Banovic says.

"Moonshine?" Crates are stacked from the dirt floor to the low ceiling, each lettered with a different name: Sunshine Dairy, Holden's Meats, Wright's Produce.

Banovic's face is proud. "I made friends, learned the widow's trade. Good money."

Bootleg money.

Banovic lifts a crate and sets it by the door. "This one is free, for Slovak friends. I said you would take to mine."

Barlow stares at the crate. "I can't."

"One case. Carry on train. Jars won't rattle—I wrap."

He shakes his head.

"No? Miners will be disappoint. Mine is terrible work—they always drink."

"If I'm caught, I'll go to jail. If you're found out... If you're found out, what will Mrs. Banovic do?" *And Alice, who would care for her?*

"Everybody here know," Banovic says.

"Police?"

"They too."

"Do you pay them?"

"Little bit."

He's glad no one knows him in Elkins. What a coward he is, when the only response he can give to Banovic's business is to leave.

19

MAY ROSE

"Mrs. Hale, you're not alone," Wanda says. "Men always leave."

May Rose is sitting in the kitchen with Virgie, Piney, and Luzanna Hale, confiding in low tones. The children are in the school room, where Alma and Evie are playing teacher to all the little ones except the smallest, who sleeps on Piney's shoulder. On the back porch, Jonah Watson waits to help his father and Simpson turn the auger. The men have pulled the pump and are dredging out their water well.

The day is foggy with mists rising from melting snow. Warm winds have brought a January thaw and encouraged Simpson and Ebert to tackle jobs postponed, like the failed well. For drinking water, May Rose and Wanda have been melting snow.

Mrs. Hale is making a ball of yarn, ripping threads from a ragged sweater. She stops to knot a broken strand. "I'd like you not to call me Mrs. Hale no more. Does it look like I'm somebody's missus? My name's Luzanna."

Alma has said her ma is forty-two. She's getting a curvature to her back and has lost most of her teeth, giving her an elderly look. It may explain why in all this time they've not called her by name.

"Will you take your husband back," May Rose asks, "if he shows up?"

"I pray he don't. I get in the family way if a man so much as looks at me." She frowns at Wanda. "Sorry, I meant nothing bad by it."

Wanda smirks and pats her belly. She expects the baby in two months, but she's tall, and even now it's almost hidden. "I guess no one will think I got this way from a look."

Only Virgie laughs.

Luzanna leans close. "Whatever you do, don't marry any old body just so that child will have a pa. My first man was no good, and though I don't like to speak ill of the dead, I hope he's safe in Hell. Albert Hale might be worse. Me and my kids is better off on our own."

If she hadn't known Wanda's dead husband, May Rose might believe men haven't the capacity to love as women do. But there's also Simpson Wainwright, openly devoted to Piney. Even Luzanna Hale might take another man if she was loved like that.

"I had no mother to counsel me about marriage," May Rose murmurs. "What will we tell our girls?" Alma, nearly a woman. Evie, now ten, who watches Jonah with interest. So frightening.

"You tell them to hold out for money," Virgie says.

Mrs. Hale laughs. "Why didn't I think of that? All I have to do is find my girl a rich man's son."

"Tell them to wait for one that's decent," Piney says.

That stops them. Young girls might talk of love, but women do not. Still, they know love when they see it.

Outside, the men reverse the auger and dump dirt from its attached cylinder. This is the first Ebert has come to Winkler since November. She knows he'll declare himself one day, unless a younger girl takes his attention or something warns him away, like the gossip that plagued her the first time she came to Winkler. From all she's seen, Ebert is a decent man. She'd have a decent life with him and Jonah, a hard-working, agreeable boy. But she already has a decent life. If it's going to change, shouldn't it be for something more?

Will has written once to Virgie about store business, but nothing to Wanda. Glory writes every month, bubbly letters about her art classes and people they don't know. She mentions Will only to say he's deep in his studies and she might as well not be sharing his apartment for all she sees of him.

Two other letters have come since Christmas, one with a Fargo postmark from a man writing on behalf of Russell Long. Russell has returned home, bringing Charlie, who's mixed up in his head. *Charlie*, after all this time. She cried, reading it, and wrote back, "If possible, bring him to us."

She keeps that letter in her apron pocket, along with one from Barlow. "Think what special thing I can do for you," his letter says. "Someday I'll come to do it."

Maybe she's foolish, but she would like to be loved again.

~

BARLOW

Working at the Jennie Town mine is Barlow's escape and punishment. He counts himself lucky to have a room of his own, though snow blows through the cracks and no one finds time during the day to come home and put coal on the fire. He shares the house with the mine boss, Randolph, and the store manager, a new man. Randolph is thinking of moving on; at this mine, everyone is either new or thinking of moving on.

"When the weather improves," Loughrie says, "watch the men light outa here." Price Loughrie is Barlow's friend and confidant, another man escaping and punishing himself. He came in December with his Bible and fiddle. The miners trust him, elected him check-weighman, their man at the scales when the company man weighs the loads of their mining carts. Loughrie also keeps the company man from throwing out slate and other rock. "This rock belongs to the company, same as coal," he says. "Give the men a pure seam, they'll dig it as well." The weight of each man's cart determines his pay. The company weighman hates Loughrie.

Some of the miners are friendly with Barlow, maybe because he's Loughrie's friend, but others scowl because he works aboveground with the boss. Also because they see him with the Slovaks—bohunks, they call them. *Hunkies.* The pages of Banovic's notebook are now smudged with coal dust, but the immigrants have made copies, and every day one or another points to a printed phrase and asks him to sound out the English.

Saturday nights, he and Loughrie sit in Roy's tavern. There's a public side that offers baths, steak and eggs, and a private side with a locked door. The private side sells moonshine and women. Roy is prospering.

Tonight Barlow has followed Loughrie from the steak and bath side to the room where they drink watered-down moonshine.

"I left a good woman for this," Loughrie says, tipping his glass.

Barlow sips. In this place, he's put aside his ideas about illegal whiskey. The drink tastes like bad medicine, but warms his gullet. "I left two, but not for rot gut." Sending his pay to Mrs. Banovic doesn't keep him from feeling like a deserter.

Loughrie raises one eyebrow, waiting to hear.

"My wife," Barlow says, "and the good woman who takes care of her."

Loughrie lifts his glass. "To good women."

Barlow doesn't mind if liquor makes him weak and heedless of the estimations of others. He bends closer over the table. "I've never been good with women. I thought because Alice chose me, I would do better."

One of Roy's girls leans on Loughrie's shoulder and leers at Barlow. "I'm good. Ask anybody." Her face is clean, but her pinned-up hair shows a streaked, dirty neck.

He straightens. "Sorry to disappoint. I'm good for nobody." It has never felt more true.

"Like that, huh?" She sways to his side of the table and ruffles his hair. "Come on, I've seen it all."

"Leave him alone," Loughrie says. "We're enjoying a moment of despair."

Loughrie's good woman is Wanda's Aunt Ruth, whom Barlow met with the rest of her family at Will's going-away gathering. Ruth seems a frightening sort, but Loughrie mentions her every day. "Ruth didn't want me to be a preacher," he says, when the whore drifts to another table. "Should a woman keep a man from what he needs to do?"

Barlow thinks too much of Loughrie to state the obvious. "That's a mystery," he says.

~

When he sees Banovic walk into the office shanty, Barlow knows Alice is dead. Banovic shakes his hand. He thanks him for coming.

The train to Elkins is already being hooked to coal cars. "I'll see if I can get the conductor to delay a few minutes," Barlow says. "If Randolph comes in, tell him why you've come. Tell him I need a week."

He doesn't need to pack, and after he speaks to the conductor, he walks for ten minutes, trying to avoid the truth. He stops at the ventilation shaft and listens to the beat of the fan. He lost their house, and Alice was in a hurry to evict May Rose. If he hadn't shown his feelings so clearly, Alice would not have been quick to move. She might not have had the stroke. He's never disliked himself so much.

Banovic has brought a new notebook of Slovak/English words and phrases that makes Randolph almost forgive Barlow for taking a week off. Before they leave, Randolph collects supply orders for him to place in the hands of Franklin managers. "Tell them we'll all quit if we can't get what we need," he says. "Timbers, rails, fuses, blankets, boots." They both know the men won't quit as long as there's food in the mess and moonshine at Roy's. Not until spring.

He and Banovic are the only passengers in a freezing car that's had most of its seats removed for freight. Barlow wears his heaviest coat, but his feet are soon stiff. He gets up and walks back and forth to warm them.

They talk of their partnership. Banovic's trade has increased in volume. "I can buy now," Banovic says. "I know you don't like this business."

"You're in danger of going to jail."

Banovic laughs. "If I go to jail, I leave missus to you."

"I won't desert either of you," Barlow says. "I'm in your debt, but I don't want to own a speakeasy."

"So I buy from you." Banovic flashes his wide smile. "I save money. Men hate this prohibition. When whiskey is legal again, store will sell best liquor." He reaches inside his coat and hands Barlow an envelope.

"What's this?"

Banovic shrugs. "Letter for you."

The envelope is from Cousin Clarence, he supposes his settlement from the Hershman estate. He's wrong. "Clarence wants to see me. He asks for a convenient time to come to Elkins."

~

MAY ROSE

Ebert's proposal is no surprise, but it comes at a surprising time. They're on the back porch, May Rose pumping water while he nails the last piece of tin siding to shelter the pump from the wind. He pauses, one hand braced on the tin, the other with the hammer ready to strike. "I think we should get married."

Wind blows back the hood of her cape. Ebert is watching for her response. She pulls up the hood and holds it shut at her throat. It's hard to meet his gaze. "I'm honored that you think so."

He shoves the hammer through a loop on his belt. "Then you agree?"

She barely knows him. "I'll have to think about it," she says. Troubled by the ruin of her marriage, she wonders if she dare inquire about his. But yes, they should ask many questions. "Did you love your wife?"

He stutters, then shrugs.

"You didn't love her?"

Wind rattles the tin, and he pounds two more nails. "No, I mean yes. Of course I loved her. She was a good woman. You surprised me. I didn't know what to say." He shouts to be heard.

She waits for the wind to die down. "I'm glad you loved her. I thought I loved my husband. I did, at first, but later I hated him."

"I'm not like Jamie Long."

Her fingers are freezing. "You knew my husband?"

"Knew of him." Ebert looks like he may have struggled with some reservations.

"It's cold out here," she says. "Let's go inside."

He looks through the door glass. "Folks are in there. Will you or won't you?"

Ebert is like Will, reliable and always working. But he doesn't know her either. She lifts the water bucket. "I'm the fool who married Jamie Long. You see why I might not trust my judgment."

"So you'll never marry?"

"I'll never say 'yes' if I don't know a man well. And if he doesn't love me, in spite of everything."

"I guess that's fair," he says.

She's glad he doesn't say he loves her. Perhaps she should say *no* before he says more.

That night she wakes to wind slamming against the house, then the smell of burning. A downdraft has filled the kitchen with smoke. Wanda opens both doors to let air blow through from front to back. It draws smoke from the house, but they're freezing in a moment, and they push the doors shut. May Rose opens the stove's draft and builds up the fire.

A great cracking drowns out the wind. It goes on and on, loud as thunder, like the sky crashing. They try to see out the windows, but all is black except the light that has come on in Piney's house. The cracking and crashing continues. Evie runs downstairs.

"It's all right," May Rose says, terrified herself. It's a freakish storm, wind from the east. The wind slams against the house and snow sticks to the back window. They sit in the schoolroom until the roar subsides and the crashing turns to a frightening silence.

At dawn, everything appears to be covered with snowdrifts. Only later does she notice that the slope across the river looks different. The tall stand of virgin forest, blackened by fire yet standing ever since, now lies in snowy mounds, as though pushed over by a giant hand.

20

BARLOW

"You gave us this chance," Banovic says.

They stand in Alice's room. His room. It's crowded with heavy furniture, their clothing, his desk and chair, her books.

"May I keep this room? I'll pay rent." It's the only home he has.

"You don't have to pay," Banovic says.

"I do. If you have trouble, send for me."

"If I have trouble like you think, no one can fix."

"Maybe not, but you're my friend. I can be here."

"And I for you," Banovic says. They shake hands.

How odd that in distressed circumstances he has found his first friends, Banovic and Price Loughrie.

Cousin Clarence comes for Alice's funeral, a small graveside gathering. Afterwards Barlow and Banovic sit in the parlor with Clarence and sign papers dissolving their partnership. His signature is shaky. He's as weak as if the funeral drained his blood, but he strengthens with Banovic's handshake, relieved of one burden. They wish each other good luck.

"Now, this other matter," Clarence says, when Banovic leaves to open the store. "The Hershman properties in Winkler. They may have some value after all."

"So it wasn't sold, like the Winkler property."

"Our uncles were dotty," Clarence says. "They never trusted you after the mill folded, not that any of it was your fault. But they were...like I said. So they put me in charge of their holdings, had me pay taxes and so forth."

Mrs. Banovic appears in the doorway and raps on its frame. "Beg pardon, visit for you."

Barlow jumps up when the visitor steps into the room. It's Will Herff, looking like a man who's seen neither sun nor rest in a long time. He unwraps his scarf and unbuttons his coat.

"Will! I didn't know you were coming. You've missed the funeral." He takes Will's coat. "Is Glory with you?"

Will swipes back his hair. "I'm sorry. I didn't know about a funeral. It's not...?"

"My wife died."

"Oh." Will's face relaxes. "I'm very sorry. She was a lovely woman. Glory said you'd given up hope of a recovery. If we'd known, we'd have come for the funeral."

"I intended to write later," Barlow says. "I didn't want her to travel in this weather."

Clarence comes forward, hand outstretched. "Mr. Herff, I'm Clarence Townsend. I've asked you gentlemen here to discuss this Winkler business."

"I almost didn't come," Will says, "but I gather from your letter that my sister and Barlow have a claim to some Winkler property. So, Barlow, is that your grocery below?"

"No longer. I've just sold my half to Banovic."

He and Will sit down, for the moment uninterested in Clarence's business. "Tell me about Glory."

"I'm a poor companion," Will says. "I think she's lonely."

Barlow inquires about Will's studies, and Will asks how he's getting along at Jennie Town. Then Clarence gets their attention by moving his chair to face them, opening a folder and taking a pen from his inside coat pocket. "Here's the situation," Clarence says. "We've an offer on the Hershman land in Winkler."

"I'm not familiar with those parcels," Will says. "They're part of Glory's inheritance?"

Clarence inspects his papers. "About forty acres adjoining your property."

"Italian Town," Barlow says, "and land downriver from the mill. You've cleared some of it, like our boardinghouse site."

"I see. I suppose the offer is from a coal company," Will says.

Clarence smiles. "Who else? The interested party has acquired other parcels near Winkler. I think the same organization made an offer for your property. It's Davis Coal and Coke."

"I turned them down."

"Yes, well, if we have no better offer, we'll be selling the Hershman parcels to them. It's likely your property will be in the midst of a coal operation. So I thought you might want to reconsider. I have a few thoughts."

Will turns to Barlow. "Are you involved in this?"

"It's the first I've heard of it. I'm one of the Hershman heirs, as are Clarence and Glory. Unfortunately, one of many."

"I've been thinking," Clarence says, "that one of you might want to make an offer for our uncles' land in Winkler. Barlow, I'll give you first refusal, though I'll have to take the best price."

"You want Will or me or both of us to buy it, or to bid up the price?"

"I don't care who buys it," Clarence says. "But Davis has offered a pittance. Here I am, obligated to liquidate the estate and pay the heirs. Competition for the land will raise the price and fatten the distribution for all. If Mr. Herff isn't interested in buying, perhaps he'd like to reconsider selling Winkler. If we bundle our properties, the company might pay more."

"I'd like to talk this over with Will," Barlow says. "When do you need our answer?"

"I'm being pressed by the other heirs. Can you tell me tomorrow?"

Will rises. "I can tell you now. I'm not selling my valley, and I can't buy anything."

Clarence turns to Barlow. "Do you still need time?"

It's not fair of Clarence to ask today, while Barlow feels weak and sentimental and has Banovic's check in his pocket. "I'll telephone your office tomorrow." He has no confidence that he'll be any wiser.

MAY ROSE

It's Friday. Ebert's boy has left for a weekend at home, and the other children are taking turns on two sleds made by Piney's husband. May Rose sits at her desk near the school room window, attuned to their squeals of delight, re-reading the letter that came yesterday from Jennie Town.

Barlow's letter repeats news they've learned from Glory: Alice has died, and he's sold the grocery to Banovic. He gives no details about these events, now a month past. She sent a note of sympathy, but it must have crossed this one.

She shared one item of his news with Wanda and Piney. Price Loughrie, who they thought was at home with Wanda's Aunt Ruth and Granny Lucie, is working in Jennie Town. Barlow calls him a good friend.

The envelope is smudged, but Barlow's letter is clean, and his message is evenly spaced on the paper, with faint traces of ruler marks. The cursive letters, too, are precisely penned, though smaller and tighter than those she sees in the schoolroom.

I'm afraid much of Winkler will soon revert to industry. The property beyond Simpson's mill, what used to be Italian Town, plus land downstream, the boardinghouse and all, has been sold to Davis Coal and Coke. I offered to buy the property, but Davis outbid me. The new branch line will travel through the middle of Will's valley.

She's proud that he tried, and wonders if he was greatly disappointed. Will wrote to Virgie about the sale, but said nothing of Barlow's offer. Virgie is excited by the prospect of new residents and greater commerce. They don't expect to see changes until late spring or summer.

The next part of Barlow's letter begins on the second page, the part she did not share.

I need to speak now of long ago. I've never properly apologized for my bad behavior. I think you may have partly forgiven me, but it would help to hear you say so. I should be saying this in person, but my faults are easier to admit on paper.

She dips her pen in ink and holds it above a blank sheet of writing paper. This is his second apology; he stammered the first long ago. Like him, she's not proud of their past.

At times she's found excuses for the harsh words she uttered then: the stress of the time, her shock. Contempt that only when she discovered the telegram did he confess. The telegram begged her to come to Fargo to help her orphaned cousins. It had fallen into his hands, and he'd kept it a day, then days and months. When she found it hidden in a filing cabinet, he tried to justify his deceit as concern and love. Until that moment of discovery, she believed his offer was the best she'd ever receive. She was starting to love him. They were keeping their plans secret, even from Hester.

She looks through the window toward Simpson's mill and the land that was Italian Town. It happened there.

The midwinter sun hides low in the sky, smearing its cloudy blanket with streaks of ivory. With all that has passed, they should at least be friends.

Dear Barlow,

Thank you for sending us your news. Perhaps you have not received our note of sympathy. In case it has gone astray, let me say again how sorry we are for your loss.

At this point she should add something comforting, but she has less sympathy for him than for Alice, who seems not to have loved or been much loved by anyone.

She writes again, easier words.

Like you, we are eager for spring. We are surprised but glad to know that you and Price Loughrie are friends. Please give him our regards.

Our most dramatic news is that Simpson slipped on ice yesterday and turned his ankle. At present it won't bear his weight, and if it does not heal in a few days, we will have to devise splints for it. How we miss Will!

I've conveyed your news to others here, for we have little contact beyond Winkler and take heart in hearing of those we know. I have not, however, shared what transpired between you and me back then. Here is my sense of it: I was as much at fault for accepting your offer as you were for making it. So I think we can forget…

She's about to write *and start again*. But start again at what point? The point where they were acquaintances, the point at which she accepted his offer to keep her as his mistress, the point at which he apologized about the telegram and offered marriage?

She adds an ending and reads the sentence again. *So I think we can forget everything. I'd like to forget my words. They shame me still.*

It will be best if he thinks she's ashamed of her rude refusal. She can't confess the lie that shames her most—that when he touched her she felt nothing at all.

In her mind, he's still Alice's husband. And she doesn't trust her heart.

Saturday is sunny, and all afternoon the children sled and play in the snow. Wanda paces from room to room and denies her time is near. When May Rose takes her letter to the store, she decides to talk with Luzanna, the only other woman in town who knows what it's like to have a baby.

The sled runs have turned into brown paths up and down the hillside, and the children have moved farther away to fresh snow. Piney comes outside and calls her children home. As the little ones trudge uphill, May Rose sees their red cheeks, the snow stuck to their hats, coats and mittens. It's time for all to come in.

The children's screams begin as she reaches Luzanna's house. Alma and Evie run downhill, calling, "Emmy! Tim!"

Luzanna runs from the house, and together they slip and stumble down the slope toward the site of the old boardinghouse.

Alma runs ahead, but Evie turns and waits for them to catch up. "They fell in! Emmy and Tim! They slid right under the wire!"

Alma stops where a post sticks from the snow, a portion of the fence Will and Barlow built around the basement.

May Rose and Luzanna shout at Alma to stay back, but she stomps down the wire fence and climbs over. Before they reach her, she disappears. Snow flies up and settles down, and timbers crash. From the pit, children's voices cry out.

Luzanna reaches the fence and goes over. May Rose turns Evie around. "Tell Piney to bring a ladder. Get blankets from your ma. Tell her I said to stay inside. Find Mr. Jonson."

May Rose bends beside Luzanna and peers into the old basement. Emmy and Tim squat in dark water beside Alma, who is lying face down under crossed floor joists. "Get her head outa the water," Luzanna cries. "Give her air!"

Tim stretches over the timbers and lifts Alma's head. They hear her choke and gasp. "Thank God," Luzanna says.

The boy is stretched beyond his height and strength. "Ma," he cries. Alma's head drops back into the water. He lifts it again. "I can't hold her! Should I crawl on top the wood?"

"No," May Rose says, afraid he'll push the timber down on Alma. "We're coming. Hold on."

Piney hurries to them with a ladder, and they lower it into the basement. "Emmy," Luzanna says. "Can you climb out?" The girl climbs up, and Luzanna goes down the ladder and takes her boy's place, holding Alma's head above water.

Evie has not returned with blankets. The boy climbs out and May Rose sends him and his sister to Wanda to get dry and warm. Then she climbs down into the basement. As soon as she steps from the ladder into the water, her feet feel turned to ice. She lets her eyes adjust to the dimness. If the timbers are moved, will they bring anything else down? Their ends seem unconnected. She puts her hands under the one on top. It's an eight by eight, roughhewn like a railroad tie, and she can't budge it. "Ropes! We need ropes!"

Above them, Piney nods and disappears.

"She's freezing cold," Luzanna says.

Luzanna is awkwardly stretched across the timbers, holding Alma's head out of the water. Alma's eyes are closed.

"I'll hold her while you rest." They change places. Her hands, like her feet, grow numb. Probing in water, she finds and clutches one of Alma's hands. It's icy and limp.

The pit is nearly full of burned wood. She and Luzanna shift positions again.

Piney returns and throws down the end of a thick rope. One end of the top timber is in water and the other rises in the air. May Rose loops the rope and slides it over the free end.

Piney calls from above. "Can you come up and help me pull?"

She climbs the ladder, but though they knot their end of the rope for hand-holds, they cannot move the timber.

"Bring me a saw," Luzanna calls.

Simpson crawls through the snow, dragging his injured leg. He lies at the edge of the pit, looks down, then points to one of Will's snow-covered piles of lumber. "See if there isn't something over there for a lever."

Jonson comes, limp-running. He and May Rose pull apart the stack of lumber, ripping their hands on splinters and nails. She finds a long two-by-four, and Jonson drags a rock to the edge to support it as a lever. As he probes the lever in the pit for a place to wedge it under a timber, May Rose climbs down the ladder to hold Alma's head. Luzanna stumbles back and rests against the ladder.

Alma has lost her knitted cap. May Rose strokes her wet hair. The girl's eyes are still closed. "Alma, honey, we're going to get you out. Just a minute now. You'll be warm in a minute." May Rose isn't sure she's breathing. She slides a hand through the space between Alma's back and the lower timber; she hopes the space means the girl's back did not break the timber's fall.

Their lever isn't long enough to lift the timber more than half an inch, but Luzanna gives a mighty lunge and push, and with a shudder, the timber crashes safely away from Alma.

Wet and freezing, May Rose has begun to shake, but with the top timber moved, she is able to squat close and hold Alma's head in both hands.

Luzanna struggles to move the rope to the last timber while Jonson prods the water with the two-by-four. "I need something longer to lift this one," he says.

The cloudy sky grows darker. Piney hands down a saw, and Luzanna starts ripping it into the timber. Jonson climbs down to take a turn. The wood catches the blade. "Oak," he says. "It's gonna take forever."

"Piney," May Rose calls. "There's iron pipe in the store basement, long sections."

Jonson's saw has dug no more than an inch into the timber when Piney returns and calls, "Here's the pipe."

"Slide it down here," he says. When the end of the pipe comes down, he digs it under the timber and hurries back up the ladder. "Get ready to pull her out."

When he bears down on the lever, the timber rises, and May Rose and Luzanna roll Alma toward them. She doesn't wake. Moaning, Luzanna squats and cradles her in her arms.

Jonson comes back into the pit. "I can carry her." He stoops, and they lay Alma over his back. Luzanna and May Rose hold her on as he starts up the ladder. When Jonson nears the top, Simpson reaches down and grabs the girl's wrists. From below, May Rose sees Piney pull Alma into her arms. Jonson climbs out and takes the girl from Piney.

"My place is closest," Piney says. "Take her there."

Luzanna hurries up the ladder as Piney and Jonson disappear.

May Rose is the last to climb out. Simpson lies on the snow. "I'll be fine," he says. "Get yourself warm."

She stands a moment in the wind as Simpson begins his crawl uphill. Freezing, slipping and sliding, she runs along the slope toward home, wondering why Evie did not come with blankets.

In the house, she finds Tim and Emmy wrapped up and sitting at school desks near the coal burner. Evie runs down the stairs. "It's Ma! The baby!"

May Rose drops her wet cape on the floor. "Get Virgie, and tell her to bring Will's doctor book."

"I already got Virgie," Evie says, "but we was too late. The baby's come."

21

MAY ROSE

"She drank some potato broth this morning," Luzanna says. "Was awake for a time, said she don't feel nothing." Luzanna's knitting needles click like her daughter's life depends on this cap she's making. The yarn is red, from the ripped-out sweater.

They sit at Alma's bedside. May Rose holds Alma's hand. "Evie's in a hurry for you to see her baby brother."

Alma opens her eyes. "I took care of a baby for Ma, didn't I? Davis, when he was born. I tried. Davis never caught on to living."

Alma's face and hands are scratched, and her hair has dried stringy, like a worn-out mop. She blinks at May Rose. "I don't remember how we got out. I remember Ma holding me."

"Mr. Johnson carried you up a ladder," May Rose says. "Everyone helped."

Alma's eyelids drift down, like a newborn who hasn't found how to hold them up. After a few moments, she opens them again. "When can I see the baby?"

"Soon as you feel like getting up," Luzanna says. She lays the cap on her knees and presses it with her fingers. They've worried since Virgie read the section in the doctor book about paralysis.

"I feel pretty good," Alma says.

Alma, their angel, John Donnelly's daughter. When May Rose thinks of the Donnellys she sees sneers and narrow looks. Remembers them attacking her and Wanda. Sees them holding

Wanda down in the woods. None of that affects how she feels about Alma, who has given the Donnellys a better name.

The girl's eyes close again and her breathing deepens. May Rose and Luzanna talk in low tones, avoiding their main worry, sharing where they've been and telling of people who have been good to them.

"I've known more good than bad," May Rose says. "And sometimes I was surprised when good came from someone I thought was bad. Like my husband's brother, Russell."

Luzanna resumes her knitting. "He was a bad one?"

"He made everyone think so. But it was my husband who was bad, and Russell turned out to be a great help. He's always been rough, and he sometimes gets things wrong, but he took in Wanda's ma when she was sick, along with a boy who grew up and married Wanda. That was Homer, Evie's father. Then Russell found Will's little brother, Charlie, though he didn't bring him home, I think because Charlie was afraid to go home."

"All o'that happened right here in Winkler?"

"I lived in Winkler at the time, but Russell's place was west of here, almost a day's ride."

"Wanda told me you all ended up way off in North Dakota."

"We did. I left here when I heard my young cousins were orphaned in Fargo. I'd have gone by myself if it hadn't been for Russell. Wanda's ma was dead by then, but she wouldn't go with me. So Russell left her no choice. He sold everything and bought train tickets for Wanda, Homer, Charlie and himself. Then he got a job at the stockyards and stayed in Fargo. Homer lived and worked with him, and Charlie and Wanda lived with me."

"Wanda says her and you haven't seen Charlie for years."

"He said goodbye when he was fifteen. It's been awful, never knowing where he was or if he was alive. But Russell went out looking for him last summer and found him somewhere. I've waited all winter to hear more. I hope if your children ever leave home they'll be kind enough to keep in touch."

Luzanna reaches out and holds May Rose's hand, and they sit linked like that, she to May Rose, May Rose to Alma.

"You have good children," May Rose says.

"Thank God. They're all I got, but they're worth the world. I pray the sins of the father will never fall on them."

May Rose nods. They've already endured too much.

On her way home, May Rose stops at the hay shed. Simpson is there, braced on a crutch. The cow and heifer, mule and horse stand in the sunshine, waiting. The animals have punched trails in the snow throughout the valley, eating dry weeds and saplings. The hay is gone. No matter how fine the days, spring is a hungry time.

"Wanda keeps saying we should slaughter the heifer," she says.

Simpson shrugs. "Grass will be growing in a few weeks."

"I know, but we can't eat grass." The store shelves are bare of almost everything but tobacco and liniment.

"I've a fifty-pound bag of cracked corn at the mill," he says. "I've been wondering which we should feed, the animals or ourselves. We've got potatoes and kraut. The cow's been giving enough milk for the baby. We've gotta have that."

"Does it look to you like our heifer is going to have a calf?"

Simpson shakes his head. "She'd have a milk sack by now. I'd like to bring that corn from the mill and keep the animals fenced up at night. Have you seen the wild dogs?"

"I've heard them."

"This old cow is weak. I'm afraid the dogs will get her."

"I can bring some corn from the mill," she says.

"That'd be fine. Whatever you can carry."

On the way to the mill, she stops at the store to borrow two five-pound sacks. Virgie is dusting empty shelves. "I don't know why I come here every day," Virgie says, "except it's someplace to go, and being here makes me glad to get home."

"Any trade today?"

"No. It'll start up soon as the roads dry. Are your hens laying yet?"

"One egg, yesterday." Hens always lay better in spring, but she has nothing left to feed them. They spend their days scratching the snow. Simpson will let her have a handful of corn.

"Will's supposed to be sending a load of potatoes and seeds," Virgie says. "With most folks' corn being froze last summer, lots has ate their seed potatoes. Almost nobody has any left over to plant."

"When you write to Will, please don't mention the baby."

"You betcha. Wanda's already threatened my life. But I don't know how she thinks she'll keep it secret. If it was me, I'd of told as soon as I knew."

At the grist mill, May Rose fills the two sacks. After delivering them to Simpson, she goes home and enters Wanda's room, where Evie is rocking the baby. Wanda looks unnatural, lying in bed.

May Rose opens the door of Wanda's clothes press. "Where's the shotgun?"

"Why do you want to know?"

"I'm going to lend the gun to John Johnson. He said he'd rather hunt than dig coal, and meat is what we need right now."

"I don't trust that man," Wanda says. "He's got a weasely eye."

"He saved Alma, and I'm hungry. He's not gonna hurt us or run off with the gun."

When Wanda doesn't answer, May Rose stoops and pulls the shotgun from under her bed. "Where are the shells?"

Wanda tightens her lips.

"Never mind, I'll get some from the store."

~

Last week, the ground thawed and every path turned to mud. Then temperatures dropped and mud froze, making roads hard as washboards but passable, allowing Wanda's granny and her Aunt Ruth to ride their mules to Winkler. Each carried a sack of corn. Wanda's baby is one week old.

They're sitting in the kitchen while Wanda and May Rose fry two skillets of squirrel. Virgie has come to write down Lucie's seed order.

"I knew it," Lucie says, when Evie puts the baby in her lap. "When we got the thaw, I knew the baby had come too. What name have you give him?"

Evie hovers near, looking like she fears the shaky old woman will drop him.

"Otis Homer Bosell," Wanda says.

"Homer for my pa," Evie says. "I picked that part."

"Bosell." Granny Lucie sniffs. "Bless you. Who's its pa?"

Virgie lifts a tuft of the baby's black hair. "Plain as the nose on your face, Old Woman."

"Nobody," Wanda says. "Don't be asking again."

Lucie grunts. "Don't matter to me."

May Rose is sure it will matter to Will.

"Aunt Ruth," Wanda says, "we hear Price Loughrie is working in Jennie Town."

"Jennie Town." Ruth turns her head toward the window. "So that's where he lit."

May Rose forks the squirrel pieces onto a platter and drizzles flour into the grease for gravy. "He's a friend of Mr. Townsend, so I'd say he's in good company."

"More like Mr. Townsend is in bad company," Ruth says. "But if the weather holds, I might ride down there tomorrow and see. Ma can visit here with Piney a few more days."

Lucie holds the baby's fingers. "First Bosell boy in a long time. You've made me proud."

"It wasn't done for you," Wanda says.

Lucie wags her head. "Otis Bosell, you and your ma come and live with me. I'll ask no more about your pa."

"We might do that," Wanda says.

May Rose turns her back and presses down on her spoon to stir lumps out of the gravy. Men aren't the only ones who leave— children leave too. It's best not to depend on any of them.

~

BARLOW

"Is this the post office?"

Barlow looks up from his tally of weights and coal car numbers. Wanda's Aunt Ruth stands in the doorway. "Miss Bosell." He rises, knocking back his chair. "Is everything all right?" He drops his pencil. "In Winkler?"

"Getting by, Mr. Townsend. I've brought the mail."

Winkler mail, he hopes. "The post office, yes. It's in the store."

"And I'm looking for Price Loughrie. I've heard he's here."

"Yes, he is. I'm pleased to see you again, Miss Bosell. Price is at the tipple, but his day's about done; he'll be washing up soon."

"Price is working?"

"He's check-weighman," Barlow says. "Supervises the coal weighing."

"Supervises." She shakes her head. "Wonders never cease."

"Would you like to wait here? Saturdays, Price stops by and we get supper at the depot."

"I'll take the mail to the store. I suppose Roy still runs the depot?"

"He does."

"And Price preaches, I'd say, when he's drunk enough to feel like repenting?"

Barlow nods. Occasions he'd rather forget.

She sorts through the bag on her shoulder and gives him two envelopes. "I'll see Price at Roy's. Don't tell him I'm here."

"Would you like me to show you to the store?"

"You sit tight. I'll spot it."

Two envelopes, both from May Rose. He stares at his name, written in careful script, the kind children learn in the schoolroom. Such foolish thoughts he has, such greed, himself a man of middle age with nothing to offer. Better that he face the truth, like Price Loughrie. Yet Loughrie's woman seems to have come for him, and May Rose has sent two letters. He'd like to believe she thought fondly as she wrote.

He slides a knife carefully along the top of each envelope and spreads the folded sheets on his ledger. One is no more than a paragraph, a note of condolence. The other has two sheets. He closes his eyes, afraid to look, trying to remember what he revealed of himself. How frightened she'd be if he wrote everything that enters his mind.

Only one paragraph refers to his apology, those words as evenly spaced and carefully formed as all others. He reads again, seeking a clue to what shames her. Is she ashamed of revealing his deceit to Hester and everyone in the boardinghouse? He deserved those words. He'd like to think she regrets what she said in private, words that left him floundering. He'd like to think her letter means those words weren't true.

When Price stops at the shanty, Barlow says, "You go on, I've got no appetite." There's another letter on his desk, from Cousin Clarence, and he doesn't know what to do about it. Banovic is in jail.

~

MAY ROSE

"I want to give the heifer another chance," May Rose says. "She may have been too young to breed." It's odd, the animals she's willing to kill, like squirrels and wild dogs, and the ones she can't, like the pretty heifer, young and full of promise.

She and Wanda are cleaning ramps, broad-leaved wild onions, smelly but tasty eaten raw or cooked with potatoes. They're the first edible greens of the year. Luzanna, Alma and John Johnson dug them yesterday in a steep dark ravine. Alma is well. Who would have expected a child of John Donnelly to be so precious to all?

Wanda pauses to chew on a ramp. Luzanna said ramps would turn Wanda's milk bitter, but Wanda said little Otis might as well get used to mountain food. Except for feeding, she scarcely holds her baby, but Evie and Alma play with him every moment they're not doing lessons or chores.

Luzanna says the new mother has the baby blues. Only on the day Alma regained the use of her legs did Wanda seem happy.

There's a rap on the back door. Wanda gives the visitor a glance. "It's that man again."

Wanda won't say his name—John Johnson. May Rose opens the door and accepts another squirrel. "You've skinned it. Thank you!"

"I'm gonna want my shotgun back some day," Wanda says.

"Yes, ma'am. Say the word." Johnson backs to the step and leaves.

"Be nice," May Rose says. "He's not only feeding us, he's feeding Luzanna and her children. We're lucky he's here."

Wanda sets the squirrel in a pot of water. "Yes, he's here, but who did he leave behind? That's what men do—they leave. Have you noticed? Not a child in this place has a father."

"Evie's father didn't leave on purpose."

"Maybe he would've, in time."

"Wanda. You know that's not true."

"Well he died. That's a kind of leaving. Even old Loughrie left Aunt Ruth."

"Your aunt said he wanted to work awhile."

"Work where he could have steady drink," Wanda says. "There's work at Granny's. But he left, and now Granny and Aunt Ruth are alone."

"I know Will," May Rose says. "It's not fair to accuse him of leaving his child when he doesn't know about it."

"Sorry, but Will left *me*. So he doesn't get to know about my baby."

May Rose pumps a pan of clean water to rinse the ramps. She tries not to judge what's best for Will and Wanda, but she's been tempted to tell Glory. Or Barlow.

"Maybe," she says, "men go where they have to be."

"They go where they *think* they have to be," Wanda says. "There's a difference."

Perhaps she's right. May Rose has never understood why Barlow is working in Jennie Town.

22

MAY ROSE

"Granny has plenty of food, and what you have here will go farther with us gone," Wanda says.

Otis is bundled like a papoose on Wanda's back. She's living up to her threat, taking him and Evie to stay with the Bosells.

May Rose reties the baby's knitted cap. Wanda hasn't said, but it isn't hard to understand why she's going. Will is due to come home. This time, Wanda wants to be the one who left.

Evie has not smiled since Wanda announced their trip, but in the last hour she's seemed brighter, learning she gets to ride Ginger, the mare Wanda bought on her first trip to Winkler. Wanda's sidelong looks have stopped every protest and caution, so May Rose hasn't asked how long she'll be away.

"This animal's not been rode all winter," Simpson says. "She's a little touchy, didn't want the saddle nor your pack."

"Ginger's too lazy to act up," Wanda says. "Besides, Evie's got corn in her pocket, and she likes Evie."

Evie unclasps her fist and lets the mare lick a few kernels of corn from her palm. Simpson boosts her into the saddle and adjusts the stirrups. She leans down for a kiss from May Rose.

Simpson hands Wanda the reins. "Piney wishes she could go along. She says you should tell your ma and Ruth to come in May for Trading Days. Or anytime.

John Jonson rounds the corner of the house, carrying the shotgun. He holds it out to Wanda. "You should take this, in case o'them dogs."

Wanda takes the gun, then hands it back. "Can't. I got enough to carry."

"I can carry it for you. If you don't mind."

"Suit yourself," Wanda says. "I suppose you know where you're going?"

"More or less."

May Rose holds in her surprise. She and Simpson watch until the walkers leave the valley, Wanda leading the horse, Jonson trailing behind, carrying the shotgun.

BARLOW

Days go by and Barlow cannot make himself reply to her letter. It's not as though she's said anything that needs a response. Every word that comes into his head seems premature. When he tries to exclude his feelings, his words look unfriendly. He has no gift of fine language, and try as he might, he's been a bungler at love. And he's lived too many months among coarse men. He hates the way they respond to the tavern's women, hates his troubled desire.

"I left a woman in Virginia," Loughrie says. "Caught her with her husband, the whore." Loughrie is in his cups. It's Saturday night, and they're sitting in Roy's tavern.

"Admit it, Price, you're a good man."

"As are you," Loughrie says. "You'll make some woman a fine wife."

Without Loughrie, Barlow thinks he'd go crazy.

"I'm sorry," Loughrie says. "You've already got a wife. Or did she pass?"

"She passed. You've drunk too much."

"That's what Ruth says. And I've got no call. I should go underground, then I'd have reason to drink."

"You should go home to your woman."

Loughrie raises his glass. "You too. Even a drunk can see there's a woman on your mind. But they've got a baby now. It's all they ever wanted, a boy Bosell."

Loughrie's slurred words hit him like a stomach punch. It's been months since he saw May Rose, no sign of anything then, but women cover up these things, and suddenly it's spring and there's a baby. Be reasonable, he tells himself. It's someone else's child. She's forever taking care of someone else's child. Still, he has to ask. *Who is Bosell?*

"Baby somebody Bosell, not a month old. Ruth saw it. Now Lucie will die happy."

"Is Lucie dying?"

"That old woman will live forever," Loughrie says. "Born on the wrong side of the blanket."

"Lucie?"

"Baby Bosell. Are you drunk?"

"Price, who is the baby's mother?"

"Wanda. *Wanda.*" Loughrie waves his arm toward Roy. "Fill this man's glass so he can clear his head."

Wanda. "Let me walk you to your bunk," Barlow says.

Loughrie stands with a wobble. "Kind of you. Good man."

MAY ROSE

Virgie hands May Rose two envelopes. "One for Wanda, today." She winks. "Guess who?"

The envelope with Wanda's name is written in a familiar hand. Will's.

"Do you want to take it or should I keep it here till Wanda comes home?"

"I'll take it." May Rose looks at her own envelope. It has a Fargo postmark.

"Something interesting?"

She's sure Virgie would like her to open both letters and read them aloud. "I've no idea," she says.

At home, she lays Wanda's letter on her bed. She's as curious as Virgie. It's impossible not to wonder what Will knows and why he's finally writing to Wanda.

The Fargo letter is from the same man who wrote about Russell finding Charlie. In fewest possible words, the letter says Charlie needs a home. Can she take him in?

Months ago she wrote something like "bring him to us," thinking they'd shelter Charlie while he recovered. He must still need help. She folds the letter and returns it to its envelope. She has no choice—even if his name didn't tug at her heart, she owes him her life. This time, though, she must tell Will.

She lays the letter on her desk and goes outside to enjoy the scents of growing grass and new-turned earth. On the slope behind the house, John Jonson is working down her garden with Simpson's mule and a spike-toothed harrow. He's not only plowed her garden, he's plowed a patch for Mrs. Hale, one for Simpson, and one for himself. Though the day is warm, he's wearing the red knitted cap made by Luzanna. May Rose has stopped accepting money for his use of Wanda's boardinghouse. Except for the sheets she launders, he's running the place.

She returns to the house with awareness that things are about to change. In the lonely evenings without Wanda and Evie, she's thought a lot about herself and two men, Ebert and Barlow.

"You might as well marry Ebert," Wanda advised before she left. "He won't be going anywhere."

Wanda is right; of the two, Ebert seems more settled. Barlow left Alice with the Banovics while he worked in Jennie Town. Before that, he left her weeks at a time to travel for the B&O. He may already be somewhere else, or he may have found a new interest, for he has not responded to her letter.

Maybe for them it's too late.

BARLOW

This morning, Randolph said he's glad to see April, March being an unlucky month for mine disasters. An hour later, they knew they had one. It's not a disaster that will not be big news—one dead man—but it's sobered them all and stopped the work. Barlow wonders why only big numbers qualify as disasters.

It's the duty of the fire boss to inspect conditions in the mine between each shift. If he finds bad gasses, weakened roof supports, or too much dust in a section, he chalks "NO WORK" on the doors that close it off. When their fire boss didn't come out this morning, Randolph went into the mine and found him dead in a passage and the flame of his safety lantern extinguished. Seeing the lantern, Randolph lowered his own lantern and backed away when the light dimmed. It's possible the man had a heart attack, but it's likely he asphyxiated. Blackdamp, the miners call it, air low in oxygen that can choke a man before he's aware. In his inspection, a fire boss is supposed to lower his lantern to the floor and check his flame. This man was always too sloppy for Randolph's liking.

Now they've shut down until the mine can be ventilated and the accident is investigated by one of the state inspectors. An inspector may not come for days. As soon as Randolph believes the noxious air has cleared, he'll take a team in to bring out the body.

No work means no pay, giving miners their final excuse to look for work elsewhere. They like new mines, where they can walk a few steps and start earning, not the kind where they walk miles to the seam. Randolph is afraid that only the Slovaks will stay.

The shutdown is Barlow's chance to visit Banovic in jail and see if there's something he can do for him or Mrs. Banovic.

He waits for the train in Roy's public room, breakfasting on steak and eggs. Loughrie sits with him. The room is dim, crowded, and loud with talk. Among these men there seems always to be a competition for the longest string of curses, the vilest stories, and the most heated complaints.

"You might as well come along to Elkins," he says to Loughrie.

Loughrie has been shaky all morning, and his grits and maple syrup appear untouched. To accommodate Randolph, Roy sells no moonshine until the day shift is done, and even though there's no work today, he's holding to the rule, not liking, he whispers, to serve men who have nothing to do but drink and fight. Roy says he's told the men it's out of respect for the fire boss.

Loughrie wobbles his fork toward the doorway. "Am I seeing things, or is that Will Herff?"

They stand and wave so he'll see them. In this crowd, they're glad for an old acquaintance.

Will edges among the tables and extends his hand. "Barlow, good to see you. Price, I'm surprised to find you here."

"I go everywhere and been everywhere," Loughrie says. "That's my trouble."

"Marshal, fiddler, preacher." Will shifts his eyes. "Bootlegger." The last word is almost lost in a roar from the next table.

Loughrie lifts his glass in tribute, then drinks and grimaces. It's a glass of water.

Barlow motions to the bench. "Sit down, join us."

"I'll stand awhile," Will says. "My butt's numb from the wagon seat. I've got a load of goods for the store. Barlow, I wish you'd bought Italian Town."

He shrugs. "My cousin is happy; my bid pushed the other one up, so we'll get a few more dollars from our cousin's estate."

"So you've come out all right. Or did you want the land?"

He doesn't know what he wanted. "It's probably better this way. If I'd won the bid, I'd be land poor, then what?"

"Land poor," Will says. "That's me." He sits and looks around for service. "Price, is the family all right?"

"Well and prospering, now they got Baby Bosell. You should've been there to catch it."

"Catch a Bosell baby? Ruth? Piney?"

Loughrie laughs. "Those old women? Wanda's baby Bosell, a 'course. Ruth says it looks like you, but I don't know why women say these things. Babies all look alike."

Though the room is cloudy with smoke, Will's face is plain to see, and now he looks like the one who's been punched.

MAY ROSE

Her school has closed for the summer, for each family needs its children to drop seeds, pull weeds, and pick bugs off potato plants.

The house seems lonelier than ever, but the benefit of being alone is a schedule that suits her preferences for bedtime and rising, meals and chores. She washes a dish as soon as it's used and sings because there's no one to object to her tuneless voice. The house, acquired and furnished while she was sick, begins to feel like her own. She's fastened hooks to the kitchen walls and hung the pots and pans Wanda kept in a box on the floor.

It's time to start the garden. She's hesitated as long as possible, thinking Wanda might return at any time and object to her decisions about what and how much to plant. Now, soon as the morning sun dries and warms the ground, she must get the potatoes in the ground and set out cabbage plants. She bought potatoes on store credit from a load traded by a hill farmer. They're cut and waiting in buckets on the porch. Ebert gave her the cabbage plants, raised over winter by his mother. To thank her for his boy's schooling, he said. He's already paid too much. She sent his mother a pair of gloves.

There's a growing accumulation of quarters and nickels upstairs in Wanda's washbasin, earnings of the boardinghouse. To fill the time until the garden dries, May Rose sets out for the store to ask Virgie if it's time to pay the boardinghouse rent and the rent for this house, too. She has no idea what Wanda has paid. Wanda doesn't mean to be secretive; she's merely careless.

Four horse teams and wagons are hitched at the store, piled high with crates. More speculators, surveyors, engineers, and sellers. There've been so many of this kind, they sleep two to a bed in Wanda's boardinghouse.

Alma meets her on the store steps. "Miss Virgie asked me to fetch you. There's men inside..."

Will opens the door, almost disguised with new glasses and skin that's too pale. He looks five years older.

He takes her hand. "May Rose. I think you are well-recovered."

"I didn't expect you so soon," she says. His letter is still unclaimed on Wanda's bed. If she's had a chance, Virgie will have told him Wanda is not here. *Will and Wanda.* She's hurt that he rejected Wanda, but glad to see him.

He draws her inside. She waits for him to ask about Wanda.

"There's some business here," he says. "A proposal you may like."

He directs her to a group of men at the table. "This is the school teacher, Mrs. Long." He introduces them as advance men for Davis Coal and Coke.

They rise at their seats and mumble greetings. Their clothing reminds her of Barlow as she saw him last—sportsmen's hats and shirts, canvas trousers tucked into lace-up boots.

One of the men reaches out and shakes her hand. "Mr. Herff says he might let us fix up the old school if we hired you as a teacher." His hand is broad and hairy, and he squeezes hers as firmly as if she were a man.

She's grateful that Will is attempting to make a deal on her behalf. But the prospect of teaching many students makes her weak. In the days of the sawmill, the Winkler school had at least three teachers. "How many children do you expect?"

"It's hard to predict, depending on the families. That's why we're eager to start with you, because you're here already. We'll add teachers as we need them. By fall, we hope to have the mine open and houses built in what you folks call Italian Town."

"Let me know when you want me to start," she says. With a real job, she'll be able to provide for herself. How surprised Wanda will be. If Wanda comes back. Then she remembers. Charlie is coming. What kind of care will he need?

Will has the same question that evening when she tells him about his brother. They're sitting in her kitchen, sharing a supper of wild greens, side meat and cornbread. He can make no more of Russell's letter than she.

"Russell is not given to explanation," she says. "But Charlie must be fit enough to travel."

"Alone?"

"Surely not alone. If Charlie needs help, Russell will bring him."

"I should be the one helping," he says. "I should be here, not off in Richmond."

She has the same thought, a selfish one for Wanda's sake. "Maybe you're exactly where you're supposed to be. For now. You do plan to come back?"

"This is my town. I don't want to be anywhere else."

They talk about Winkler, Glory, and medical school. He's already heard that Wanda is with Lucie and Ruth. From the careful way he says Wanda's name, watching her face, she suspects he knows more.

"Wanda left before your letter came," she says. "Do you want me to keep it until someone goes to the Bosells?" For Wanda's sake, she'd like him to say the letter is too important to wait, that he'll go and deliver it himself.

"Give it to me, then," he says. "The letter was hasty. I'll write again and do better."

When she brings the letter, he folds it into his pocket. "I spoke with Barlow Townsend in Jennie Town," he says.

So he's still there. "How is Mr. Townsend?"

"He's tired of Franklin Coal and Coke. Loughrie is too. Price Loughrie, you know who I mean? I thought there for a while he was gonna marry Wanda's Aunt Ruth. He's been working in Jennie Town."

"We know. I've met Mr. Loughrie."

While they finish coffee, he tells of a man asphyxiated by bad air in the mine. "Barlow says the Franklin company doesn't give this mine enough support. He plans to leave."

"I suppose he has other ambitions." She wonders where they'll take him next.

Will rubs his eyes. "I'm looking forward to my own bed. Is some of that coffee left?"

She adds a bit of water from the hot teakettle, swishes it with what remains in the coffee pot and fills his cup.

He takes a sip of coffee and briefly closes his eyes. "I remember Barlow Townsend when he was boss here. He's different now."

"Maybe not. You saw him as your father's employer. And you were just a boy."

"You're the same as you were then."

"You and I have always been friends. That's the only thing that hasn't changed." It's hard to look at Will and not see the boy hunched against the wall in the boardinghouse, crying about his lost brother. Or the boy stamping out sparks in the sawmill. Or the boy bent over, holding his ankles, waiting for his father's strap.

He reaches across the table and covers her hand with his own, a man's hand, grown strong and capable. "May Rose, since you're my oldest and best friend, you should tell me about Wanda's baby."

She hasn't cleared the table, and when she draws back in surprise, she knocks her fork and knife to the floor.

He bends and retrieves them, gets up and lays them on her plate. "Ruth Bosell told Price. He called it the Bosell baby. I know how you all collect children, so I'm wondering if this baby fell into Wanda's lap or if she got it the regular way."

She wants him to know but is sorry to be the one who must answer his question. She avoids his eyes. "The regular way."

23

BARLOW

They've ridden the train to Elkins together, Barlow, Loughrie, and Randolph. Randolph has come to strengthen his recommendation that one of the Slovaks be made fire boss at the Jennie Town mine. Barlow's mission is to see what he might do for Banovic, to pay his rent to Mrs. Banovic, and to give Loughrie something to do besides drink. They part from Randolph at the depot, agreeing to meet there in the morning.

He and Loughrie walk first to the grocery, which he is surprised to find open for business. Though the shelves are nearly empty, they shine as if waxed, as does the floor, the windows, and the glass and steel of the meat display case, which contains not meat but a beautiful assortment of pastries. In place of Banovic, Mrs. Banovic presides, and she's wrapping baked goods for a small crowd of housewives. The yeasty aroma in the store sets his mouth watering. There's also a scent of simmering chicken soup.

"Umm," Loughrie says, like he's about to faint.

Barlow inhales. "I know. Why didn't I think of this? She's a wonderful baker."

They wait their turn, but when they reach the head of the line, he decides not to try to talk with her now, for more customers wait behind him. Mrs. Banovic's broad, brightening face makes him glad he's come. She glances nervously toward the other customers.

"I'll come back. I'm on my way to see him," he says.

"Wait. She reaches into the case and wraps three flaky pastries with berry filling, his favorite. "One for each. I close soon to make for tomorrow. You come later to house."

Never has Barlow eaten on the street, but like Loughrie, he munches on his pastry as they walk to the county jail. He holds one hand under his mouth to catch the crumbs, and when he's finished, wipes his lips with the back of his hand.

"You two look like shit warmed over," Banovic says, when they're taken to his cell.

Barlow laughs. Banovic's description is the only improper utterance he's made in all their years together. Barlow has only to look at Loughrie to know that he himself isn't particularly clean. The stain of coal dust never quite washes out.

"You, on the other hand, appear to be king of this castle," he says. Banovic is freshly shaved, his hair is slicked back, and his shirt is starched and ironed.

Banovic winks. "All good. I have sixty days to rest and make strategy. Let my wife feed you. Stay with. She misses."

When later they reach the apartment, Mrs. Banovic impresses him with her deposit slips and her assurance that she'll not let her husband sell illegal whiskey again. Two young women work under her direction, and her kitchen has a second oven.

Seeing Banovic has restored Barlow's spirits, and eating Mrs. Banovic's chicken and dumplings makes him long for the comforts of his past life. "We all need to do better," he says.

She insists he stay in his old room, and makes up a couch for Loughrie. In the morning, Loughrie asks, "So now, where?"

"It's time to do better," he says.

~

The door to the office shanty opens and closes, admitting the current delights of the atmosphere, always smoke and dust, and today, wind-blown rain. Men in dripping oil suits and gum boots come and go, signing up for work. It's Barlow's last day. He has no destination, except that before anything else, he needs to see Loughrie home to Ruth Bosell.

The shanty has two desks crowded together and almost no standing room. The next man to step to his desk is Will Herff, and the wrinkle on his forehead makes Barlow set down his pen.

"Will. Is everything all right?"

"Never," Will says, but his face relaxes. "I'm heading back to Richmond. I hoped we could have a word."

"Turn and see if there's an end to that line."

Will counts. "Four more."

"Get a bite down at Roy's. I'll see you there."

He stays fifteen minutes longer, then finds Will drying out beside Roy's pot-belly stove. Today they have the public room to themselves.

"Did you see everyone in Winkler?" It's a pointed question, meant to draw out news of May Rose.

"I guess I saw everybody." Will's forehead wrinkles again. "Not Wanda. She's staying with her aunt and granny."

Along with Wanda's name, he expected a word about her baby, confirmation or denial, but Will's lips are tight. There's another aspect to his report that spurs Barlow's concern. With Wanda gone, May Rose is alone. "Has Wanda moved for good?"

"When I see her, I intend to ask." Will shakes water from his hair. "Life was a lot simpler before my ideas started working out."

Barlow's laugh is short. "That's how it goes. Best not have too many ideas."

"Roy's bringing stewed potatoes," Will says. "You want to sit and have lunch?"

He's always hungry. Roy's food isn't always good, but it's the best reward for living here. Barlow and Will take the most private table, the one in the corner, though they're still the only ones in the room.

"Here's the newest rock in my road," Will says. "Two rocks. Store business is getting too complicated for Virgie, Ebert is too busy on his farm to help, and my brother is coming home. *Charlie*. He was nine when he ran away. I guess you know he ended up with May Rose in Fargo."

He nods. "May Rose kept my sister informed about you and Charlie so Glory would grow up knowing something about her brothers. This is good, isn't it? Glory is eager to see him. He's coming to Richmond?"

Will's expression is grim. "He's coming to Winkler, to May Rose. Russell wrote, said Charlie needs looking after."

"Your brother is sick, and May Rose is to take care of him?" The repetition makes him feel dim-witted, but Will seems equally perplexed.

"That's what she says. I don't know how she'll manage, especially without Wanda. And Davis Coal is gonna fix up the school—May Rose is supposed to be the first teacher."

Will's brother. Wanda's baby. Endless children. Once again, her life will be robbed by other people's needs. But what does he want, except to have her fill his own?

"Whatever happens, she'll manage," Will says. "We'll manage together when we see what Charlie needs. I'd like your advice on another matter." He lowers his voice. "You said you could point me to a good engineer if I wanted to develop my coal mine."

Barlow pushes back a jealous thought about May Rose and Will managing together. "You've decided for coal? Or are you still thinking?"

"No matter what I do, my valley is going to change. Mines are starting up beyond the mountain, and there's going to be mine works in Italian Town. I'd like an opinion I can trust. Someone to tell me if my coal seam is worth anything, and what I'd need to start up a mine."

Roy kicks open the swinging door to his kitchen and carries two bowls of stewed potatoes to their table. "Fresh made, and more if you want it. How's things in Winkler?"

"Booming," Will says. "We'll soon be busy as Jennie Town."

"Glory days, again!" Roy lingers. "Any news in particular?"

"They say spring is coming," Will says.

Roy laughs. He looks like he's about to sit down to chat.

"I'll have coffee if you've made fresh," Barlow says.

"I'll make it now."

Barlow waits to speak until the kitchen door swings shut. "I've met no better coal man than Randolph, the boss here. But I don't know when he could get away to look at your mine. I'm leaving him short-handed."

"So you're going. I'm surprised you stayed this long. Where now?"

"I don't know. Banovic's in jail. When we failed at the grocery business, he took up selling moonshine. Now Mrs. Banovic is selling pastries and showing us how to be a success—do what you do best. I used to think I knew what that was."

Will smiles, and Barlow starts again. "About Randolph. I'll relieve him in the office and send him to talk with you. He's not happy here."

"You could help me in Winkler," Will says. "I'd like to increase my stock, add miners' gear until the new mines get their stores up and running. And I need someone to make sure squatters and speculators don't so much as pound a post on my land. Think about it. I've two more years in Richmond."

He doesn't have to think. "I got nowhere special to go." And Winkler is where he'd like to be.

~

MAY ROSE

It's May Rose's turn to bring in the cow and heifer.

Simpson and his mule are plowing the pasture they fenced in the fall, where he intends to plant corn. His cow has had her calf, now safely enclosed in Will's fenced field above the store. The other animals range free, but always return before dark, the cow to her calf, the mule and Glory's heifer to the shed for a lick of salt.

Today the animals have feasted on bright new grass across the river, and now they stand at the river's edge, hesitant to step into the swift water. It hasn't rained in Winkler this week, but it's rained somewhere nearby, for in the last few hours the river has risen. In the fenced field, the calf is bawling for its mother.

"Wear my boots," Simpson says, "and bring the cow and heifer across at the ford. Or do you want me to go?"

A bank of black clouds has hung all afternoon in the western sky, a slow-moving storm. On the slope beyond the river, streams and waterfalls splash in crevices unnoticed in dryer times. Rain will soon fall on the valley. If Simpson doesn't finish plowing tonight, he'll have to wait until the ground dries out again.

"I'll go, and I accept the offer of your boots." She and Piney stuff the boot toes with paper. The tops reach to her knees, making walking awkward, but not impossible.

She crosses on the footbridge, ignoring its sway and the swirling water below. It's an undependable river, shallow most of the year, but today it foams and roars over its rocks. Upstream, the cow has put one hoof into the water. If the mule were here instead of plowing on the other side, it would lead the cow and heifer to the ford. Cows aren't shrewd thinkers.

The ground along the river is soggy as a swamp. When she reaches the animals, she lets the heifer lick a bit of corn from her palm, then offers the same to the cow. The cow comes up the bank and takes the corn, but turns back and stands at the shortest distance from her bawling calf.

"Sook, sook," she calls, holding out a hand of corn. Drops of rain fall on her nose and cheeks. The heifer follows her downstream toward the ford. Even the ford can get too high to cross, but the animals don't like the footbridge, which moves underfoot. She keeps calling, "Sook, sook," and finally the cow turns and runs to catch up.

When she wades into the water she is almost knocked off her feet. The animals push behind her. Water swirls over her boot tops, tugs at her skirt and threatens to pull her over. In a moment she's dragging extra pounds of water in her boots. She's brought no walking stick, a foolish oversight.

"May Rose!"

Ebert splashes into the water, reaching first her hand, then bracing her with an arm around her waist. The cow and heifer rush past, leave the water and trot off toward the field with the calf. Ebert tightens his arm, nearly lifting her with each step.

Simpson comes running. "Can I help? I shouldn't have let you go."

"I'll get her home," Ebert says.

As they step out of the river, rain pours down. Her legs shake and her feet are numb from the chilly water. She rests a hand on Ebert's shoulder. "Will you help me off with these boots?" He pulls them off and turns them upside down to drain.

He doesn't scold. When they reach her house, he brings in coal and wood and builds up the fire in both kitchen and school room while she changes to dry clothes.

"I'll fix supper if you can stay," she says.

"I'd like that another time. Ma's waiting."

They pause at the open door. "Thank you," she says. "It seems I'm forever in your debt."

"Good."

Ebert doesn't smile often, but when he does, it's nice.

~

BARLOW

Construction is underway for the railroad branch, and there's steady wagon-freight traffic on the road to Winkler, so Barlow and Loughrie have no trouble hitching a ride. Otherwise, he thinks Loughrie would not make it. Loughrie no longer has his fancy riding horse. When he came to Jennie Town in December, he sold it to Randolph.

"Ruth won't want me like this," Loughrie says.

"You'll get straightened up." If not, maybe Loughrie will be lucky enough to die with someone who loves him.

The man lies curled in the wagon across crates of canned food, tobacco, and miners' boots. "Put me off anywhere," he says.

"This load is going to Winkler," Barlow says. "We'll get off together."

When they reach Winkler, Barlow and Loughrie set down their packs among unopened cases in Will's store. Ebert Watson is there, arranging gum boots on a shelf.

If Barlow were hiring a miner or mill hand, Ebert would be his first choice, a clean, strongly-built man with a direct gaze, square shoulders and large hands.

Ebert doesn't hide his doubt. "Will's put you in charge? Nobody's told me."

"Will and I talked on his return trip to Richmond. He said the job has grown, and Virgie doesn't want to work so much."

Loughrie sits at a table. "Got anything to drink?"

"We don't serve liquor," Ebert says. "Water is free. You can have coffee for two cents."

Barlow looks at the store with new purpose. Will has set up a cooking area in a front corner and built a wall across the middle of the room with a door at the side. Shaded lamps still hang on long cords from the ceiling, though there's been no electric for more than a decade. There's almost no merchandise, but other things are the same—oiled floors, high ceilings, high windows. He feels at ease. *At home.*

Loughrie puts two pennies on the table. "Hell of a place."

Ebert pours a stream of dark coffee from the pot on the cook stove.

"Will said I should live right here and sleep in his room," Barlow says.

"Did he tell you where his room is?"

"Through that new wall to the back."

Ebert kicks an empty crate aside. I don't guess you got anything in writing? I'm supposed to hand you the keys and walk off?"

"He must have thought you'd take my word."

"Because you was boss here," Ebert says.

"You must agree Will needs help. He has a load on his mind, and his brother is coming."

"Yeah. Sick brother." Ebert nods toward Loughrie, whose head is bent to the table. "Is the marshal supposed to stay here too?"

"He'll stay till he feels better. A few days."

"I don't know," Ebert says. "Will is my friend."

"He's my friend too. I'm not here to take advantage. Will knows you have your own work. He hopes you'll continue to help when I need it."

"We'll see," Ebert says. "Do you mind if I finish out the day?"

Thunder crashes. The door blows open, and a woman under a hooded cape rushes in. She throws back her hood. "It wasn't raining when I left the house!"

He knows why Ebert's face softens. It's May Rose.

~

MAY ROSE

She hates to be caught revealing more than she's ready to admit. Like her pleasure and surprise at seeing Barlow, followed by embarrassment to find him and Ebert together, two men who keep changing places in her thoughts.

"Hello." To hide her confusion, she looks toward the third man, who sits with his head resting on the table. "Is that Mr. Loughrie?" Loughrie's eyes open briefly, then he turns his head to rest on the other cheek.

Barlow comes forward. "Price Loughrie, indeed it is. We've traveled together today. Let me help…"

She needs no help, but fumbles the bow at her neck, and with an awkward sense of the past, lets him lift the wet cape from her shoulders.

"Has Glory come too?" Glory's name deflects other personal awareness, like the reminders in Barlow's last letter and the fire she sees in Ebert's eyes.

Her cape lies over Barlow's arm. "Just us," he says. "Will has asked me to manage things here while he's in Richmond."

"Truly," she says. "How nice."

Ebert sends her a long look as he drags a crate to a shelf in the middle of the room.

Thunder rattles the windows. There's static in the air.

24

BARLOW

Each morning Barlow rises from bed with the thought that he's planted his two feet in the soil of a slower, better life. When he looks over the valley, he sees more green than anything else, a color restful to the eyes. As yet there's no noise, no pressured heat or gray growth of industry. Most days, he's free to choose his tasks. He feels younger, more vigorous. Anything is possible. He sees May Rose every day.

In those few minutes, he forgets the obstacles that remain. He's managed distance and been pardoned for his past. He's no longer married. He thinks she has gone out of her way to welcome him to Winkler, stopping at the store every day on her way to visit one or another of her friends, asking if there's news from Glory or Will.

When he's not with her, his path seems more difficult, for he has no advantage, and she has established an independent life. Nearly independent. She has wood and game from John Johnson, and this week Ebert Watson repaired her door latch and replaced a window glass cracked by winter wind. He does not know if she favors Ebert, only that the man is uncommonly attentive and wears a worried look. He's worried too. She has no reason to need Barlow Townsend.

Today the valley shines. Rain has slackened, the sun has come through the clouds, and beads of water sparkle in the air and on every blade of grass. The store bell jingles and she comes in, carrying a loaf of bread. He's afraid he wears the smile of an idiot.

She stops by the door. "I'm your cook today. Imagine—Virgie has caught chickenpox from the Hale children!"

"Very good. I mean, I'm sorry for Virgie. It's good you've come."

"Poor Virgie," she says, unwrapping the bread. "The children are not sick with their spots, but Virgie is suffering. Have you had chickenpox?"

"I believe I did. Mother said Hester and I had everything—measles, mumps, scarlet fever."

"Mothers endure so much. With the baby teething and fussy all the time, Piney is taxed to the limit. And the chickenpox has yet to reach her house!"

It may be his imagination, but this chatter makes May Rose seem as nervous as he is. She sets her loaf on the table. "There are no boarders at present. Have you and Mr. Randolph had breakfast?"

"Randolph left at dawn. I cooked his breakfast." The skillet is still on the stove, full of hardened grease. The prospect of time with May Rose makes Barlow relieved to have him gone. His friend seemed to be caught, as he is, by the way her eyes lift and how her lips part when she smiles. Randolph inquired about her circumstances, prompting Barlow to confess, "If you intend to know her better, it may not be possible for us to remain friends." Randolph's laughter made him feel worse. He has not declared himself. If he can't risk rejection, he may lose her without trying.

"So you don't need me," she says. "Need a cook, I mean."

"I'll be happy to have you cook something for me. I'm here, always hungry."

She looks through the door glass. "You may need my help after all. I see men on horseback. They've stopped outside. I think they're coming in."

"Perhaps you could do something about a noon meal, then."

They part, she to the cooking corner, he to meet the strangers, three of them.

"We're looking for Will Herff," one says. His tailored jacket, riding trousers and polished boots identify him as a speculator. Men like this typically look wealthy but seldom are. They must spend everything on clothes and horses.

He gives them Will's Richmond address, points toward the Davis holdings and tells them the extent of Will's property.

The branch line has reached the northern boundary of Winkler and turned west toward mines now under construction a few miles away. Any day, he expects Davis Coal and Coke to start laying track up the valley to Italian Town. Winkler will have only a distant view of the mine works in Italian Town. But if Will decides to develop his own mine, they'll see more changes— another railroad spur, miners' houses, a closer coal tipple. And if he wants to ship on the Davis-controlled line, Will may have to trade some of his valley.

The speculators ask for directions to other properties, including Ebert Watson's farm, and he tells them about Wanda's boardinghouse and meals in the store. When they leave, he goes back to May Rose.

"How will you feel," he asks, "if Winkler becomes a coal town?"

She sets a pan of eggs to boil on the stove. "Coal, lumber, or something else, the important thing is to keep it a good town."

"We could have electric power again, maybe paved streets."

"Wouldn't we like that! Even better, we might have a sanitary system with flush toilets. Our wells are in danger of pollution from the outhouses, don't you think?"

He agrees. "A good town. I'll do my best." It's a feeble promise, but he loves making her smile.

~

MAY ROSE

When she was ill, May Rose was certain she wanted nothing more than to be free of pain. She supposes that Luzanna, in her most desperate times, wanted no more than food for her children. In the silence of her house, May Rose knows she wants more than absence of pain, more than food and warmth. She feels ungrateful to admit it.

Each day she finds a reason to spend a few hours away from home. This morning she sits in Luzanna's kitchen, cutting gloves from leather.

"You've been restless since Wanda left," Luzanna says.

"I suppose that's it." When Simpson and Piney returned from delivering Price Loughrie to the Bosells, Piney said Wanda is cooking and helping Ruth plow and plant. Evie sent back a carefully penned letter about dogs and geese and a fishing pond. Wanda sent nothing.

Luzanna bites off a thread and puts a knot at the end. "You can't pin your happiness on other folks."

"I know it's true, and I know Wanda. Once she decides something, she doesn't think she needs to explain to anyone."

"From what you've said, Will Herff must be an upright man. If you told him about the baby, surely he'd do the right thing."

"He knows. I think he's waiting for Wanda to tell him."

"And she's waiting for him," Luzanna says. "Waiting far away, so he'll have to make an effort to get to her. If she was mine, I'd slap that girl."

May Rose has to smile, though the truth is sad. "Wanda doesn't want him if he doesn't want her."

"I suppose there's something in that."

They work on in silence, May Rose marking and punching small holes in the leather for Luzanna's stitches.

"I just hope these new mines doesn't spoil things by bringing back Albert Hale," Luzanna says. "He tries them all you know, looking for one where the work's light."

"If he comes, will you turn him away?"

"I'll sure try. We was never legal married, common law, you see. I figger by now he's took up with some other fool woman. That'd be my wish."

Luzanna does not ask if she's happy. Perhaps Luzanna has never known the crushing, dizzy joy of love. She feels foolish to want a feeling that may fail in the hard winters of married life and disappear, like snow. Even so, she can't push away the desire to try again.

Her wishes may have to be postponed. Charlie is coming, and he's mixed up in his head. That could mean so many things.

~

BARLOW

No one has come to the store this rainy day, giving Barlow time to complete his new set of account books. When he first looked at the store's records, he understood why Will asked him to help. Like the Elkins widow, Virgie and Ebert tossed invoices and bills of lading in a box, kept brief notes about credit sales in a long continuous list, and made no reconciliation of income and expenses. There's no record of rents, how much they are or what anyone owes. Virgie says people pay as they can. She says Will doesn't care, he's glad to have his friends here. Simpson is the only tenant who pays regularly. He's made improvements to his house and wants to buy it, also the land on which he built his grist mill.

Barlow has sent a letter with Simpson's request and an offer of his own. If Will decides to partner with Randolph, Barlow will invest his Hershman inheritance in the mine and co-sign for other financing.

He'd like to build a house for May Rose, but sees no sign that she likes him better than anyone else. He tries to look his best, shaves and washes every day and keeps his shoes shined. Virgie trims his hair, and Mrs. Hale does his laundry.

Everyone loves her. If ever she asks why she should choose him, he can only say he's loved her for the longest time.

Rain ends and the sun comes out. On the other side of the valley, white water cascades in rocky runs to the river. On the town side, brown water floods the street, gushing downhill from newly-planted gardens, carrying pebbles and soil.

He draws on a new pair of gum boots and sets out with the excuse of seeing the damage to her garden.

Ditches that used to line the terraced streets have long since filled in with dirt, and water now finds and deepens its own paths, creating jagged gullies in the steep lanes, some nearly a foot deep. He walks with his head down, watching his step. From somewhere comes the scrape of a shovel. He needs to do what Will would do, go back, get a hoe, and start filling in the gullies. He's about to do that when he hears crying.

He stops, uncertain whether the sound is coming from left or right. Alice cried easily, and he never knew what to do. Hester seldom cried, but worried him when she did. This crying comes with a sound of exertion—someone shoveling with sobs and grunts. The shoveling stops with a soft howl. It's from May Rose's house.

He finds her in a slick of mud that begins in the garden and ends at her back door. She wears a gum boot on one foot, but her other foot is bare and held above the mud. An empty boot is stuck in the mud beside her, apparently sucked off when she tried to take a step. Two days ago, he sold her those boots at the store, a bit large, for the store has none in ladies' sizes. That time might have been his opportunity. He could have said, *Rely on me. You'll never need to wear boots made for a man.*

"May Rose! Wait there!"

She leans on her shovel. Mud has splattered her face and coated the skirt and hem of her dress.

"Thank you," she says, as he lifts her arm over his shoulder. He winds his arm around her waist.

She leans against him. "I can't hop in this boot; I might as well take it off and wade."

"Here." He bends and lifts her in his arms.

She doesn't resist. "Look at my garden. Look at my porch. Mud came under the door. It's in the kitchen!"

"Only the center of the garden has washed down," he says.

She points to bits of green in the brown muck. "Look at my cabbage plants."

"We'll replace them."

She is warm and soft, and he thinks he could carry her forever. He sets her down at her front door and wipes a smear of mud from her nose.

"Barlow…"

She presses her cheek to his and does not resist as he draws her close and wraps his arms around her back.

They stand this way for only a moment, then she pulls away. "Thank you. I…you…" Her face begs him to understand. "You should not come in."

They've been alone in her house before. Something has changed. He doesn't know if he should worry or be glad.

~

MAY ROSE

Upstairs, she washes in the basin while watching Barlow through the window. He's at her garden, holding her shovel. Then he walks through the mud toward the back porch and she doesn't see him but hears the shoveling.

The dangerous feeling has not passed. Her clean dress lies across the bed. She might go down in her shift, open the back door and bring him inside. Be loved again; seal her fate. They are two people who care for each other. They do not have to be alone.

She hears voices; he's talking with John Johnson. Someday soon she'll have to say yes or no. She's promised Ebert to visit his farm after Trading Days. Meet his mother.

With Ebert, she'd share another woman's house. If she chooses Barlow, she'll have him to herself. If he asks her. She hates that her way isn't clear, that she distrusts herself. It would be better to have no choice. She liked leaning on Ebert when he helped her from the river. She felt cared for in Barlow's arms. Perhaps both times what she felt was gratitude and loneliness. Perhaps her answers should be *no* and *no*.

25

BARLOW

In the five days since he lifted May Rose from the mud, Barlow has walked with her every evening, careful not to touch, trembling from the effort. He comes at suppertime, when Luzanna and Piney are feeding their families and Virgie is cooking for boarders. For people alone, especially those accustomed to a full house, evening is a lonely time. She no longer invites him inside. He hopes it's herself she fears.

This evening she carries a basket. "Egg salad and bread. I thought we might picnic over there." She points to the grassy slope across the river where her heifer and Simpson's animals are grazing. Some evenings they herd the animals back to Will's field.

Another spell of sun and wind has dried the ground. She chooses a knoll and spreads a cloth from her basket. "Right about here, Wanda and I saw Charlie run from the ashes of a fire."

Almost always, their talk comes back to memories of Winkler. He sets down a pint bottle of fruit liquor, sweet and only mildly alcoholic. The sadness in her voice makes the fire sound serious. "A big fire? Little fire?"

She sits on the cloth and curls her legs to one side. He'd like to sit close, but he'd also like to sit opposite and watch her. He chooses the nearer place, where they can share a view, and he can turn and watch her eyes as she speaks.

"It was a campfire, down to coals and pieces of unburned wood. I think he'd been there all night. Or maybe he was only sneaking after his stepbrothers, those Donnellys. Will worried about that, said sometimes Charlie didn't sleep at home. Charlie was years younger than those boys, but he meant to pay them back for hurting Will. And for other things."

He remembers some of that, especially the day Charlie disappeared and she confessed her fears about the Donnellys and what they'd tried to do to her. He wishes he'd battered those boys himself, instead of sending them away.

"What's always bothered me about the fire," she says, "was the half-burned pieces of his father's carvings. Do you remember when Morris Herff came to the boardinghouse and accused Wanda of stealing them?"

"I remember Morris was a hothead. We never told Glory."

"I hope she'll never know. When I first went to their house, the boys were sleeping on the floor because he'd sold their bed. I can hear Will yet, saying his father wouldn't sell a single one of his carved birds and squirrels."

"Charlie burned them?"

"I wanted to think it was the Donnelly boys. Morris whipped them too, after he married their mother. Will wouldn't steal; he's always tried to do right. But Charlie..."

"Charlie burned the carvings and ran away."

"He didn't run away then. He ran away the night he rescued me from the laurel, where his stepbrothers left me tied up. Or the next morning. You remember..." Her voice breaks. "The next morning, all this was on fire."

Another vivid memory. The slope is pasture now, but then it was dense with logging debris, brush and stumps.

"I think Charlie burned more carvings that night, and his fire got out, and he ran from it and kept going. Or he ran to keep the Donnellys from killing him."

"He never explained?"

"Not to me. He may have told Russell."

"Poor boy." Barlow pulls the cork on the bottle of fruit liquor. "I've forgotten glasses. Can you drink from the bottle? It's not strong."

"I don't mind." She tilts her head, takes a swallow, and passes the bottle back. She's quiet as he drinks. He offers the bottle again, but she shakes her head. "Barlow, I'm afraid. Charlie is coming, and Russell says he's mixed up in his head. That could mean so many things."

"Do you know when he's coming?"

"It's been months since the last letter. They've left me great room for imagination, whether Charlie is coming alone or with Russell or someone else, where they are, what is happening. Will wants to help, but what can he do in Richmond?"

Only inches separate them. He feels the warmth that radiates from her body. "I'll be here," he says.

"I know you will. Luzanna will help too, and John Johnson, and Piney and Simpson. But you all have your own work. I'm sure I'll feel better when I know more." She takes a slice of bread from the basket and spreads it with egg salad. "Imagination can be a terrible thing." She holds out the bread.

He takes it from her hand. "Terrible and wonderful." He lets his imagination go no farther than picturing her unrestrained and as compelled as he is now.

He's held back too long. He studies the finely chopped egg, the bit of green onion and the vinegary-smelling sauce. "I also have a problem. I hope you might advise me about marriage."

She spreads egg salad over another slice, this time more slowly. "Advise you, as Hester did?"

He cannot see her eyes. "I believe you would give better advice."

This earns her smile. "I'm afraid to trust my judgment. You know I was not well married."

"Where marriage is concerned, I'm not sure I've ever had good judgment, only feelings. But I've never misplaced them." He stops. "I suppose that's not true. Alice and I..."

"You should not blame yourself for Alice's unhappiness," she says. "She told me she was not the type to be married."

"Did she?" His eyes water. "Do you suppose we're all failures? That we have no chance to be happy?"

"I hope there's still a chance."

They eat for a while without talking, sharing the fruit liquor. The sun dips behind them, leaving them in the chill of the mountain's shadow. She stands and folds the cloth into the basket.

He looks up. "I can't stop thinking about it. If you won't marry me, I'll have to leave this place."

"I know." She takes his hand to pull him to his feet. "Can you wait? Alice has not been dead a year, and there's so much ahead that's uncertain."

"When will I know?"

"Soon. I should not commit to anything until I know about Charlie."

"I think you love me," he says. "But I'm afraid you love everybody."

"Only the good ones," she says.

At least she hasn't excluded him.

~

MAY ROSE

Wanda and her children come home the day before the full moon, dominating the house with attention to infant needs and blocking May Rose's lonely impulses.

"I like Granny's, but I miss Alma and everybody," Evie says.

Wanda says nothing about how long they'll stay. Granny Lucie is lodging with Piney, and Ruth and Mr. Loughrie are setting up a tent among others near the river. It's the first Trading Days of the season, sure to be as crowded as in the fall.

She follows Wanda upstairs and watches while she changes Otis's diaper. "Will is here. I saw him yesterday with Barlow Townsend and Mr. Randolph. They walked up and down the valley, pointing and talking."

"Is Will going to sell his land? Or his coal?"

"Maybe. Barlow says the town is going to change no matter what Will does. Davis Coal and Coke is opening a mine in Italian Town. From here you can see the rail line where it turns up the creek toward your uncle's old place. We have so many travelers, you could fill two or three boardinghouses."

Wanda looks up with a wicked smile. "*Barlow says*?"

"Mr. Townsend is living in Winkler. Will asked him to take over the store. Until the coal companies are ready to supply their own stores, ours is stuffed with everything from canned milk to carbide lights."

"Now you say *Mr. Townsend*. It's all right, you can say *Barlow* to me. Poor Ebert."

"Nonsense," May Rose says. "No one needs to be pitied." In the rush of preparations for Trading Days, her daily walks with Barlow have ended. At this moment she has a note from him in one pocket, and one penned to him in the other. His says his work days are too busy. He says he wishes he could come home to her. For the first time, she's annoyed to have Wanda in the house. To be more exact, she's annoyed to be living in a house that suddenly is not her own.

She drops the dirty diaper in a pail of suds. "Will arrived yesterday with Mr. Randolph, a mine engineer."

"Busy, busy," Wanda says.

It's true. Will is the busiest man in town. Everyone needs his attention—Virgie, Simpson, Ebert, and people with ailments, who have somehow discovered he's here. She supposes Wanda would also like his attention, but Wanda doesn't say.

"He wrote to you. The letter came after you went to Lucie's."

"Did it, now." Wanda pulls down the baby's dress, unbuttons her bodice, and sits in the rocker to feed him. Her head is bent, hiding her face.

"He took the letter when he was here last month." She says it quickly, wishing it weren't true. "I'm sorry. He asked if you'd got his letter, and when I said it was still here, he asked to have it back. I couldn't decide if it was yours or his."

"Doesn't matter," Wanda says. Otis wraps his fist around his mother's finger and looks into her eyes as his mouth tugs on her breast. Wanda now seems completely devoted. Perhaps she no longer cares so much for Will; mothers often seem more attached to their children than to the children's fathers.

"Did Will say anything about me? Say what he wrote in the letter?"

"He knows you've got Otis. But I don't think he knew that when he wrote the letter. Shall we invite him to meet the baby?"

Wanda runs her hand over the baby's thick hair. "I can't think of a reason in the world to do that."

~

MAY ROSE

"There'll be no sleep as long as this ruckus goes on," May Rose says. They're sitting outside, May Rose on the front step, Wanda and Otis on a blanket in the grass. With the full moon, their hillside seems bright as day. Evie is running from house to house with Alma and other small shadows, playing chase. Fiddle music rises from the low-built stage on the street below. Visitors' campfires dot the valley.

Wanda sits up. "Someone's coming." A walker approaches, shadowed, but they know his stride.

"Good evening," May Rose says.

Will looks unusually formal in a white, wing-collared shirt and a bow tie. "May Rose, Wanda." He hunches beside the blanket. "I'm sorry I couldn't come sooner."

"Busy-busy," Wanda says.

He tweaks the baby's toe. "Who's this?"

"I guess you know who he is," Wanda says.

May Rose stands up. "I'll call Evie to come in."

"Let her play awhile," Wanda says.

"Otis Bosell, is he? Could we take him inside? I can't see good out here." Will's voice is calm, the even tone she remembers from her sickness. His doctor voice.

"Suit yourself," Wanda says. "Take him in, give him the once over."

Will lifts the baby like an expert and turns to the door. "You're not coming?"

"I know he's fine. I don't need your say-so."

May Rose waits until the door closes. "There's no need to be disagreeable, unless you're trying to make an enemy."

"I'm disagreeable when I feel disagreeable," Wanda says. "I've only two temperatures, hot and cold. I can't be in-between."

"Don't we know. But maybe you could try, for Otis. Will would be a wonderful father, even if it turns out he can't be with him all the time."

Wanda rises and shakes the blanket. "What about me? It feels a lot better to hate him. If I give in, I'll feel awful, 'cause he don't want me."

"Maybe he would again. Go inside and say you're sorry."

"He's the one should be sorry, dropping me without a word. Six months later he sends a letter. Then takes it back!"

"For Otis," May Rose says. "Go in and apologize. For the baby's sake."

"I'll go, but I'm not sure I can say *sorry*."

May Rose has had enough of the jostling crowds, has spent all day relieving first Luzanna and then Virgie at their market tables, but now she needs to be where she won't hear Wanda and Will.

In the lane, she meets Ebert. "I was coming to see if you was awake," he says.

"I thought I'd go down to hear the music."

"Then if you don't mind, I'll go with you. The crowd's got rough. I don't know where they've come from. Miners and railroad trash, I guess. Foreigners, hunkies."

"Is that bad? Foreigners?" She doesn't know the other word, but his tone is disparaging.

"When you can't tell what they're saying, how can you know what they'll do?"

Torches burn along the street, and tables cleared of sale goods are being used for dice and cards. People congregate around the stage.

"Wait here," Ebert says. "I'll see if I can spot a seat." He edges away through the standing crowd.

There's a touch at her elbow. "May Rose."

Barlow. Like Will, he's smartly outfitted in a white shirt and tie. He also wears a black satin vest and a policeman's badge.

"The badge isn't real," he whispers. "Will needs some of us to look official. I declined to wear a gun." He nods toward the stage, where Price Loughrie is fiddling. "John Johnson and Price are also wearing badges, but Johnson's the only one of us with a gun."

"I hope it's not necessary." She reaches into her pocket and hands him her note. It says only that she too is looking forward to their next walk together.

"Thank you. This helps." He grips the note like it's gold. "Will's never had a crowd like this, people he doesn't know, men wearing guns. It's why I haven't been to see you. The sheriff didn't come, so Will organized us. Johnson is ordering anyone with a gun to leave it in the church with Ruth and Lucie Bosell or to get out of town. Have you noticed how Johnson has a way of looking mean? When he pulls a face like that he reminds me of Wanda's granny." Barlow takes her arm and draws her close to his side. "Let me see you home."

Ebert comes through an opening in the crowd. "What's this, Townsend? Arresting my lady?" Ebert's voice is jolly but gruff.

Barlow does not let go. "Pardon me?"

"Ebert met me in the lane and walked me down."

"She wants to hear the music," Ebert says.

"It no longer seems like a good idea," she says. "Virgie and Luzanna are just over there. I'll walk home with them." With a nod of thanks to each, she pulls her arm from Barlow's and goes to her friends, embarrassed by the way he and Ebert are staring at each other.

Virgie and Luzanna giggle like school girls. "Them two," Luzanna says. "I thought they might get into it."

"I do like the look of Barlow Townsend," Virgie says. "May Rose, if you don't want him, maybe you could pass him off to me?"

It's no use saying she doesn't know what they mean. When they giggle again, she clamps her lips and hurries on alone.

In the lane near her house, she's stopped by Will. "May Rose, before I go back to Richmond, we need to talk about Charlie."

"That would be good."

"And please say something to Wanda. I don't want my boy raised by the Bosells. She says she won't marry me. Help me out."

May Rose sighs. "Will, she wants a man who loves her."

"And who would that be but me? Hell, I love her! Sorry, May Rose. I do love her. I just don't always like her. You know?"

She does.

26

"Get ready—Ebert's got his eye drilled on you," Wanda says.

May Rose has already seen him pause on the store steps, locate their table among other sellers on the street and turn their way. She arranges their remaining pairs of gloves. It's the lull of the afternoon, and they've sold none for the past two hours. "I suppose I need to talk with him. I may have to leave you here. I won't be gone too long."

"Take your time." Wanda wiggles her eyebrows. "Virgie said there was a tug of war last night—you between Ebert and Mr. Townsend. I'm sorry I missed it."

"I'm sorry I was there," May Rose whispers. "But it was misunderstandings, no war."

"Us girls are enjoying the suspense, so don't decide too quick," Wanda says. "Virgie's betting on Mr. Townsend, says he's got a prosperous look about him, but Virgie's not the best judge; she likes most anything in trousers, don't you know. I told her you've loved that man forever, spite of the fact he's old. But just look now at Ebert's arms, they're busting out of his shirtsleeves."

She does not need to look at Ebert's arms to remember how he steadied her in the river's current.

"If you won't have Will, maybe you should consider Ebert," May Rose hisses. They've not talked about Will's visit. She wonders if he's relieved today or unhappy about Wanda's refusal.

There's no use trying to influence Wanda, who now seems as peaceful as a woman whose persistent headache has passed.

"Ebert would never have me. He thinks he's too good for a Bosell. And how do you know I won't be marrying Will?"

"He told me you said no. I was surprised."

"It ain't over. He's awful proud of Otis." Wanda waves a glove in the air. "Ebert Watson, come over here. Look at these gloves, fur-lined. Be good for you or your boy."

Ebert takes no notice of the gloves and barely looks at Wanda. "I'm well supplied with gloves, thank you anyway. May Rose, can you walk for a while?"

"'Deed she can," Wanda says.

May Rose comes from behind the table, and he uncorks a small bottle and sets it in her hand. "Ginger tea. Ma makes it."

"Just the thing—I'm parched." As they walk away she sees Wanda in the corner of her eye, sidling over to Virgie's table. Watching and talking about her, she's sure.

Ebert guides her through the crowd. They turn uphill.

"Trading Days is out of hand," he says. "Will and I used to manage everything, but no more. I'm for ending it unless he gets more crew. And gets the sheriff here."

They pass her house and garden and go on to the highest terraced street, a grassy shelf with a vine-covered stone wall but no houses. She stops to drink her tea. She's been thinking this high street would be a nice site for a house. The nearby masses of laurel no longer look thick and formidable, possibly thinned by the goats Will kept.

"When the mines open, Trading Days will be worse," Ebert says. "And Winkler won't be such a nice place to live. Some o'these miners will be types you won't want for neighbors."

From here they have a long view of the valley and the mine construction at the upper end.

"You'll see, it's a lot nicer on my farm."

She hands him the empty bottle. "Tell your mother I like her tea very much."

"You should visit soon and tell her yourself. She'd be here now only Trading Days has got too rough for her liking."

"It's certainly noisier and more crowded," she says. "I think the miners will be better behaved when their families come and they have something like a regular life. The church will start again, and there may be a lawman. Do you remember Winkler when the mill and logging camps shut down? Men from the camps moved into town and lived in tents. They soon settled down."

"I saw some of it, but I had a farm and a family to go to. I never wanted to live in Winkler. Folks get along better when they don't live too close."

She's been grateful for lights in nearby houses and friends ready to help. "You have no neighbors?"

"I have the best neighbors, just a few miles away."

"I don't know what I'd have done this winter without Piney and Simpson, the Hales, John Johnson and Virgie. Or without my school."

"That's another thing," Ebert says. "You don't have to teach strangers and foreigners. You can teach Jonah at home. It's getting to be a busy time, and I'll soon be working in the hay, but we can get married soon as a preacher comes. Or go to Elkins for it."

"I'm sorry, Ebert."

His eyes crinkle when he smiles. "Sorry? But you haven't seen my farm. If I was a girl I might say no to me, but not to my farm. And the house. It's lots better than any here."

Wanda might not be welcome to visit Ebert's house, and certainly not Barlow. That friendship would have to end. And what about Charlie?

"There's something else," she says. "I've made a promise to do what I can for Charlie Herff, Will's brother. We don't know yet what kind of care he'll need."

Ebert shoves his hands in his pockets and shifts from foot to foot, raising scents of crushed grass. "You're to care for Will's brother? Did you promise this before I asked you, or after?"

"Before, I think, but it doesn't matter. We've old ties, Ebert. He's my boy."

"*Doesn't matter?* Is he your son or Will's brother? Or both?" He snorts. "Good God, woman!"

Somehow she knew he would not tolerate her taking care of anyone else. Perhaps Barlow will not, either. "I raised him, Ebert, but I'm hardly old enough to be his mother."

Ebert moderates his voice. "Where will he live, then?"

"I don't know. Perhaps with me, maybe with Russell, my brother-in-law. I think he must be bringing Charlie. I thought they'd be here by now."

"Russell Long? The crazy man?"

"He's not crazy."

"Nobody ever thought he was normal. It ain't right. Will shouldn't expect you to do this."

"Will had nothing to do with it. I can't say *no*."

"You're saying *no* to me."

"Ebert, you and I have not had much time together. I'm only starting to see my way clear. I admire you, and I like you. It's not enough."

He studies her like a man convinced he's right. "We had our first love. We don't need that again, do we? I favor you. Jonah likes you. Teaching other people's kids? Taking care of some invalid? That's no life. Come and see my farm."

"I shouldn't. It won't change anything."

"I may not give up. That bit last night—you're not going for Townsend, are you?"

"He's a good friend. We have old ties." Her face heats with memory.

~

Will is staying and Wanda is leaving. May Rose follows her around the house as she picks up the booties, sweaters, and caps knitted by Luzanna and Piney. She's going back to the Bosells with her aunt and granny.

"Think, for once, of Will," May Rose says. "What he needs. The kind of wife who will be good for him."

"Somebody else, I suppose you mean."

"*Not* somebody else. He said he loves you. Stop trying to hurt him."

"Now where's that girl?"

Carrying Otis, May Rose follows Wanda outside. "Evie doesn't want to leave her friends. You could let her stay with me."

Wanda calls, and Evie appears in the doorway of the Hale house. "She's not staying this time, Ma." Wanda motions Evie to come.

"And when school starts?"

"We'll see. Send word when Charlie gets here. If you need help, I'll come."

"Thank you. I may need it."

"I don't always think about myself," Wanda says.

"I know you don't." Otis is a plump baby, and May Rose shifts him to her left hip. "I'm sorry Will is giving up medical school. He said he might go again next year, after his mine is up and running, and if Charlie's all right."

Evie dawdles along the path from the Hale house. Wanda rotates her hand to make the girl hurry. "Yeah, the mine and Charlie. It'd be nice if me and Otis was one of his reasons to stay."

"Maybe you're his main reason and he just doesn't want to advertise it."

"Advertise? Everybody knows who Otis's daddy is."

She loves Wanda, but living with her is not easy. "Sometimes you make me so mad," she says.

Wanda holds out her arms for her baby. "I do that with everybody, don't I? I'm sorry, but it's what comes of being a Bosell."

~

BARLOW

To Barlow, the knoll across the river where they picnicked is a quiet and reflective place that separates him from daily cares. Each evening since the end of Trading Days he's walked May Rose here with growing hope.

The terrain is not as he remembers. It has burned, regrown, and in recent years been turned to pasture by Will's goats. The ground is covered with wild strawberries and tiny violets.

"Come winter," he says, "we won't have walks like these. Then how will I see you?"

"You may walk me home from school," she says.

"A hurried walk in the cold, ending with goodbye at your door. It won't be as nice as this."

Her gaze is steadier and unafraid, if a little sad. "I know," she says.

He lifts her hand and directs it across the river to a spot on the highest street. "Today Simpson and I staked out my house. You see the place?"

"I do. I saw you there."

He lowers her arm but keeps her hand in his. "I'll build with good dry lumber. The house will have a furnace, inside plumbing, nice wood finishes. I don't suppose you could go with me to Grafton and help choose what I need?"

"You'll make good choices. I need to be here when Charlie comes."

The uncertainty of Charlie. He hopes it's their last barrier.

They halt at the top of the knoll, startled by a drama on its other side. Simpson's cow stands between her calf and two watching dogs. Barlow releases her hand and picks up a rock.

The dogs dodge his rock but turn and sit back down. He searches for another rock.

"Wait," May Rose says. "They don't look mangy like wild dogs."

He lifts his arm to throw. "Look how the cow stomps her feet. She doesn't like them."

May Rose touches his raised arm. "A cow with a calf is always suspicious of a dog. Let's just move the cow."

When he and May Rose reach the cow, the dogs run around them in a wide circle, then splash through the river and race toward town.

"They act like herd dogs," she says.

In front of the store, the dogs set up a wild yipping. It's too far to see who is coming down the steps, but he understands what's happening as the dogs leap up. The man stoops between them.

"There. That worked out," she says. "I think Will's dogs have come home."

He takes her hand again. "I love being with you."

She stands very still. "Someday I need to tell you about my marriage," she says.

"I'm ready anytime." He's not. He's afraid he might hear that her husband beat her, or that she'll never love anyone as she loved him.

27

BARLOW

Barlow doesn't give the two strangers a second look. They sit on spotted horses, watching a railroad crew lay ties for the branch to Italian Town. They're travel-worn like all who stop here, miners who wander in from their camps, strangers seeking opportunity.

He's absorbed in the arrival of his own goods from Grafton, a few pieces of stored furniture and six wagon-loads of lumber, glass, and pipe. Also a box of architect's specifications. He's neglected to ask Simpson if he can read blueprints, but Simpson is quick to learn, and Randolph can explain anything he doesn't understand. Simpson has hired strong young carpenters from mountain families, but they've built only cabins, pole barns and fences, and know nothing about turning spindles or joining fine woodwork. He trusts Simpson and Randolph to make them do the job right. His house must be perfect. It's for her. He hopes it's for her—she has not committed.

He now sees her only occasionally in the store and alone no more than a few hours on Sundays, because these days he stops work long after dark. He's become a partner and front man in their new Winkler mine, hiring workers, carrying out Randolph's purchasing orders, negotiating with the Western Maryland Railroad and submitting the proper paperwork to the state office of mines. Fortunately, Virgie is willing to clerk in the store, though she talks longer than necessary with the abundance of new young men. Ebert has not worked in the store for some time. Barlow thinks he knows why.

Simpson has come to meet the wagons. He talks to the mule handlers and points toward the building site. As the wagons turn around, Barlow notices the two strangers for the second time. One has a bushy gray beard. The other is younger and black-bearded, with the upper part of his face shadowed by a western-style hat. They're crossing the street, leading their horses and a pack horse. In spite of his high-heeled boots, the younger man walks with a familiar bouncing step. The stride makes Barlow take another look at his face. Will's walk, Will's eyes.

Will is not here to greet his brother—he's gone to Richmond to give up his apartment and bring Glory home.

Barlow extends his hand, though it's a courtesy less common in Winkler. "Charlie Herff? Russell Long?"

"That'd be us," the older man says.

They ignore his hand. Russell takes off his hat, showing a bald top, a ring of gray hair over his ears, and a swath of white skin across his forehead. The rest of his skin is dark and leathery. Charlie, too, is suntanned and slender as a post. He wears tooled leather boots with high heels and a holstered handgun, and he looks everywhere but at Barlow.

He's relieved to see Charlie doesn't look sick. The older man, though, breathes with noticeable effort. "I'm Barlow Townsend." He shoves his hand into his pocket. "May Rose will be glad you're here."

Charlie mounts and turns his horse. Russell seizes the horse's bridle. "Charlie, this is where we stay. This is home."

"We've been expecting you for months," Barlow says.

Russell mops his face with a red kerchief. "Been riding here and there. The boy likes to keep moving. He's more himself, riding." Russell looks around. "Where do we light?"

"Follow me," Barlow says. May Rose has been apprehensive; he doesn't want her to meet them alone.

~

MAY ROSE

May Rose finds it difficult to ignore an altercation, even when the shrill voices come from adults and not children in her charge. Still, if the argument flared among strangers, she might lower her head and continue hoeing weeds around her bean plants. But this anger sets her in motion, for it comes from Luzanna, her closest friend, and it includes the roaring voice of a man. She's afraid she knows who.

Lifting the hem of her skirt, she runs with her hoe toward her friend's house. At the sound of a crash, she hurries through Luzanna's open front door. Emmy and Tim sit at the scarred kitchen table as if frozen. Alma is helping Luzanna from the floor, where a chair lies shattered. A man kicks through the chair parts and reaches for Alma. She has no distinct memory of Mr. Hale's appearance, but it's likely he is this thin, scruffy-bearded man.

He halts as she rushes between them, holding her hoe like a barrier. "You kids," she says, "run for Mr. Johnson, anyone." Alma scoots past and hurries through the back door. Tim and Emmy hurry after.

She has the advantage of surprise only a moment before the man pulls the hoe from her grasp. "Don't be interfering in my family. Get out."

Unbalanced, she stumbles toward Luzanna, who holds her arm like it's hurt.

"Albert, we're done," Luzanna says. "Might as well say you left me and my kids to die. Well, we didn't. And we're not taking you back."

"That's for me to say." Albert Hale backs with the hoe to the stove, slides the bean pot close and digs in a spoon.

May Rose slides her arm around Luzanna. "Mr. Hale, Luzanna and her children have a home here. I'm sorry, but you do not." She doesn't know how she manages to make her voice come out firm when her stomach is fluttering. At their last standoff he didn't take Wanda's gun seriously, and he doesn't look like he'll be moved by mere words.

She tugs on Luzanna's sleeve. They should get away and not excite him further.

Luzanna does not heed her warning, but puts one foot on the broken chair, pulls off a rung and raises it like a club. With a roar, Mr. Hale drops his spoon into the pot and swings the hoe toward her. The hoe's forward movement is stopped by someone who runs between them. *Barlow.*

"Here, now, stop this," he says.

As she expects, words are not enough to stop Hale, who pushes the handle against Barlow's chest. Barlow grabs it with both hands and pushes back.

With the men jostling for the hoe and crowding the floor space, May Rose pulls Luzanna to the wall. She picks up a shattered chair spindle at her feet, for Mr. Hale looks like he's about to smash the hoe into Barlow's face.

Barlow gives a downward push on the handle, and its metal end strikes the table and rebounds. Mr. Hale yelps, releases his hold and shakes his hand like it's burned. "This is a damned unfriendly place!"

Barlow lifts the hoe like a club. "Get out."

Mr. Hale is already headed for the front door.

Barlow's hair is drenched in sweat. He turns around. "Are you all right? May Rose? Luzanna?"

May Rose's heart pounds like she's been running.

"He didn't hit us," Luzanna says.

"I'm sorry, I didn't intend a fight. Do you know that man?"

"Albert Hale," Luzanna says. "We was together for a while."

"He's your husband?"

Luzanna drops her chair rung into the wood box. "No, thank God. I need to see him gone, and I need to find my kids."

May Rose and Barlow follow her outside. Her children stand at the corner of the house, watching Mr. Hale trot down the street.

Two horsemen wait at the steps below the house. May Rose's breathing has settled, but now it stops like she's been struck in the chest. One is Russell. And the other?

"Charlie?" The black-bearded man gives no show of hearing.

Barlow takes her hand. "It's Charlie. We were coming to find you when Alma called me inside."

She feels light-headed. "He looks fine. Wonderful."

Russell's shoulders slump, but Charlie sits erect. He's watching Mr. Hale, who is turning down the street toward the store.

She can't take her eyes from Charlie, so different with a full beard, no longer a boy. He's not yet looked at her.

"Virgie's alone at the store," Barlow says. "I should make sure that man leaves town. Then I'll come back and stay with you until we know more about what's needed."

She hurries to greet them, but as Barlow reaches the place where Mr. Hale disappeared from view, the man who must be Charlie flicks his reins and his horse starts down the street. With a look of weary patience, Russell rides after him, leading a pack horse.

Luzanna comes and watches the men leave. "One thing after another," she says. "I'm sorry you had to get messed up with us."

May Rose touches the arm Luzanna holds against her chest. "I care about you. Is your arm alright?"

"Good as the rest of me, I suppose. So that's your Charlie?"

"I guess it is. I'm not sure he knows me."

~

BARLOW

Barlow reaches the store when Hale is halfway up the steps. He grabs the center rail and takes the steps two at a time, keeping the rail between them.

The air rings with the sound of steel on steel, the railroad crew pounding spikes.

Barlow shouts. "Just a minute."

Hale keeps going. "This is a public place. I got a right."

"You're on private land. You're welcome in the store as long as you behave yourself."

Hale turns, leans across the rail, and gives him a shove. Barlow stumbles but catches himself on the rail. He ducks as a rope swirls through the air. Its loop falls on Hale, tightens around his chest and pulls him down. In the street, Charlie sits on his horse, winding the end of the rope around his saddle horn, pulling Hale down the steps. When he nudges the horse forward, Hale falls in the dirt.

Barlow hurries down the steps, because Charlie is riding away dragging Hale, and the man is clutching the rope, shouting, cursing, and trying to get to his feet.

Russell rides up and grabs the bridle of Charlie's horse. When they stop, Barlow runs to them and loosens the lasso from Hale's chest. Straightening, he sees May Rose near the church steps. Her face is pale and her eyes are wide. He knows what she must be thinking.

Hale's nose gushes blood. He pinches his nostrils with one hand and swipes blood from his mouth and chin with the back of the other. "Crazy people," he says, passing May Rose, rubbing his scraped elbows and brushing himself off. He spits in the dust and walks away toward Italian Town, holding his nose, spitting blood and glancing back every few steps.

There's no one else in view but the distant railroad workers, whose mauls continue to ring.

Charlie's horse prances.

"Charlie. We're staying here," Russell says.

Barlow meets May Rose and walks her to the middle of the street. "Charlie, here's May Rose."

Stepping closer, she stops squinting and gives him a wide smile. "I'm so happy to see you."

Charlie tips his hat, then turns and watches Hale. Russell keeps his hold on the horse's bridle. "The boy's about got me wore out," he says.

What Barlow has seen is sufficient for belief.

May Rose approaches Russell. "Come and sit down. Let us get something for you to eat."

"That'd be fine. But we'll eat out here," Russell says.

Barlow and May Rose go into the store to tell Virgie.

"Will's brother? I gotta get a look," Virgie says.

"Look, but don't go close," Barlow says. "He seems shy of people."

When Virgie goes outside, he and May Rose ladle stew onto tin plates.

"I know you have other things to do," she says. Her voice and hand shake.

"It's fine. I can do my work anytime." He'd like to give her a comforting hug, but Virgie returns.

"I didn't see nobody on horses," Virgie says. "I guess they've gone somewhere."

They find Russell and Charlie sitting on foundation stones by the footbridge, watching the river while their horses graze nearby.

Russell accepts both plates and hands one to Charlie. "Thanks for this," Russell says. "Best leave us for a while."

Barlow takes her hand. "Why don't we sit over there? Shade or sun?"

"The sun feels good," she says.

They sit at a distance with their backs turned to Charlie and Russell. "He doesn't know me," she says.

"I'm not sure he looked at you. We'll have to give him time."

"Yes. I've known children like him at the orphanage."

"Did they get better?"

"Sometimes." She cries into her handkerchief, then blows her nose. "I'm fine," she says. "I'm glad he's here."

Russell brings the empty plates. "I'll try to keep him here. We'll ride around now. It's what he likes to do."

"I've an extra bed in my house," May Rose says.

Russell shakes his head. "The boy won't sleep in a house. I found him in jail, battered senseless. Took a while before he'd trust me."

May Rose bows her head, then looks up and touches Russell's arm. "Thank you."

Russell grunts, walks away and turns back. "There ain't no bullets in that gun."

"Good," Barlow says.

He walks her home and sits with her on the front step. They can see across the river, where Charlie and Russell sit near the grazing animals. He wonders if Charlie started the fight that put him in jail.

"I've never heard Russell talk so much," May Rose says. "Making up for Charlie, I suppose. He was a sweet boy. I don't think he'd hurt anyone."

Barlow can't agree. "I think he would have dragged Luzanna's man to death. Maybe he heard the argument in the house, and saw him push me at the store. At least we haven't seen him react violently to anyone else."

"I worry about him wearing that gun," she says. "People won't know it's empty."

Barlow imagines her following Charlie on a horse as Russell does. "He's only been here a few hours. Tomorrow will be better."

The din of railroad construction has stopped for the day, but hammering echoes from the upper end of the valley. New houses are going up for the Davis mine, named the Barbara. His distant view of the valley and mountains is peaceful, denying the existence of discord and sorrow. A distant view always pulls him away from troublesome thoughts.

"Thank you for rescuing Luzanna today," she says. "And me. And for helping with Charlie."

A stranger might be afraid of Charlie, but she and Russell see a little boy they loved. He holds her hand. "Let's warn folks to keep their distance for a while. Until we all know more."

She nods. "Can you be with us at mealtimes?"

"As long as you need me," he says.

~

At dusk Barlow crosses the footbridge and speaks to Russell about herding the animals back for the night.

Pointing across the river, Russell says to Charlie, "Time to get 'em in."

Barlow leads the way to Will's fenced field. The cattle and mule turn through the gate with no urging, and when Barlow opens the horse shed door to get them a bit of salt, he finds a place

Charlie is willing to sleep. It's the shed behind the store. It has a box stall, hooks and nails for tack, and enough space on the floor for two bedrolls. It smells like leather and horses.

When he returns to May Rose, her house is dark and she's sitting outside on the step. "They're settled for the night," he says. "I showed Russell where to come for breakfast."

"Thank you. I'm so glad you were here to help." Her voice sounds weary.

He sits beside her and ponders the starry sky. He once thought there were as many trees as stars. Maybe there were, before the logging.

They talk quietly in the dark. "I've yet to hear him speak," he says. "I wonder if he'll recognize Will, or remember he has a sister." By now, Glory and Will should be traveling from Richmond. She will be sad to find her lost brother in this condition.

"Will can be hard-minded," May Rose says. "They were quarrelsome as boys, but he was upset when Charlie disappeared. I'm glad he didn't see what Charlie did to Mr. Hale."

Tomorrow Barlow needs to hire builders to help Randolph and Simpson stake out plots for miners' houses. Unfortunately, houses for miners are more necessary than his own house. It's a bad time to worry about a wayward boy.

28

She thinks she's risen early, for the sky is still dark, but when she peers from her door she sees the dark forms of two men by Simpson's field of young corn. They've tied their horses to posts and seem to watch the sky for day to begin.

Yesterday Russell said Charlie has to have a campfire, even when the weather is hot. She hurries to the stove and starts coffee, trusting the aroma will draw them, then slices bread and dips the pieces in beaten egg. Charlie always liked fried bread. It may be necessary to bake every-other day, as she did when he was a boy. She hasn't much flour, but Will may bring some when he returns.

Last evening, while Barlow and Russell were trying to find a sleeping place to suit Charlie, she cautioned her neighbors not to approach him and to warn their children. She hopes he'll start to feel at home and become comfortable with everyone. She worries that he'll draw his unloaded gun in fear or irritation and a stranger will shoot him. These days the store draws too many strangers.

When she brings out the coffee, Russell and Charlie come to the benches she and Barlow placed in a circle, just boards laid across bricks. They laid wood in the center for a fire.

The men eat with good appetite, but do not sit long at breakfast. Charlie gets up and walks off while she's pouring Russell's second cup of coffee. The coffee sloshes in his cup when Russell sets it on the bench. He hitches his trousers and trudges toward his horse. "Come back for lunch," she says, worried each time Charlie rides away that she'll never see him again. She gains some confidence later when she sees them move the animals across the river. But Russell is a concern, for he's stooped and short of breath, and he groans sitting down, standing up, and getting on and off his horse.

Like a miracle, Wanda and her children arrive that afternoon. Wanda rides her ginger mare and carries Otis, and Evie rides behind Price Loughrie on the brown plow horse they call Old Henry. A dog trots along with them. Evie barely says hello before running off to find her friends.

"Price has come to work at Will's new mine," Wanda says, as he tips his hat and rides away. "He says he's tired of being bossed by Granny. I'm sick of her too, especially how she talks to Evie. I wouldn't be surprised if Aunt Ruth gives up on her someday."

May Rose holds out her arms to take the baby. "Charlie is here. She nods toward the slope across the river.

Wanda shades her eyes. "Finally! That over there is Russell and Charlie? Yeah, I can tell Russell from here. Riding herd, are they? Charlie's all right?"

"He doesn't seem to know me. I'm not sure he remembers Russell. He's given no sign that he knows where he is."

"Might be good that nothing here looks the same," Wanda says. "He ran away from Winkler once already. Does he know Will?"

"He hasn't seen him. Will should be on his way from Richmond by now. He's bringing Glory."

"I'm glad to see Charlie's not bed-rid," Wanda says. "I'll just ride over there, see what he thinks of my mare."

"Maybe not yet. He's shy of everyone and doesn't seem to like direct looks."

"It's all right. I'm that way myself," Wanda says.

May Rose shifts Otis to her other arm. "When have you ever been shy?"

Grinning, Wanda tucks up her skirt, puts a foot in the stirrup and swings her leg over the mare's back. Under her skirt, she's wearing trousers. May Rose sits on a bench with Otis and watches her cross the river, meet the two horsemen, and ride for a while between them.

The second miracle is that when Charlie and Russell come to the campfire for their evening meal, Charlie gives Wanda a glance and says, "Wanda."

"Hey, Charlie," Wanda says, like acquaintances who pass every day in the street.

May Rose turns her head to hide her joy. *Charlie has a voice. He knows Wanda.*

He speaks again, now seeming to study the ground at his feet. "Where's Homer?"

Wanda hands him a plate of ham with eggs fried hard, his boyhood preference. "Homer's dead."

Nodding, Charlie folds a fried egg in quarters and spears it with a fork.

Even Russell seems overcome.

Barlow and Loughrie come to the house near dark and join their campfire. There is no talk. Loughrie plays sad melodies on his fiddle. May Rose sits on the front step, hidden by night, but watchful.

The third miracle is that when Russell yawns and says "Let's turn in," Charlie goes to his horse and leads him in the direction of the shed where they slept last night. Russell follows. Loughrie stretches, says goodnight, and walks downhill toward his tent. Evie comes home, and Wanda carries Otis into the house.

Barlow kicks dirt into the ashes of the fire, and May Rose goes close to thank him again. The strain of Charlie has left her exhausted. They stand quietly in the dark, one step between them. He takes that step, puts his arms lightly at her waist. She rests her head on his shoulder, and he draws his hands tight at her back.

"I think," he whispers, "this will give me strength for another day."

"Yes. Me too." They stand like that until it's clear they must do something stronger or something to break them apart. They decide in unison, letting their cheeks, and then their lips touch before taking a step back. She holds his hand until he says goodnight.

~

MAY ROSE

"You need to give that man some relief," Virgie says.

May Rose does not need to ask what man or what kind of relief Virgie has in mind, though it takes her a moment to absorb the shock. Virgie has said this, not just to her, which would be embarrassing enough. She's said it in the presence of Luzanna and Wanda. Ordinarily she joins them in laughing at Virgie's talk, even when it crosses the line of propriety. It's not as funny when she's the butt of the joke.

Barlow has just left the store, but aside from a greeting, they didn't speak. While she and the others waited in the sewing corner, he talked at length to Virgie and left her with a long hand-lettered list of tasks.

These days he seems harried and anxious. She would like to defend him, say he only wants Virgie to take care of business, but Virgie would say she knows the kind of business he needs.

Virgie stuffs Barlow's paper in her pocket without a look. "May Rose, how red you are!"

Grinning, Luzanna ducks her head and inspects the darts and collar of Virgie's half-sewn blouse.

"It's not my fault you're not doing your job," May Rose says. "I should take care of the store and let you carry on with your fashions."

Virgie knots a thread, takes the blouse and bastes across the bottom of the tucks to hold them in place "You in the store? You're too soft to manage all the rough trade we got coming and going."

"I can handle the work as well as you," May Rose says. *Better*, she thinks.

"Is that right? You got the shell of an egg. For this job you gotta be tough as a gourd, like me and Wanda."

Wanda has been unusually quiet, but now she sets Otis on the floor and digs her hand into Virgie's pocket. "So here's the best idea yet."

Virgie squirms away, but Wanda pulls out Barlow's list and presses the crumpled paper on the cutting table.

"I'll keep store. You go home and sew. Ma and Evie can take care of Otis and bring him here for feedings."

Virgie slips on the bodice of the blouse, finished all but the sleeves. She pulls it together in the front and looks at herself in a free-standing mirror. "That's good by me. I keep telling Will I want to quit." She winks at Wanda. Won't he be surprised to find you here! You and the baby might as well go ahead and move into his room."

Wanda retrieves Otis from the floor. "I'll not go that far."

May Rose would rather keep the baby than work in the store. "You could have Alma here to keep the records," she says. No need to mention that Wanda is impatient and careless about adding long columns of numbers.

Luzanna flashes a look of approval, takes a pin from her lips and marks a spot for Virgie's collar button.

"Suits me," Wanda says. "I'll share my pay with Alma."

"Well," Virgie says, "it happens I get no actual money in pay. It's my rent, you see, and some credit for groceries."

"I'm all right with that kind of pay," Wanda says.

It's a good idea. They're all in Will's debt.

Virgie arches her eyebrows and gives everyone a wicked look. "Now that's settled, let's get back to what May Rose can do to settle Mr. Barlow Townsend. And when she's gonna do it!"

May Rose holds out her arms for the baby. "Wanda, get busy on Barlow's list. I'll take Otis home."

Reaching the steps, she can't help smiling, though her face is hot. Her friends are still laughing.

~

May Rose keeps telling Wanda she doesn't have to do everything in one day, but since replacing Virgie at the store, Wanda seems to be in a race with Barlow. The more she accomplishes, the longer his list grows. "My choice," Wanda says. Virgie is happy, Wanda is happy, and Barlow seems to be impressed.

She remembers a long-ago conversation when she tried to convince him that Wanda, then thirteen, could keep house for Morris Herff and manage his motherless children, Will, Charlie, and Glory. She's glad Wanda has finally won his approval.

It's probably good that she and Barlow have almost no time together and are exhausted by work. More and more, she's wishing they could be alone, but she does not want to sneak to the woods like kids. Virgie blatantly offered her house, but May Rose ignored the suggestion. She has not acknowledged these feelings, not even to him.

Whatever Wanda is doing now, she needs to stop and feed this baby. May Rose sets him on her hip and leaves the house. He's a plump four-months old, mildly cranky with teething, but with no sign of Wanda's temperament. Wanda has chosen good fathers for her children, Homer and Will, calm and steady men.

She wonders if it's too late for a child of her own.

When she reaches the street, she sees the wagon, notable because of how high its crates are piled, and exciting because of the people stepping down. Will and Glory. *At last.*

Glory sees her first and runs forward to squeeze her and Otis in a hug. "Oh, I love him," Glory says. "This *is* him, isn't it? Otis? My nephew? Has to be, he's as pretty as me!"

May Rose lets her take the baby, but Will immediately claims him, looking proud. He brings a silver baby rattle from a pocket, puts it in Otis's chubby fist, and laughs at the baby's gurgles. After a few minutes of play, he says, like he's forgotten, "Where's Wanda?"

"She's working in the store. Barlow says she's doing wonders," she adds, to ward off any objection. He hasn't actually said *wonders*, but she wants Wanda to look good. The baby begins to fuss. "Otis is hungry. I was just taking him for his feeding."

Glory runs ahead and opens the door, and Will carries the baby up the steps. May Rose follows, wishing she could alert

Wanda. Hopefully Glory's admiration will help Will see Wanda in a better light.

Inside, it does seem that Wanda has worked wonders. The store area looks almost as it did in the days of the sawmill. For the abundance of new merchandise, Wanda has created shelves in aisles where customers might walk through and select for themselves. To keep them from walking out without paying, she's moved the counter and cash register close to the doors.

Otis cries when he sees his mother. May Rose stands back as Will puts him in Wanda's arms. "How I love your baby," Glory says.

Otis' mouth roots at the cloth of Wanda's bodice. She smiles at Glory. "Alma, watch business, he's gotta eat." She carries the baby toward the rooms at the back of the store. She's barely looked at Will, but he follows. The door shuts after them.

May Rose and Glory are left alone with Alma, who sits on a stool by the cash register. "Well," Glory says. "*I hope.*"

There's no need to say what they hope. She walks Glory outside. From the steps, they have a good view of the slope where their animals graze. She points to the two horsemen, now standing under the shade of a tree. "Over there is Charlie. He's come home."

Glory grips the railing and gives her an anxious look. "Is he all right?"

May Rose doesn't know what to say. "He's no bother, but he won't come inside or look at anybody. That's Russell with him. He stays close and keeps him from straying. Morning to night, Charlie does nothing but ride around those animals."

Glory shades her eyes. "What's he like? Will said he might be mixed up."

"He's shy and quiet. As far as I know, he's said exactly three words since he's come. You must not rush him."

"Keep away?"

"Perhaps stay at a distance for a day or two until he's used to the sight of you."

The two horsemen and the small grazing herd are a quiet contrast to the hammering at the other end of the valley.

"Is our heifer over there? Did she have a calf?"

"She's there, but she had no calf this year. Maybe the next."

Glory gazes up the valley. "Things here have sure changed."

"They change every day." The Barbara Mine has opened, and coal cars stretch from there to the tracks in front of the store. Gradually, they've stopped saying Italian Town, adopting the name used by all the new people: Barbara Town. On the Winkler side of the river, Simpson and a dozen helpers are building workers' houses for the new mine owned by Will, Randolph and Barlow.

Glory links arms with May Rose. "Will wants to marry Wanda and raise his baby. Can we help?" Glory is as lively as Virgie but sensible and forthright, like Hester.

"With you here, I feel more hopeful. Wanda won't say yes until she knows Will wants her for herself. I don't know if we can help with that or not."

"Sometimes Will is as slow as Uncle Barlow. I'll put a bug in his ear." Glory smiles. "And how *is* my uncle? He hasn't written in a long, *long* time."

~

Glory and Will come that evening and wait with her and Wanda on the benches in the yard. Wanda has said nothing to May Rose of what may have passed between her and Will, but they seem to be on amiable terms.

They watch the horsemen cross the river and then the railroad track, riding behind the mule, Wanda's mare, Simpson's cow and calf and the young cow they still call Glory's heifer. "He's relieved us of that job," May Rose says. "He takes them across in the morning, stays there all day, and brings them back at night."

"He could manage a lot more cattle," Wanda says, "if we could cut enough hay for winter feed."

Will raises his head like he's heard something he likes. "We wouldn't have to feed them long. We're going to have four mine camps nearby. The Winkler Company used to bring in steers and hogs. There was a slaughterhouse here. We can do that again—in fact, we'd be fools not to." He stops, like he's correcting himself. "That is, if Charlie and Russell want to do something like that."

"I don't know about Russell," May Rose says. "When he comes you'll see how tired he is. Half the day he lies over there under a shade tree." They've explained to Will the little they know about Charlie, his distance, his silence, and his one act of violence against Mr. Hale.

"Being here with us may improve him," Will says. "It's a good idea for us and Charlie too. He could have wages, maybe cattle of his own."

Soon Russell and Charlie appear, quiet shadows announced by the slow clop of their horses' hooves. As usual, they tie the horses to fence posts by Simpson's corn field. Several paces from the benches, Charlie stops. Russell takes a few more steps, then seems to realize Charlie isn't with him. He turns and goes back.

"I'm sorry. Charlie's not going to join us while you're here," May Rose says.

Will and Glory get up and move to the front steps, but Charlie doesn't come to the benches until they go into the house. Then he bends and assembles the fire.

Barlow and Loughrie arrive and sit in their usual places, and Wanda brings out a water bucket and tin cups. While they wait for the flames to burn to coals, May Rose asks Russell how the animals are, and he says, "Same as usual." In quiet tones, she directs questions about the day to Wanda, Barlow, and Loughrie, repeating their names and glancing to see if Charlie is paying attention. He gives no sign.

Will has contributed fat sausages for their evening meal, and Wanda spears them on sticks and hands them to the men to roast. Grease drips from the sausages and sizzles in the coals.

When everyone around the circle has sausage on their plates, she takes some into the house for Will and Glory, who are sitting just inside the doorway. "I hate to keep you away, but he gets used to people a little at a time. I still don't know if he recognizes me. He said Wanda's name once, and asked about Homer."

"It's all right," Will says. "He lived with them at Russell's that winter when he ran away. I wonder if that's where he is in his head—nine years old. If it is, maybe he'll remember me too."

~

That night, Wanda comes to May Rose's room as she's brushing her hair. Wanda takes the brush and pulls it through her own tough curls, now as long and bushy as ever. "About Will. I'm not sure I can be as good as he wants." She gives the brush a hard jerk. "And I've never told him about my fits."

It's been more than a year since Wanda confessed these outbursts of temper, the last one most frightening because it was directed at Evie.

"I haven't had one since last summer," Wanda says, "but I worry. It's feeling helpless that sets me off, then I get so crazy I can't stop myself." She sits on the bed, still holding the brush. "Piney says my ma was like that too, so you see how it worries me. And here's something I don't want my kids to know, same as I don't want them to know my ma was a whore. In one of her fits, she shot her pa. Shot him dead."

Shot. Yet Wanda was not afraid to buy a gun. May Rose can't speak.

"Granny, Aunt Ruth and Piney—they was there, but they never told on her. That was right before Ma came to Winkler and started whoring."

Wanda rakes the brush through her hair. "I didn't know till last summer. If Will ever saw me in a fit, he might grab up Otis and leave. Which might be the right thing to do."

"Don't think about your ma," May Rose says, though she knows this revelation will keep her from sleep, along with the worry that Wanda, who has never seemed to fear anything else, seems once again to be afraid of herself. "You didn't get out of control on the road when Mr. Hale tried to take our wagon."

"I know. The last couple of times I started into a fit, I held it off. Back there on the road, I was trying to use my head and think of things one at a time, like how tight he was wrapping those reins around his hand. How they'd leave a mark if I spooked the horses and they ripped the reins away. Course I didn't want to spook the horses with all of you in the wagon. And I was wondering how I could get my bullets from your pocket into the Colt." Wanda's laugh is short. "Glory saved us, didn't she?"

"You need to tell Will," May Rose says. "Tell him, tell him about all those times, and how you're trying to right yourself. If he doesn't care enough to help, he doesn't deserve you."

Wanda sets down the brush. "Easy to say, ain't it?"

29

"Charlie can't herd cows through the street during Trading Days," Will says. "And he's got to stop wearing that gun."

May Rose is helping Will and others unload a freight car of cook stoves, bed frames, chairs, and tables—used furniture he'll sell in the store. In the hot car, she and Alma push and carry pieces to the door. Outside, Will and Wanda lift them down, and Luzanna and John Johnson carry them to Will's market tent.

May Rose slides the last piece to the door, a Victrola player in a tall cabinet. No one in town is eager for Trading Days. This morning they set up tables of boards and sawhorses in the street. With all the activity brought by the new mines, Trading Days seems like too much work.

Will helps her and Alma down from the car, and they pause to look toward the slope where Russell, Charlie, and Will's dogs are minding the cows.

"He's smart enough to drive them where they need to go without getting near people," Wanda says. "But I don't know what we can do about the gun. Russell says he sleeps on it."

Remembering last month's rowdy crowds, May Rose fears no place in town will be safe for Charlie. And with the noise, he won't want to sleep in the horse shed, because it's just a few steps from the main street.

"I'm wondering if it's right to keep him here," Will says. "Maybe we should put him in the asylum at Weston."

"No," Wanda and May Rose say together.

Will wipes his forehead with a red kerchief. "We got no idea what he'll do. He doesn't know me and won't look at me. In fifteen years, he didn't come home or write. I don't feel like his brother. I can't take care of him."

"Nobody's asking you to take care of him," Wanda says. "The rest of us can do that. What about your idea of getting him a real herd of cattle?"

"I got too many ideas and not enough people I can trust."

"Please, give him time," May Rose says.

Will sets the Victrola on the ground. "If you want him to be safe, find a way to take away his gun."

That night Barlow and Price Loughrie do not come to the campfire, but Will and Glory are there, accepted by Charlie, or at least no longer identified as strangers. She hopes no one will try to take Charlie's gun.

She hands Charlie a plate of bread and beans, encouraged because for the first time he glances at her face. Maybe if she asks, he'll let her keep the gun during Trading Days. Having known so many orphanage children, she thinks Charlie was different even as a little boy, heedless and prone to do whatever came into his mind.

"We'll have lots of people in town tomorrow," she says. "It will be noisy, so you might want to keep the animals on the other side of the river and camp over there. We'll carry supper, same time."

Charlie takes a bite of bread. Russell nods.

"I don't know," Wanda says. "With Barbara Town and the Winkler mines building up, there's less room to camp. Some who come for Trading Days might want to set their tents over there.

"We'll keep away from 'em," Russell says.

May Rose sits down with her own plate. "The market goes on for three days and nights. No guns are allowed. Anywhere."

Around the campfire, no one takes a bite or says a word, like they're all listening for a sound from Charlie.

Wanda sets her plate on the ground. "I don't much like guns. I've always been better with a knife." She goes to Charlie and opens her pocket knife. "This is my new one, what do you think?"

Charlie peers at the knife and nods. Wanda gives the knife a flick that sticks the blade in the ground. She bends and pulls it out. "Remember how we played mumbly peg?"

Charlie lifts his head to the fire's red glow.

"We played about every day," she says. "Till I stuck my foot, and Ma took my knife away. Come on, Charlie, let's throw. You win, I'll give you my mare. I win, I get your gun." Her voice teases.

Nobody moves but Russell, who stretches out a leg and kicks a half-burned log back into the fire. Sparks fly. Slowly Charlie stands and unfolds his pocket knife. He faces Wanda with his feet spread wide.

"This isn't a good idea," May Rose says. "It's too dark." She looks to see if Will or Russell might interfere. They sit motionless with their hands on their knees and blank expressions on their faces.

"We can see fine," Wanda says. "Charlie, set your feet closer, same distance as mine. I'll go first. We each get three tries to stick the knife in the ground. Closest stick to our own foot wins."

May Rose would protest again, but she's held by the fact that Wanda is influencing Charlie. Both are wearing thick boots—maybe a knife won't go through the leather.

Glory moves to sit beside May Rose where there's a better view of the contest.

Wanda positions the blade end between her fingers and gives the knife a hard flip. The blade sticks safely between her feet. "All right," she says. "Match that."

Charlie flips his knife with the same result.

Glory claps her hands.

On their next throws, Wanda's blade doesn't stick in the ground, but Charlie pins half the distance from his first toss.

"Good stick," Wanda says. "Now watch this."

This time when Wanda hurls the knife May Rose closes her eyes. She opens them when Glory murmurs approval. The knife is stuck close to Wanda's boot.

Charlie's grunt sounds like admiration. He pauses a few moments, then throws. When his knife sticks, its handle wobbles from the force of his throw.

"Don't move," Wanda says. "Ma, you judge."

May Rose stoops and measures the distance of each knife with her finger. Wanda's knife is one knuckle from her boot; Charlie's is one and a half. Silent as ever, he unbuckles his gun belt, hands it to Wanda, and sits back on his bench.

Will exhales, a tense, audible swoosh of air.

"Time for apple dumplings," May Rose says.

Glory and Wanda follow her inside. "That was wonderful," Glory says.

Wanda reaches high and places Charlie's gun and belt on a shelf. "No it weren't. Charlie always did let me win."

~

BARLOW

At the end of the day, Barlow wants to come home to his own home. Or anywhere, as long as he can come home to her. But without a dedicated work crew, his house won't be finished before next spring. It hasn't even started. He and Loughrie have erected a floorless pole building to shelter his stacked furniture and lumber. The building is partly sided with old tin from the store basement, and is open on the side facing town.

Last night he spent the remaining hour of light sawing and sinking posts for a sleeping platform. He and Randolph are tired of their small hot room at the back of the store, though it has access to the only inside plumbing in Winkler. Randolph has set up a tent above the store. Come winter, they'll all need something better. Come winter, he wants to be in his new house.

He wrote Banovic, asking if he might find carpenters willing to travel. Mail is faster now, for it comes by train to the Barbara Town post office, but Banovic hasn't responded. Barlow saw him last when he stopped by the grocery on his buying trip. He was helping his wife in the store, and as usual, seemed full of strategies that made Barlow worry.

This is the second night he's stayed away from the campfire. He's finishing the platform with oak planks purchased for the house. Each board he nails in place makes him grieve for its original purpose. He's not blind to the fact that he wants a grand house to make up for his deficiencies. He must have something fine to offer her, must not bore or disappoint her. She loves him a little. He must never let that turn to disgust.

From here he can see the roof of her house and smoke from Charlie's campfire. Charlie's routine has not varied from the first day. Everyone on this end of Winkler is used to him herding the animals from one side of the river to the other. The children watch curiously but keep their distance. Will's dogs trot along with him. As yet he's not interacted with miners or other strangers.

Now the full moon is on its way, and whether Winkler is ready for them or not, people will come for Trading Days. When Will started this market, there was no railroad separating the street from the river, no coal tipples and no tent camps upstream. He doesn't know where visitors will park their wagons and pitch their tents, but there's no cancelling the full moon.

He drops his hammer on the platform when he sees her drawing near. Her skirt sways and stops. Her arms are full. "I've stuffed a pillow," she says. "I've brought you a quilt."

He unfolds the quilt and lays it on the platform. She puts the pillow at one end. "We could stuff a mattress tick," she says. "As it is, this will be a hard bed."

"I'll get used to it. Thank you." He takes her hand to ease her down to the platform, for it's a low seat.

The moon lights her face. "I think Will and Wanda will marry," she says. "She loves him. He loves her. They may have troubles, even so." Her voice is quiet.

Barlow sits beside her. "Will is impressed by what Wanda achieves in the store."

"He loves Otis. They should be a family. They should try."

"We're going to share a doctor with the Barbara Mine," he says. "Will hopes to work with him this year, since he's not going back to medical school."

"I hope he'll be happy."

"What about me?"

"Of course," she says. "I want you to be happy too."

"Are you going to be my wife?"

"You're building a house. You must think you know."

"I'm building in hope." Even now, he can recreate the sensation of carrying her from the mud, the weight and feel of her arm around his neck. He bends his head and touches his lips to her cheek. She inches closer, and he slides his arm around her waist. "I will take such care of you."

"I want to tell you something about myself," she says.

"I don't need to hear anything. I know who you are."

"You don't know this. Jamie left me alone on the mountain, weeks at a time. It was a terrible time. I had nobody. I don't mind living alone as long as I have friends and neighbors. But if we marry, if I join my life to yours, if I care for you more than anything, you can't leave me."

Can't leave? He wants to smile, but cannot make light because her voice is unusually solemn. "Not for work?"

"If you're home every night."

"No traveling?"

She rises. "If I can go with you."

He holds onto her hand as she starts to move away. "But you're leaving me now."

"I haven't said 'yes'. It will depend on you."

~

MAY ROSE

The full moon market is over, and though everyone is exhausted, they're happy because they sold every piece of furniture to miners and hill people, and Charlie stayed safely away.

"All done till next time," Wanda says.

They're celebrating with the first campfire in her yard in three nights, and tonight Virgie, Evie and Alma are sitting with them. With his face hidden under his hat and beard, it's not possible to be certain about Charlie, but May Rose thinks he might be pleased to be back.

Will and Barlow come late to the campfire, carrying something between them.

When they draw near, Wanda rises and latches onto Will. "Will Herff! You've built a baby crib! You rascal, you never said a word!"

Will's voice and face don't change, but even in firelight, she sees his pleasure. "Guess I've done one thing to suit," he says.

Wanda turns to Virgie. "There's been a couple of things. So far." Virgie laughs.

Will and Barlow carry the crib inside, then come back to the fire. "Sit with us," May Rose says.

Will takes his customary place beside Glory, but Barlow says goodnight to all. May Rose walks with him a few steps toward his construction site, and he presses a folded paper into her palm.

"Oh, dear," she says. "We're back to notes."

"Read it soon," he says.

She puts the note in her pocket and returns to the campfire, now dying to ashes. "Charlie," she says, sitting beside Glory. "Do you remember your baby sister?"

Even the cricket drone seems to stop. Charlie makes no sign that he's heard. Then he says, "Morning Glory."

She's not the only one who takes a sharp breath. "That's right. Which one of these girls do you think she is?"

Charlie lifts his head and stares across the smoldering coals. She has no idea if in past weeks he's registered the identities of Glory, Virgie, Alma and Evie, but after his usual spell of silence, he nods toward Glory.

Glory straightens and leans forward.

"Exactly right," May Rose says. "She's all grown up."

Someone sniffs. Will, she thinks. Maybe Wanda.

Will puts his arm around Glory. "That's what Ma called you. *Morning Glory*."

"Charlie, you have a brother, too," Wanda says. Her voice sounds choked. "Do you remember?"

Charlie gets up and kicks dirt over the ashes. "Will." He leaves, as though he's said enough.

No one at the campfire speaks. May Rose lifts her apron and wipes her eyes.

~

A light rain begins as she walks uphill in the dark. "I've news," Barlow's note said.

Clouds obscure the waning moon, but he's tramped an easy path from her house to his building site. She does not hurry. She's thinking of Charlie, Glory and Will, who may become a family again. But now as she nears the darkened site, she thinks of Barlow.

He steps from the shed into the rain, holding out his hand. "Here. I'm here."

"I see you."

He draws her under the roof. His arms are bare—he's wearing an undershirt, as laboring men do in the heat.

"Sit over here. Watch your step."

They sit at the edge of the sleeping platform. "I've had a letter from Banovic. He's bringing workmen to build our house, some of the Slovaks from the Jennie Town Mine."

"Our house. You're not going to leave me, no matter what."

He squeezes her hand. "I won't leave you, no matter what. If you forgive me."

"You're not hard to forgive."

"I hope that proves to be true," he says. "When you said there was something I didn't know about you, I knew I had to tell you something you don't know about me. I shamed myself. But in the same circumstances, I might do it again."

"Barlow, we've put that behind us."

"This isn't about my indecent proposal, and it's not about the telegram. It's about Morris Herff and his children."

"Whatever it is, it's all right." She doesn't want to hear anything that might change her mind.

He turns her hand over, kisses her palm, closes her fingers and holds on. "When Mrs. Donnelly took over your job, that was because of me. I told Morris you weren't coming back, that you did not want to take care of his children any longer."

Because of him? The bad things that happened to Will and Charlie when their father married Mrs. Donnelly took place because *Barlow lied?* She'd wondered, at the time, but had dismissed her suspicious thoughts because he'd been concerned and helpful in other ways.

She feels sick.

He grips her hand like he will never let go, and though it grows sweaty and limp, she does not want to be released. She wants to hear that what he just said isn't true.

Rain pounds the tin roof. Minutes pass while she tells herself he meant well, that he did not have to confess. He wants no secrets between them. She struggles to keep her mind on that, and not the past. "You're brave to tell me."

"I hate what happened to that family." His voice breaks. His hand is hurting her fingers. "I told myself I had good cause to lie to Morris. When you started taking care of his children, a lot of crude jokes went around at the sawmill about the two of you. He was going along with all of it, letting the men think that he and you... I knew it couldn't be true."

"You encouraged him to marry Mrs. Donnelly."

"I said I'd pay her to take care of the family. She must have done the rest. With her husband dead, she had nothing. She was a desperate woman."

He could not have predicted that living with the Donnellys would magnify the family's troubles. She rests her head on his shoulder. "I think Will and Charlie are going to be all right."

"And you?"

"I lied too, but I'll tell you about that tomorrow. Since you've promised not to leave me, I've decided not to leave you. My friends will be relieved to know that starting tonight, I will sleep wherever you are. I hope your friends will not be scandalized."

"Sleep? May Rose, I want to do what's right."

She stands and unbuttons her bodice, steps out of the dress and feels along the platform to the pillow, where it's too dark to see anything. She turns and waits. "This is right. Please. Show me how you love me."

Rainwater falls in sheets from the roof's edge, splashing the ground and further darkening the interior. Unable to hear his steps or see his shadow, she flinches when his hands touch her skin. Her hands wrap behind his neck. He's shed his clothing. For a moment they stand cheek to cheek, then press lips to cheek, to neck, to lips. Their hands slide lightly until the pressure is too strong, and they lie down on the quilt.

Later, curled against her back, he murmurs, "You could do better. You could have any heart you want."

She presses his hand to her heart. "It's too late. I'm already caught by yours."

Thank You

Thanks to Bob Summer, author of *Breaking East* and *Alone But Not Lost*, and to Diane Plotts, Jill Bitner, and Michele Moore for your careful reading and excellent suggestions.

Thank you, reader, for selecting *Midwinter Sun*. I'd love to hear from you.

Email: carolervin2012@gmail.com.

Facebook: https://www.facebook.com/carolervin.author

Website: www.carolervin.com

Follow the lives of May Rose and her friends in *The Women's War*, available from Amazon and other retailers.

#14.99

LONGWOOD PUBLIC LIBRARY
800 Middle Country Road
Middle Island, NY 11953
(631) 924-6400
longwoodlibrary.org

LIBRARY HOURS

Monday-Friday	9:30 a.m. - 9:00 p.m.
Saturday	9:30 a.m. - 5:00 p.m.
Sunday (Sept-June)	1:00 p.m. - 5:00 p.m.

64270472R00151

Made in the USA
San Bernardino, CA
21 December 2017